Dictates of the Heart

WHERE THE HEART BELONGS

CHINYERE OBINNA ONWUCHEKWA

ADORE PUBLICATIONS

Note: Some portions of the dialogue in this book are italicized. This is delibertely done to delineate the different language structures and parlance that abound in Nigeria. Some of the characters converse in Pidgen English, while some speak in broken or restructured English. The italics are done to empasise these aspects of the Nigerian lingo.

FOREWORD

In the study of anatomy, we learn that the heart is an important
organ in humans which pumps blood through the blood vessels of
the circulatory system. But it is more than that. In this literary
fiction, Dictates of the Heart, Chinyere Obinna Onwuchekwa
demonstrates that following the dictates of our heart can lead one
to fulfillment of life's desires. Thus, whereas the blood that the
heart pumps assures the human of life, following the dictates of
the heart can propel one to desired accomplishment in life. Such
a connection made in the context of this well-conceived storyline
makes it a must-read for everyone.

Long before our in-person meeting about a year ago, I had been
an avid reader of a blog which, unbeknownst to me, is hosted by
Ms. Onwuchekwa using a pseudonym. Our meeting occurred in
the context of her being introduced to, and becoming a member
of, the Nigeria-based non-governmental organization (NGO) of
which I am the USA-Diaspora Chapter Coordinator. Her presence
and the level of progressive inputs she brings to the entity's
deliberations so impressed me that I encouraged her to serve on
more than one committee. I have come to appreciate Ms.
Onwuchekwa's virtues of critical thinking, intellectual
assertiveness, compassion, and most especially her literary
adeptness in such a short time. Soon, we began to share a
mutual feeling as if we had known each other for decades, which
made it easy for me to honor her request that I pen the Foreword
for this amazingly audacious work of fiction.

Set in the postmodern era in Nigeria, the novel tells the story of Adora Amadi, a beautiful young girl coming of age and learning to navigate the world, and in particular her society's traditional norms, on her own terms – following her heart. The entire novel abounds with evidence of Adora's determination, persistence, and tenaciousness despite the shocking reality of the death of her mother, her most endeared confidant, in a tragic car accident and facing initial apparent old-fashioned "protectionist" mentality of her father, Dr. Chidi Amadi, and his antimodern world perspective. On full display in this novel is Ms. Onwuchekwa's steadfastness as a "wordsmith," a master storyteller with a higher-order sense of humor and her ability to parsimoniously transition from chapter to chapter; keeping the story line synchronized to the end.

The novel embodies numerous heartwarming episodes about relationship dynamics, not only between Adora and her father, but across the entire multitude of the book's characters. Ultimately, by the time you reach the end of the book, you will find that you cannot but totally agree with the author that the novel is "an endearing love story about waiting for the right thing."

You are invited to read it!

Dr. Ifem Emmanuel Orji, PhD, JD

Public Law & Policy Scholar and Consultant,

Fellow, Institute for Research on the African Diaspora in the Americas and Caribbean,

(IRADAC), The City University of New York

New York City, New York, June, 2019

CONTENTS

Dedication

This book is dedicated to my late sister Joy Nkechi Onwuchekwa Osazee who made me believe that I can achieve anything I set my mind to. A more beautiful angel inside and out has never been born. Also, to my late mom Mercy Ngwamma Onwuchekwa who inspired me to discover my latent gift when I picked up her completed manuscript as a teenager.

To my brother Enyinnaya Onwuchekwa whose constant feedback and encouragement kept me grounded and updated about the current realities of Nigeria. To my wordsmith friend Bryant Rowe, whose invaluable advice helped me to streamline and simplify my excessive prose. To my learned friend and and advisor Dr. Orji for your encouragement and feedback and to Dr. George Onuorah for believing in me. To my Senior Pastor, Dr. Olu Fadare, who has been my spiritual and moral compass. To my wonderful sisters Vanessa Ekeke and Emily Akuabia for your constant feedback, encouragement, love and support. To my big sisters Crown Princess Olubunmi and Lynn, Chidimma and Tochi whose unconditional love kept me going, and my beautiful sisters Pastor Annie Onwuchekwa and Hanah Crandon for your prayerful support. To my sis Ugodibeze and my brother Dr. Sam, you never stopped encouraging me. Thank you also to all my family and friends who never gave up on me even when I had given up on myself.

DICTATES OF THE HEART

"Nobody can teach me who I am. You can describe parts of me, but who I am - and what I need - is something I have to find out myself."

Chinua Achebe, Nigerian Author

Chapter 1

Adora paced barefoot around the spacious living room of her father's massive stone mansion, her footfalls noiseless on the pristine white marble flooring that ran the entire length and breadth of the sunny downstairs rooms. Stopping for a moment, she drew her light blue cotton robe tighter around her slender frame and glanced anxiously at her father, who stood stock still by the west window, staring glumly through the hazy blue veil of the sweeping floor to ceiling French window, at the spectacular vista of the impeccably manicured garden that he had named "Christina's garden, which was alive with the verdant colors of life, vivid in the early morning sun that was rising through a curtain of fluffy clouds.

He stood there, tense as a tautly stretched wire, his fatigue etched deeply across his tired face that still held strong traces of his handsome features. His hair had turned gray at the temple, where a vein throbbed visibly, accenting his red-rimmed eyes, where the tell-tale lines and puffiness revealed signs of advancing age and the overwhelming weariness that he seemed to wear like a mantle lately.

"So different from the fun dad that she knew some ten years ago," she thought wryly to herself. She was a young kid then, and to her eleven years old eyes, her father was an amalgamation of all the childhood heroes that she had read about and seen on television, rendered in one handsome, clever and resourceful package. That was also before the accident that changed everything - torn her mother away from their lives in such a cruel sudden manner, and turned her father into this brittle, embittered shell of what he used to be.

As though sensing her thoughts, her father turned slowly towards her; his eyes held a strained expression, as though the burden of going through life was a physical load that dragged him down with every faltering step. She felt a rush of pity towards him; if only she had a magic wand that could ease his suffering which even the march of time had not been able to eradicate.

A raspy, barely audible sigh escaped his lips as he lowered his long, almost bony frame on the pale blue sofa that faced the wide screen television, and faced her with the same guarded, stiff stance that seemed to embody him now.

"Adora, I already told you my reasons," he said in a voice that sounded as dead as the echo of the mahogany side table, where he dropped his briefcase and the stethoscope that he had been clutching tightly in his hands the entire time. Adora sank into the loveseat that faced the entrance foyer, and dropped her head in her hands, more from deep despair and sheer mental exhaustion than from any physical limitation.

Her father maintained his mechanical posture and sat there, an immobile, stone wall that seemed to defy her every effort to penetrate it.

"Dad, I am twenty-one after all. Can't you see I can take care of myself?" Her voice sounded strained, almost shrill in her vain effort to reach her father.

"Nonsense my dear," he countered. "I already told you what I think, and I don't want you in Lagos."

"Dad, I know what you think," she persisted. "But this is a great opportunity."

"Nonsense Adora," he repeated. "You do not have to go to Lagos. Enugu University has a perfectly good program that rivals the English program at the University of Lagos. Your brother Chike is doing perfectly fine at the Enugu campus."

"Dad, I know that, but he's taking law and I'm doing English. UNILAG—the University of Lagos has one of the best English programs in the country, and dad, don't forget the scholarship they offered-------."

"What about the scholarship?" he snapped. "I work very hard so that I can pay for my children's education."

Adora sprang from the chair like a tightly coiled spring and began to pace the floor again. Despite the artificially frigid air that poured out from the vents of the house's centrally controlled air, she felt an almost suffocating wave of heat that spread quickly across her face and neck; she fanned futilely at her face with the open palm of her right hand and walked towards the shuttered glass window that let in a stream of light through the gaps in the sweeping curtains.

On the windowsill, a lone bird perched and began to peck at a berry that rested on the outside ledge, fallen from the clump of trees that provided cooling shade from the searing tropical sun that launched its fiery attack in the dry, harmattan season, and the violent deluge of the tropical storms of the rainy season.

A sliver of sunlight sliced through the sheer window curtains and bounced off the glass surface of a wall clock that adorned the wall by the mantelpiece. The clock showed that it was six-thirty - almost time for her father to leave the house for work. As if on cue, he glanced at his watch, signaling that the conversation would soon come to a screeching halt.

Sensing that her father was losing patience with her Adora sighed wearily but stood her ground. She was not going to give up that easily. The scholarship that she had won into the University of Lagos meant that she would not have to ask her dad for money for any of her sundry student expenditure. Despite his great wealth, her father was prudent with money, and always required a detailed explanation for each Naira that trickled out of his pocket. But deeper than the money issue was another that lay buried deeply in her heart. Maybe the break would provide an escape from the pervading guilt that she carried about her mother's death like an almost physical weight, a dead weight that lay like a live thing in her heart, souring the joy and pride that should have accompanied all her academic triumphs.

From the distance came the proud crow of a rooster heralding the dawn of another day, piercing through the early morning quiet and the palpable tension that had settled in the air like a living, breathing thing. Her father glanced at his watch again and rose slowly from the couch.

"Six forty-five. I have to be at work at seven fifteen," he declared in the somber tones that had come to characterize him in recent years.

"And I believe I made myself clear; there won't be any more talk about Lagos will there?"

Without waiting for her response, he grabbed his briefcase and stethoscope from the side table and headed towards the front door. Adora watched in dismay as he marched purposefully down the cobblestone driveway, sat behind the wheels of his gray Porsche, revved the engine into life, and steered the car slowly towards the distance gates that protected the vast property.

◆ ◆ ◆

Clara Umeh paused before a table piled with an array of colorful produce ranging from fruits and vegetables to various assortments of dried fish. Behind the table sat a thin, graying woman wearing a brown caftan style blouse over a two-tiered georgette wrapper set, comforting a cranky, fidgety toddler.

"Oh Jacinta," she cajoled, "food is coming—you should drink some water first," she consoled the baby.

She offered a colorful plastic cup to the baby, who scrunched up her face and let out a loud wail; arms flailing in indignation as she spilled fat goblets of water down the woman's brown-checkered wrapper, drawing an instant reprimand.

"Jacinta, look what you've done," the woman complained as she dropped the baby on the floor. Her cross frown punctuated her complaint, as she rubbed briskly with the edge of her wrapper at the rapidly darkening spot on her brown wrapper. She reached for a plastic baby bottle, which was warming on a deep metal bowl set on the tabletop and shook the bottle hard, wincing as the white-hot liquid squirted onto her wrist.

The toddler reached for the bottle; her frustration evident on her face as her voice rose higher. The woman snatched her off the floor with a quick impatient motion and thrust the cup at her again.

"Too hot Jacinta, drink some water, food is coming," she instructed. In response, the baby scrunched up her face and let out another yell, as she snatched the bottle from the woman's hand and proceeded to nurse hungrily from it. The next instant, she dropped the bottle and let out a loud yelp, causing the woman to drop her on the bare floor again and spank her on her plump thigh.

"Didn't I tell you too hot? Why you no listen?" she scolded in Pidgin English.

The baby's loud wail sailed above the clamor of the outdoor market and the woman picked her up and thrust the water cup at her again, her face pinched into a tight frown of disapproval. The baby gulped down the water and coughed and sputtered, her face twisted into a mask of consternation. The woman's face softened as she rocked the baby and rubbed her back with slow, gentle movements. The baby's voice rose to a piercing crescendo and the woman's shoulders stooped in weariness.

Just then, a girl of about fourteen appeared from nowhere and stood hesitantly by them. The woman looked relieved and handed the baby to her.

"Mary, take care of your niece, what took you so long?" she demanded.

"Good afternoon mami, I went, I stopped at Nneoma's shed to-," Mary began, but the woman thrust the baby bottle in her hand and dismissed her with a quick wave of the hand.

"You know that you have to help me after school, and not gallivant off to some place or another. Now take care of your niece. I have work to do."

Mary disappeared behind a curtain that led off to an inner chamber, singing in a high-pitched voice, which soared above the clamor of the outdoor market.

"My little baby girl, when you cry you break my heart, you cry and break my heart, I will cry along with you. I cry along with you, it will break my mother's heart, I break my mother's heart, she will cry along with us. If mother cries with us, it will my make me very sad, If I am feeling sad, who will give you love and hugs?"

The baby's high-pitched voice blended with Mary's voice as she giggled and cooed and babbled along with Mary's lyrical jargon.

Clara shook her head and chuckled lightly, tickled by Mary's creativity.

"*Ewee*," the trader woman sighed. She sank on her chair and dabbed at the sweat trickling down her tired face with a checkered white handkerchief. Looking up, she noticed it seemed for the first time, the stout woman standing in front of her table. Her face took on a bright smile and she greeted Clara warmly, like an old friend.

"Madam Clara. Is it you? **Welicome**. You did well to come. I have everything you need. Dried fish, plantains, maybe some beans eh?"

Clara dropped her black canvas bag on a corner of the table and leaned towards the trader woman.

"Mama Maureen, how are you, are the children well?" she asked.

"Ah, the children are well. The baby is okay," the trader woman responded smiling brightly as she rearranged the piles of fruits on her trading table.

Clara smiled in acknowledgement and her eyes went to the curtain that separated Mama Maureen's stall from her private back room. The sounds of Mary lilting sing-song voice and the baby Jacinta's giggles came at intervals, intermingled with the sounds of the bustling market place.

"Mama Maureen, I see the baby Jacinta, she is certainly looking well, thank God for that, she is growing so fast," Clara remarked as she surveyed the table and pointed to a rack of dried asa fish piled high on a round red tray next to a large plastic pan half-filled with uncooked red beans. "How much for those?" she asked

Mama Maureen pulled out a stack of tin cups of various sizes from behind the pail. "Don't worry Madam Clara, I will take care of you."

"Good," Clara said. "And how is the baby's mother?"

A cloud fell across the woman's lined face and her brows knitted into a frown. "Maureen? Hah I have not heard from that child of mine since the day she left Jacinta here and ran off with that--- no good army man ----- I hear they got married in Abuja last month, but she didn't even tell me. Can you believe it? Never came home to seek my consent----- no wine-carrying or bride price offered by her so-called husband. Ever heard of such a thing? If only papa Maureen was alive, this kind of thing would never happen."

Clara shook her head in sympathy, and the trader woman continued, encouraged by Clara's commiseration.

"I didn't raise my daughter Maureen to behave like this. Such modern ideas. I worked so hard to send her to beauty school and she came back with a big stomach instead of a certificate. Madam Clara, my sweat and tears for nothing."

"No dear Mama Maureen," Clara said sympathetically. "You gained a lot. Look at that beautiful baby Jacinta."

"Oh yes, I thank God for her, but my daughter Maureen disappointed me. I was making plans for her to apprentice with Madam Fine Face Beauty Palace but she never even stepped foot in that place. My daughter changed before my very eyes. Started sneaking around and the next thing I knew, I was a grandmother. But the worst part is the way she dumped the baby with me and didn't even look back. I can't cry enough."

"Eeyah, I'm so sorry to hear that, Clara said, clucking her tongue. "What possessed her to do such a thing?"

"Madam Clara, I don't know," the trader woman began, shaking her head vigorously, which caused her headscarf to loosen and cascade to the floor in a bedraggled heap.

"I don't want to complain too much," she continued, picking up her headscarf and twirling in in her hand. "I thank God for my grandbaby, she's a blessing but my daughter is so heartless. Just dumped her with me three months ago and ran off to Abuja with that man. He never came to seek my consent or to see the kinsmen. Can you believe that? Well, as far as I'm concerned, she is still a spinster. I still pray that she will come to her senses one day soon," she concluded as she re-tied her headscarf.

"Oh, what a pity----children of nowadays," Clara remarked with genuine concern.

Mama Maureen rose from her stool and retied her over-wrapper, which was hanging loosely about her waist after her emotional outburst.

"Never mind my dear." She sighed. "God knows best. I am coping. I thank God for Mary, she is helping me with Jacinta, otherwise, I would have been in serious trouble. And what about your husband and the family, Madam Clara?" she asked in the same breath.

"Ah James, he is fine," Clara responded with a broad smile. "I cannot complain--."

"And your mistress's children? Eh, what a pity. Those poor children, motherless so young," Mama Maureen interjected.

A shadow flickered across Clara's face, so fleetingly, that one could have imagined it. The face that she turned to the trader woman was wearing a bright smile.

"My mistress's children? Those children, they are doing very well without the madam. In fact, they are just brilliant," she crowed with pride, as though the children in question were products of her own womb.

"Yes, I heard," the trader woman stated with a smile.

"My madam was a blessed woman although God saw fit to take her away from us so young and full of life. But, he knows best," Clara said, glancing skywards. "Her children are a real blessing - the oldest, Chike, he's studying law at Enugu University."

Mama Maureen nodded her head vigorously "So I heard. I heard the daughter is in University too."

"You mean Adora?" Clara planted her feet more firmly on the floor and leaned towards the trader woman.

"Adora graduated already. She graduated with full honors you know? And now she is ready for her Masters degree, and with a full scholarship -- a full scholarship, I say."

"Ndi okpokpo akwukwo, those book people. Mama Maureen stated in Ibo. "I don't blame her. If I went to school instead of marrying so early, I would have — who knows. But that is really good to hear," Mama Maureen remarked.

"Yep, that's my Adora, and only twenty-one," Clara boasted. "And don't even ask about the youngest one," she added for good measure. "That boy Uchenna is another story. He will probably end up a doctor just like his father.

"That is perfectly good," the trader woman stated, jangling the metal cups. signaling that she was ready to do business. Clara retied her wrapper around her waist and stood arms akimbo. "How much for the beans?" she began.

"This one is twenty Naira a cup, and this one is fifty Naira a cup," the trader woman replied, pointing at the smallest and the largest cup. Clara shook her head and lifted the larger cup. "I want this one, but fifty is too much."

The woman shook her head vigorously and ran the cup through the pile of dried beans.

"Ah Madame Clara!" she exclaimed. "These are premium beans, madam, from Abam. My customers love it.

"Hmm," Clara smiled and rifled through the big black handbag, tucked under her arm. She pulled out a wad of bills and rolled them tightly, then stuck them into her ample cleavage.

"Thirty Naira is more reasonable, and I want twenty cups," she said. Mama Maureen's face creased into a frown.

"Thirty Naira? How can I feed my children at that rate? That is below my cost price. I can only give you two Naira discount per cup. That is quite a lot Madam Clara."

"Thirty-five is all that I'm willing to pay," Clara insisted, glancing at the teenage boy, who was helping her to carry her groceries from stall to stall. The boy had stopped to chat with a young brown-skinned girl of about fifteen, who was wearing beaded braids and blue and white school pinafore. The girl noticed Clara's gaze and cast her eyes downwards. She mumbled something to the young boy, who laughed out loud and raucously, causing the young girl to hiss disdainfully, before flouncing away, her braids bouncing behind her.

Clara shook her head slowly and made a grimace. The young girls of nowadays are so forward, she thought sadly. It was a good thing that her Adora was nothing like those fast girls.

Mama Maureen cleared her throat, running the measuring cup through the pile of beans.

"I will buy thirty cups, but thirty-five Naira is all that I will pay," Clara told her. The woman made a face and started to measure the beans into a black plastic bag. "Madam," she said, looking pained as she measured.

"I have taken off a great deal of money. I will give you for forty-eight. That is almost my cost price.

"Then make it forty, and we are in business."

"No, no, no, I can't," the trader said firmly. "I am losing a lot of money already, believe me, Madam Clara."

"Then I will go to mama Obi," Clara said deliberately. She motioned to the young boy, who stood by, listening intently to the exchange between the two women; a toothpick sized chewing stick bobbing up and down in his mouth.

"Get my bags, we're leaving," Clara said to the boy. He hefted the huge bags into a makeshift cart, but the trader woman stopped him.

"What? That charlatan? She will cheat you; I know her very well. Did you know that she had a smithy place a false bottom in her measuring cup? Come back and I will give you at forty-two per cup. Clara smiled and pointed to the stack of dried fish on another table. "Good, I want some of those too."

◆ ◆ ◆

The metropolis of Enugu was beginning to make the usual transition towards dusk, bustling with activities, with people returning home from offices, shops, and the markets after another hectic day of enterprise. The street hawkers were beginning to come out, lured by the promise of a cool evening breeze, spreading their colorful wares on the side of the streets, calling out to passersby and motorists in sing-song voices,

"Maltex, buy my ice-cold delicious Maltex™."
"Oranges, look at these ripe and succulent oranges."

"Suya, who will buy my Suya?"

The distant call of the street vendors reminded Adora of the steady gnaw of hunger that she had tried to ignore all afternoon; she had raided the fridge earlier, and only came up with fresh fruit salad. She was tired of fresh fruit. Clara was still at the market, and dinner would not be served till eight.

The roman numerals on her watch indicated that it was four twelve p.m. Almost four hours to wait for a home cooked meal. The thought propelled her to her feet, and she grabbed her white straw hat and dashed out of her room, and down the back staircase that led to the kitchen. Her sandals on the parquet covered stairs clattered noisily and echoed across the silent house.

She stopped briefly at the foyer as she caught a glimpse of her reflection on the ornate gilt-framed mirror that hung near the entrance door. Her face stared back at her, exquisite, an almost flawlessly perfect oval framed by a cascade of dark wavy hair that grazed her bare shoulder blades, forming a stark contrast to her copper colored skin, which gleamed almost translucent in the softly waning sunlight that filtered through the window shades. Deep set, almost leonine eyes, framed by a fan of lush dark lashes underneath high arched eyebrows lent her face an almost feline grace, balanced by high, regal cheekbones and lips that straddled a fine line between sensuously seductive and perkily innocent.

Her eyes showed a bit of puffiness from lack of sleep and the tension that had settled inside her, coiling up in the pit of her stomach like a venomous snake ready to strike, forcing her to confront the unease that she had tried to conceal, even to herself about the fact that each moment that passed by spun her dangerously closer to the day that filled her with dread, the day that she would depart from the protective enclave of home and face an uncertain future. Would she fall on her face and return home a complete failure? Would she ever meet up with her father's high expectations of her?

Frowning, she flicked off an unruly lock of jet-black hair from her face with an impatient finger, and it sprang back to her face like a coil of tightly wound up black silk cord, falling over one half of her face as she ran out the door, past the driveway, and towards the entrance gate that guarded her family estate. She waved at the gate man, who sat motionless at his post, nodding before an open magazine.

Adora rattled at the gate and the startled gate man rubbed at his tired eyes, peering at her over the magazine, and frowning.

"Where are you going at this time?" heasked gruffly, trying unsuccessfully to sound alert.

"Nowhere far. Don't sleep too deep," she threw over her shoulders.

"Sleep?" he responded in a voice that smacked of defensiveness.

"No sleep for these eyes for the next six hours at least. My shift ends at ten," he said as he swung the large, ornate iron gates open, and Adora passed through.

"I'm going to Mama Franca's. Do you want me to bring you something?"

"Oh, no, I just ate," he stated, rubbing his stomach, which was bulging slightly under the loose drape of his dashiki.

At the end of Park Lane Road, tucked in a cul-de-sac, stood a wooden kiosk, painted garishly green, with a handwritten sign hanging from the wall, proclaiming the phrase, "MAMA FRANCA'S GARDEN OF EDEN, in large letters, and in smaller letters, "the best food in your life." The front awning of the kiosk was decked out with gaily-colored streamers. The sounds of African highlife blared from the interior, underscoring the most delectable aroma of mingled dishes that wafted out from the kiosk.

Without hesitation, Adora walked through the narrow entrance and stood on line behind a young boy in khaki shorts. A rotund, yellow-skinned woman in her late forties stood behind the counter, sweating profusely and ladling white rice and plantains onto a plastic bowl. She added chicken stew and handed the dish to the boy, who chewed his lower lip and shoved his hands deep into his pocket.

"Fifty Naira", she informed him in a loud voice that matched the yellow colored synthetic blouse that stuck to her ample bosom and competed with her bright yellow complexion.

"I have t,t,t,twelve mama F,F,F,Franca," the boy stammered hesitantly, shifting from foot to foot.

"Then pay me the rest tomorrow, **underless**, I won't serve you again." "T,Thank you mama Franca," the boy stuttered.

He grabbed the paper bag from the counter and dashed out of the kiosk, running smack into a stray dog, which wagged a mangy expectant tail and endured a swift kick at the ribs. The dog let out a yelp and jumped away, running into the path of an oncoming car, which careened towards the unpaved road shoulder, amidst a shrill shriek of brakes and a swirl of dust. The dog ran across the street and the boy threw a rock at it.

"One day, I will **raport** that bad greedy boy to his mother," mama Franca complained loudly to no one in particular, as she lifted the till and hid away the bulk of her money under a flat plastic board in the drawer.

Adora chuckled to herself at the quaint way that mama Franca manipulated the English language. Equipped only with a primary four education, mama Franca had managed to build a flourishing business out of her love for cooking. Her canteen had been a fixture in the neighborhood for as long as Adora could remember and was her regular haunt along with other kids from her school, who would throng into the kiosk after school and spend all their pocket money gorging themselves on mama Franca's delectable delicacies. Over the years, nothing had changed about Mama Franca's cooking, and Adora often found herself wandering into the canteen on those evenings when the hunger pangs gnawed at her stomach and she couldn't wait for the housekeeper to return from the market.

Mama Franca turned around from the till and saw Adora. Her eyes danced with merriment as she roared in her high decibel voice.

"Hey! ***Look who here today. Why you no come regular my dear?***"

"No particular reas-- - just a bit busy," Adora responded, looking around at the small room, illuminated by colorful lanterns that hung suspended from the canteen's low-slung ceiling. Her eyes wandered to the hand scrawled chalkboard menu riddled with spelling errors hanging on the wall behind the till and she skimmed through the special, wondering as she usually did why nobody had ever tried to correct Mama Franca's spelling on her menu, and then realizing that it didn't matter anyway, because her food was always delightful.

TODAY SPESHAL

'Rise and steu with plantens. Goat, foul or beef extra.
Rise and bins with plantens and fish.
Goat, foul or beef extra.
Very dilishos mai-mai with steu or
rise and fish.

Dilishos pepper soup with goat meat or fresh fish. Speshal prize.
Seek and you shall find. If you don't see it on the menu riqest for it.'

Mama Franca's eyes followed the direction of Adora's eyes and she smiled.

"What you want today?"

"Let me see, you have banana fritters?"

"No, my dear, no faritas today. What about Akara? They fresh. I just finish a batch."

"Sounds good," Adora said, sniffing the pungent air appreciatively.

"What else you want?" mama Franca goaded her.

"Only akara today thank you ma."

"Only?" Mama Franca exclaimed in a loud voice that filled the small space. She glanced at Adora's slim figure, clucked her tongue, and wagged a fat finger at her.

"My dear, I can't remember the last time I looked like this. Maybe never. *Anyway, you no go add weight, in fact, you need more meat if you ask me*."

"I'm not that hungry, just wanted to patronize you a bit," Adora retorted.

"Thas right my dear," Mama Franca exclaimed in her mixed-up English. *"Now you talking. You need to come more often. Mama Franca cook the best of everything. Better than those fancy restaurants in town*." Adora shook her head as Mama Franca bustled about and hummed a tune as she packed the golden and crispy balls of akara bean cake.

"*I hear say you get scholarship*," she began in Pidgin English. "*That is good my dear. You smart girl.*"

Adora's eyes widened slightly in surprise as she accepted the food wrapped neatly in a small brown paper bag, wondering how Mama Franca knew about her plans.

"Mama Franca, how did you know about this?" she verbalized her thoughts.

Mama Franca's eyes danced merrily, and she chuckled as she bustled around the tiny space.

"My daughter, good news is like pregnancy. You can keep it hidden for a while, but the belly will tell the story."

"So, whose mouth is the belly?" Adora was on the verge of asking, but she hesitated as Mama Franca turned her attention to a fresh group of customers, three young men in business attire who thronged into the small space and crowded around Adora. Although they were not directly in her line of vision Adora, could feel their lusty eyes drilling a hole through her. Ignoring them, she held her head high and waited for Mama Franca to ring up her order

One of the men planted himself beside Adora and eyed her boldly, grinning broadly from ear to ear. He opened his mouth but snapped it shut as Mama Franca's strident voice rang out, cutting across the room like a whip.

"Are you here to feast your eyes or is it your belly?"

Mama Franca's brusqueness suggested that she brooked no nonsense, customer, or no customer.

The man's mouth grew slack and his eyes grew round. He swallowed hard and kept staring at Adora, who paid mama Franca and made a hasty retreat, thankful for the woman's aggressive interjection. The three men stepped aside to let her through, but their eyes followed her.

"You want today's special or should I get you something else?" she heard Mama Franca say. The sounds of the men's voices followed her as she stumbled out of the canteen and stepped out on the street

"Wow! She is a beauty!" one of them exclaimed.

"My oh my, who is she? I have never seen her around here before," another said.

"Well, she is something else," came another, followed by Mama Franca's harsh voice. "When you ready to order, let me know."

Chapter 2

The strident ring of the telephone startled her as she stood over the kitchen sink, scrapping the remnants of the food into the garbage bin in a corner of the kitchen. She dried her hands hastily with a faded blue napkin that she snatched off a wooden peg by the sink and hurried up the staircase to her room, where she picked up her room extension.

The voice on the other end was young and excited, breaking as a result of approaching adolescence.

Adora settled on her pink covered bed and kicked off her slippers. "Uchenna! Where have you been?"

"At my friend Olu—you know – Oluyinka."

"I know, but what are you doing there so late?"

"We are studying Adora – but not to worry, I'll be home soon. Olu's mother just called from the office. She is on her way home and she promised to drop me off when she gets here."

"Okay, but don't keep her waiting either."

"No, I'm already all set to go, but hey! Guess what, guess what?" Uchenna began in the next breath. His voice rose sharply by several octaves, piercing through Adora's eardrums.

Adora almost dropped the phone, responding to the urgency in his voice.

"What?" she asked, half expecting her thirteen years old brother to spill out of the phone receiver and emerge in her bedroom, dancing from his live-wire excitement.

"I've got smashing good news, listen to this------."

"News- what news?" Adora interjected in a voice fraught with anxiety, visualizing her little brother's wiry body prancing around his best friend's room in his excitement.

"Oh, Adora, you won't believe this. Daddy said it's okay for you to go. Can you believe it? He actually said that you could go!"

His excitement was infectious, and Adora flipped off the BET broadcast beamed via satellite on the flickering television set in the corner of her room and stepped out barefoot to the balcony, squinting slightly as she caught sight of the brilliant orange orb in the sky dipping lower into the horizon, turning the fluffy clouds a translucent blend of cotton candy shades.

She lowered herself on a white wicker balcony chair and tapped impatient fingertips on the glass-topped patio table by the chair. "You see, I pierced through daddy's indifference. I broke his resistance. I persuaded him to let you go," Uchenna's excited, almost lyrical tone broke into her muse.

"Go where, Uchem, what are you talking about?" she addressed him by her favorite endearment for him, an abbreviated form of his name Uchenna.

"UNILAG, that's where, the University of Lagos."

"Wow! But how did you manage that?" Adora asked, making an effort to hide her amusement.

"Oh I was relentless Adora. I told dad that it would be a mistake not to let you go. I told him that letting you take the UNILAG offer would be in your best interest for your graduate studies, considering the scholarship."

"Nice touch Uchem," Adora said.

"Yeah baby," Uchenna crowed in a singsong voice.

"I reeled him in there------I told him that UNILAG's offer was by far-- more comprehensive than the one that Nsukka offered you. I was so persuasive that dad agreed with me--- just like that. Can you believe it?" "What? You persuaded dad. How did you manage that?" Adora muttered,

feeling a stab of guilt at the deceit that she was practicing against her little brother. But his triumph at his conviction that he had helped her battle her father was so contagious that she did not have the heart to let him down and reveal that she had finally pierced through her father's resistance. Her father had relented only on the condition that Adora would stay with her mother's sister Aunt

Agatha, who happened to be a History Professor at the University of Lagos and had indicated on the phone that she would be thrilled to accommodate her niece. Adora was secretly pleased since Aunt Agatha was one of her most favorite people, with the added bonus that she lived in a beautiful villa overlooking Lekki beach.

"You made Dad proud, you know," Uchenna said suddenly, breaking into Adora's train of thoughts

"Proud?" she found herself echoing Uchenna's words incredulously, feeling relieved as she realized that her little brother had relieved her of the burden that she had been carrying around for days, the burden of breaking the news to him that she would be leaving home soon. He had discovered it for himself in the process of trying to fight her battles for her. Buoyed by the incredible feeling of relief that pervaded her entire being, she felt lighter than the pure cleansing air that she pulled into her lungs as the leaden weight that she been carrying in her heart floated away in the wind behind Uchenna's words.

The tension, which had settled over her shoulders like fingers of ice for the past few weeks, melted like magic, and her heart soared with a confluence of conflicting emotions culminating in a feeling of giddiness.

"Yeah, dad really is proud of you, and did you know that the kids at my school are all talking about you?"

"Talking about me?" Adora echoed.

"Yep! Only yesterday, Elota Uwakwe was holding court with a bunch of kids during

lunch at the canteen. Do you know what he said?"

"No, what did he say?" Adora mumbled, feeling a mixture of amusement and puzzlement.

"Well—he said that his big sister Chinasa went to under grad school with you. He mentioned that she is kind of jealous. Do you know her?"

"Know who?"

"His big sister Chinasa. She went to your schoo---."

"Nsukka is a large campus," Adora said evasively, barely containing her amusement, tinged with a hint of ironic contempt. Did she know Chinasa? Did she know Chinas Uwakwe with the pinched bird face and the horsy laugh? The question was who didn't? Known as the campus know-it-all, Chinasa had her nose in everyone's business, and knew all the latest news and gossip even before they happened. Adora still had a bitter taste in her mouth thinking about Chinasa.

"Well Elota said she knows you," Uchenna continued excitedly.

"She went to your school, and she knows about you. You should have heard Elota go on. Do you know what he said?

"What did he say"? Adora asked.

'Hear this. He said, my big sister's stupid anyway; all she thinks about is clothes and boys. He really said that about his sister Chinasa. Can you believe that?" Uchenna said with a light chuckle and Adora joined half-heartedly for she was feeling far from gay - she literally had to bite her tongue to keep from speaking her mind about Chinasa, who had tried to spread a rumor about her to the effect that she slept her way to good academic ratings. If only Chinasa knew, the irony was that she had not even kissed a man yet. And she couldn't say the same of Chinasa, but like her friend Chiaka Ndukwe always said, "It takes a slut to know a slut."

Uchenna was still chattering about Elota Uwakwe's rendition of his sister Chinasa and Adora made all the appropriate noises, strongly resisting the urge to rip into Chinasa's character. One thing was clear to her- she stood in complete agreement with Uchenna's friend Elota's assessment of his sister's stupidity.

A tiny black speck whizzed past her face, buzzing most annoyingly close to her ears. It was nearing the end of the rainy season and rain always brought those pesky gnats towards nightfall. Their sting often left an itchy rash that was even more annoying than the resulting scar that marred the skin for a few months before disappearing. Thankfully, the cool, centrally controlled air that circulated around the house kept most of them out save for a few strays that always managed to find their way inside the house only to expire at the vents of the air conditioners.

Adora waved her hand in front of her face and the insect zipped off in a zigzag pattern, brushing against her cheek and perching on her bare knee. She picked up a magazine from the patio table and swatted firmly at it, thinking of Chinasa as the insect escaped and whizzed past her face, perching on the railing of the balcony. She rose from her chair and swatted at it again, and it flew gleefully towards the sunset.

Adora went inside and shut the door against the tropical fauna that were beginning to gather around the house, drawn by sweet smelling nectar of the tropical flowers that surrounded the house.

The increasing sounds of a car engine reached her ears, and she rushed to the window, leaning close to the pane. She parted the curtains and leaned forward, craning her neck to get a better view of the driveway through the thick tangle of climbing plants that always filtered the brightness of the morning and kept her room cool.

A gray Porsche shot to the west part of the driveway and stopped abruptly amidst a spray of gravel in front of the two-car garage by the guesthouse.

"Daddy's home. I don't believe it," she told Uchenna.

"Dad home? You sure about that? It's only some minutes after six."

"I don't believe it either, and you won't believe the way he was driving, but I have to go now - come home soon," she instructed Uchenna, and pressed the off button, dropping the cordless phone casually on the window ledge.

She clambered off the window seat and ran to her spacious closet, where she picked out a baggy pair of jeans, and jumped into it, leaving the short skirts that she had been wearing, folded underneath her pillow.

Sitting on the pink-carpeted floor of the closet, she pulled on her sandals and hurried downstairs to greet her father.

Chapter 3

He strode past the white-painted foyer into the cool teal living room, taking long, confident steps, pausing briefly to survey the room, and then walking towards the white leather sofas arranged in a hexagonal pattern around the large room. His build was lean and athletic, and his bearing was proud, and erect. He wore a tailored blue denim shirt, tucked into carpenter's jeans, and his feet were encased in blue and white Nike joggers. A tan leather overnight bag crammed nearly to over flowing was slung casually over his shoulder.

He was tall, about six feet three, in his early twenties, with the chiseled good looks of a brown-skinned Adonis. His face was handsome and rugged, and his smile, when he looked up and saw her on the stair landing, was bright and infectious. His evenly spaced, white teeth flashed as he quickened his steps towards her and she bounded down the stairs in his direction, letting out a shrill shriek of excitement.

He tossed his bag casually on the carpet and it flew open, spitting textbooks, rolled up clothing, and a green bottle of after-shave lotion all over the place.

He sidestepped the mess on the floor and faced her with a big grin on his face and his arms wide open.

"Chike! Oh my gosh, what are you doing home?" Adora shrieked gleefully, hurtling into his strong, waiting arms.

"Hey little sis," he said breezily, as he swept her easily off her feet, whooping exuberantly; he swung her around in the air like a child, making the room to spin around in a dizzying circle. She clawed at his shoulders and he placed her down gently, holding out a steadying hand as she swayed unsteadily; she clutched tightly on to him as the living room whirled crazily around her.

"Sheesh, Chike, you know I hate that," she breathed, leaning heavily against him.

"You used to love that remember?" he said teasingly.

"Yeah, back when we were kids," she shot back.

"And now you are so old huh sis," Chike chuckled.

Adora threw him a searing glance and shook her fist at him in mock anger.

"Wait till I get my hands on you Chike Amadi. You won't know what hit you," she

said tersely, jabbing playfully at his taut stomach. He lurched forward, keeled over and dropped heavily on the white sofa, groaning low in his throat, his face contorted into a mask of agony.

Adora's heart skipped a beat and she dropped to her knees in panic. Chike slid from the sofa to the carpeted floor and his limbs jerking spasmodically and Adora dropped on her knees beside him and instinctively placed her fingers on his pulse as she often saw her father do when a person was in medical trouble.

"Chike, you okay?" she blurted anxiously, feeling for his pulse, which beat strong and steady under her thumb.

Chike's body continued to quiver and Adora realized in that split second that he was shaking with laughter.

Relief flooded through her tense body, replaced quickly by a white-hot anger as Chike suddenly stood up and pulled her up alongside him.

She regarded him with narrowed eyes and shook her index finger at him.

"How dare you Chibuike Amadi? You've gone too far this time," she remonstrated in a voice that was tight with anger, calling him by his full appellation, which she usually did when she was angry with him.

"Oh c'mon now, lighten up a bit," he chuckled. "Lighten up? Is that all you have to say?"

"You used to enjoy a joke or two," Chike shot back. "Now I see you've changed in more ways than one."

He let out a low whistle and studied her, his eyes twinkling with amusement. "Who are you? And what have you done with my little sister Adora?"

"And what have you done with that skinny boy that used to be my brother?" she shot back.

Chike stroked his neatly trimmed mustache thoughtfully and looked directly at her.

"Seriously, sis, you've grown so beautiful. Dad may be right about his stance of not wanting you to go you know, someone may steal you away at that University."

Adora dismissed his words with a quick wave of her hands.

"Isn't it a little early to be home?" she asked. "I thought your final examss aren't over till Friday."

Chike rubbed his stomach and grinned.

"Clara's cooking?" she exclaimed. "I knew it, you greedy brother of mine."

"Baby sis, you don't understand. I grew tired of the mush that they call food at the campus cafeteria, and Clara's food is going to make up for all my suffering," he chuckled.

"But your exams, you haven't completed your finals," Adora countered.

"I know that, but did you actually think that I'd just let you go like that? I got your message and I rushed right over – to persuade you not to leave - okay - the truth this time, I came to give you my moral support – and don't worry, I'm done with all my exams – except for Prof. Odili's course – I explained the situation to her and she agreed to let me take a make- up when I return. But two things

– how did you pull this off, and why are leaving so soon?" he asked in one breath.

Adora found herself chuckling at the look on her brother's face.

"It was a major battle for dad to let me go," she began. "We went through a sort of face-off, but in the end, I had to fight for what I believe in. I'm twenty-one and I have to stand up for myself. I know it's hard to believe, but dad finally caved, and I didn't want to push it."

"Oh, so that's why you are leaving so soon?" Chike asked, stroking the hair on his chin thoughtfully.

"Exactly. I don't want him to give him the chance to change his mind. Besides, I also wanted to give myself time to settle in before school starts."

Chike threw himself at her feet and grabbed her ankles.

"Please don't go. I will be a better brother, I promise," he said dramatically.

"Hey Chike, cut it out," Adora remonstrated.

But Chike clutched tighter at her ankles.

"Was it anything I did? Is that why you are running to Lagos? I need you at Enugu campus. You don't understand-----I used to be so popular in campus because of you – the prettiest and the brainiest girl in campus--- my sister. Now I feel so abandoned."

"C'mon Chike-------," Adora began, "Enough of the drama Mr. Chike drama king. Chike's eyes lit up as he rose and settled next to her on the couch.

"Sis, on a serious note, I'm really happy for you –of couse I have to admit that I will miss you a lot, it just won't be the same without you."

His voice betrayed the tenderness that he had been hiding under his jocular attitude and suddenly, the tight rein of control that Adora had erected so carefully over her emotions slipped, and she found herself fighting tears. As though sensing the turmoil within her Chike held her close and gently ruffled the thick, shoulder length hair that swept over her tear-streaked face. Tenderly, he wiped a tear that had found its way down the bridge of her nose and patted her shoulder.

"Don't worry darling," he murmured. "Lagos is not the North Pole - besides, there's always the holidays, the postman, the telephone, email, cell phone, and if possible, I'll use mental telepathy."

Adora giggled, feeling a sudden wave of shame at her bout of self-pity. She rose from the chair and grabbed Chike's overnight bag.

"I'd better take these up to your room before Clara finds this mess and lays an egg," she said in a voice that she hoped sounded light, as she gathered the remainder of Chike's possessions that lay scattered on the couch and crammed them into the bag.

Chike stood next to her and placed a hand on her shoulder. "Relax sis, I'll take care of that later---."

"Shh," Adora interjected as she headed towards the staircase with Chike's bag. "I won't stop taking care of you now."

His bedroom was a masculine contrast to her airy, pink-carpeted one. The neutral shades of the gray carpet and the black lacquered dresser on the corner against the stark white wall gave the room a Spartan look. It was bare, except for the full-size bed in the corner, the black dresser that abutted the wall across from the bed and the big study table that was positioned next to the bare window. Chike loved a lot of light, and as a heavy sleeper, he needed the first rays of the sun to wake him up every morning.

The room smelled faintly of old leather and starched sheets, and the musty, closed feel of an unused room lent the room a slightly claustrophobic feel, despite the airiness. Adora went to the window and rotated the louver handle to let in some air. A cool breeze wafted in from the garden and Adora leaned closer to the

window and raised her face towards the sweet caress of the gentle wind, drinking in the sweet-scented air.

The roof of the guesthouse was closer to Chike's window and looked like an undulating sheet of russet glass in the orange glow of the sunset. The guava trees beside the guesthouse waved a lopsided salute in the evening breeze and the green fruits dangled heavily from the branches.

The sun was making a lazy descent from the sky, setting ablaze the glorious scenery with a fiery display of vibrant color. The flower hedges that brimmed with the blooming colors of tropical plants seemed to burst into flames in the brilliant glow of the tropical sunset. In the distance, clumps of green covered dunes huddled in clusters, edged by tall slender trees that swayed gracefully to the drum roll of a cool breeze, which whistled in occasionally from the surrounding Udi hills. Beyond the lush stretch of the cultivated green lawn near the entrance gate, a slender seedling stood proudly in solitary magnificence, dancing to the beat of the wind, like a silent dancer twirling and taking his bow amidst the whistling applause of the wind.

In the distant gatehouse, the gateman was leaning against the fence, chatting up a fruit vendor. From that distance it was difficult to make out her face, but Adora suspected it was Adamma, the pretty daughter of the local seamstress. Everyone in the neighborhood knew that Sani was getting more than just fruit from her. Adora wondered if Adamma knew about Sani's wife and three kids living in Sabon Gari in the North, but then, it was none of her business.

The sound of laughter drew Adora's attention as she made her way downstairs from Chike's room. In the living room, she found her brother engrossed in conversation with a beautiful girl of about twenty, who sat across from him, sipping a citrus colored ice-filled liquid from a tall fluted glass and munching on some homemade pastry from a hand painted ceramic bowl on the console table. She was wearing a very tight black tank top embellished with a scattering of a glittery material that threw off iridescent lights, over a pair of skimpy jeans, rolled up at the hem, showing off her shapely brown legs.

"Hey Adora, I'm glad you're home," she said airily, as soon as Adora descended the last rung of the staircase.

"Amaka, what are you doing here, how did you get here? I thought you were supposed to travel to Umuahia for your big sister's traditional wine carrying," said Adora, who suspected strongly that her friend was there because of Chike.

Amaka Ohaneme was Adora's friend from the time that they were both at Ekulu, an exclusive grade school near the Okere mansion. Lately, she seemed to have developed a sixth sense radar that always drew her to the Amadi mansion whenever Chike was around.

Adora knew that Amaka harbored an unrequited crush for Chike for as long as she could remember, she and an army of girls from Adora's undergraduate university days, and Adora sensed that Chike knew it, even relished it; but his heart was somewhere else. A mystery girl named Karen whom Adora had never met.

Amaka rose from the couch and placed her drink on the marble console table by the wall, and did a little pirouette that displayed her lean, lithe figure.

"Yay," she jubilated. "Iheoma is finally getting hitched, thank God. No more sharing space with a mean, bossy half-sister, and I won't have to hear anymore of her moaning and groaning about her bad luck with men – if you ask me, I think that she created her own troubles. Anyway jare, I'm still traveling to Umuahia, but on Monday; and, I trekked over here from the gate, my aunt dropped me, and your brother was standing outside when I got here."

She pulled Adora away from Chike, close to the sweeping window that gave a panoramic view of the garden and leaned close to Adora. "Swear, don't tell this to a soul," she whispered conspiratorially. "I know that you can keep a secret otherwise I won't tell you. The real reason that Iheoma is getting married is because," she stole a glance at Chike, who was now standing on the stairs landing, talking into his cell phone. "The real reason that she is getting married is because she is pregnant for Okechukwu."

Adora's head snapped towards Amaka, and her mouth formed a silent O. "Okechukwu – the one from America? Didn't she just meet him in May, just three

months ago, and wasn't she going with---?"

Amaka clapped her hand over Adora's mouth and glanced nervously at Chike, who was now sitting on the stairs landing, scratching his neatly trimmed beard thoughtfully as he spoke into his flip phone.

"Shhhh," Amaka cautioned. "Don't let him hear. Ihuoma dumped the Professor a while back because – get this. She says he does not have enough income and she does not trust him with the campus girls. I guess she doesn't want the same thing done to her that she did to his ex. Anyway, their affair is now ancient history."

"But she hardly even knows this dentist American Naija guy. Wasn't it just three months ago that she met him?"

*"**Na she sabi**,"* Amaka remarked in Pidgin English. "Anyway, she is an adult. She wants to go to America – and she says that Okechukwu is very a successful, elitist--."

Amaka stopped mid-sentence and glanced coyly, out of the corner of her eyes at Chike, who had just concluded his phone conversation and was now striding towards them.

Adora was brimming with questions about Amaka's half-sister, Iheoma, the first daughter of Chief Ohaneme's first wife, fondly known as Mama Iheoma. Amaka was the product of a polygamous family and her mother, the third and the youngest wife of Chief Silas Ohaneme was by nature competitive and petulant – always wanting to outdo the chief's other wives and their children. Adora was sure it was only a matter of time before Mama Amaka would begin to mount pressure on Amaka to find a richer and more educated husband than her rival's daughter. What puzzled Adora most was the fact that the chief would give his daughter away to a total stranger. It couldn't be the financial gain - Chief Ohaname was independently wealthy and did not need the money or the bride price that would come with the betrothal.

But her questions could wait for another time as Chike was standing right next to them, full of his own questions.

"What are you ladies whispering about?" he asked with an easy smile. "Nothing, just girl business," Amaka said demurely, shrugging her shoulders.

"None of your business, and who were you on the phone with," Adora asked saucily.

"None of your------," Chike began, but Adora glared at him, and his handsome face melted into a disarming smile.

"Guess who? Our little bugger," he said fondly. "You mean Uchenna?"

"Yeah, Uchem. And he's on his way home now."

"Great, I love your little brother," Amaka gushed. "He's so brilliant.

"And what does that make me? Pounded yam?" Chike asked and Amaka giggled.

"N—no, you kidding? It's not so easy to be a law student," she remarked.

"Then you should see my grades," Chike began. "A pathetic C in trigonometry. That's what my test scores say." He winced and sank slowly into his chair.

Adora stared at him hard, noting for the first time a barely perceptible hint of dark shadows lurking beneath the sparkle of his brown eyes. She sat next to him and patted him gently on his arm. Amaka sat on the seat across from them and nodded sympathetically.

"But that's not so bad Chike, just one C," she said.

"That's right, Adora agreed. "A C in one subject is not exactly the end of the world," she stated in a voice that she hoped sounded reassuring. "Considering that you cleared your other papers – didn't you say that professor Odili would let you do a make-up test? That should boost your average I'm sure."

Chike shot her an annoyed look "Well go tell that to dad. You should have been there when I broke the news to him at the clinic – the first thing he wanted was a rundown of my results."

"So that's how you got his car?" Adora asked. "I was so surprised and happy to see you earlier that I forgot to ask."

"Yeah, I took the bus in from campus. The fares have gone up drastically and I was a bit short of cash."

"Inflation – story of life in this country," Adora declared.

"Why do you think I went to see popsy first? Asked him for a bit of cash and all I got was the third degree about how no son of his should be a failure and blah blah blah, he couldn't even wait for us to get home to start with the lectures.," Chike announced tersely as he rose abruptly from his chair and began to pace nervously around the spacious living room.

"I am so sorry Chike," Amaka offered.

"Hopefully, he'll cool off by the time that he gets home, which may be never at the rate that he's going," Adora added.

"Of course, I got the standard lecture, about how no firstborn son of his should be a loafer etc. etc.," Chike complained.

A vein throbbed at his temple and he wandered aimlessly to the window where he stood, staring out morosely at the vista of rolling green lawn and the brightly hued flower hedges, now shrouded by the waning orange purple light of dusk. Beads of perspiration stood in tiny clusters across his temple and he made to pull off his shirt, but glanced at his sister and her friend, and thought better of it.

He walked instead to the air conditioning unit that stood on the window, whirring softly, and turned it on at full tilt. A blast of cold air poured out of the vents and struck Adora's bare neck and arms with frigid fingers of ice. She shivered and rubbed briskly at the goose bumps that stood out on her bare arms as she rushed to the west window and threw the panes open, leaning into the warm air of the gathering dusk.

Outside, Musa had finished mowing the lawn, and was clipping the hedges, stopping to wave at them. Adora waved back and turned to find Amaka and Chike by her side.

"I think that your dad is a bit hard on you guys. One C should not be a big deal," Amaka began. Adora shook her head and flicked a rogue shock of hair off her face.

"You don't know the half of it. You don't know my dad. Did you know that today is his day off?"

Chike gave her a look as if to say, 'poor thing, you don't even know your own father.'

"And you're surprised because?" he stated.

"My point exactly," Adora responded. "You can't blame dad sometimes. He got this far because he worked super hard. I guess he can't help but judge us by his own standards."

"Standards!" Chike blurted in a voice oozing with bitterness. "His standards are too high."

"I wouldn't lose too much sleep over this. One solitary C should not bring the world crashing down around you. And trigonometry's not even a required course for you. You're studying law for peace sakes."

"Try telling that to dad. If I didn't take trig' I'm not challenging myself enough, so I caved in and took trig and what happens? My points go crashing down and now I have more problems than I started out with. God forbid that an Amadi child should come home with less than perfect grades. You forget what happened when I chose Law instead of the Sciences?"

"Now, really Chike, you need to stop this. You know that you gave it your best shot. That's the important thing," Adora said in a voice that she hoped sounded soothing.

"Oh yeah-- of course I forgot, my little brother Uchenna, the genius more than made up for the disappointment that his first son turned out to be," Chike said in a self-depreciating tone.

"So why don't you make that work for you?" Adora asked. "How do you mean?".

You know how good Uchenna is at the sciences." "So, what has that got to do with my dilemma?" "You should make him your plan B."

"Plan B?"

"Yeah! Why don't you let him coach you in trig? If you can make up for the C next time, that will push up your scores again."

Chike peered at her like she had lost her mind. "You've got to be kidding me right?" he exclaimed.

Amaka fluffed up her hair and patted her pert hip. She gave Chike an encouraging smile

"No, I think it's a good idea. A prophet is not recognized in his own country. You know the gift that your little brother has."

"She's right you know," Adora agreed. "You know that Uchenna can do it if anybody can,"

"I really think that he should be your plan B," Amaka suggested.

"That's really swell. Now I've got to swallow my pride and let the little runt talk me my head off."

Adora glared at him. "Now enough self-pity – pull yourself up and shift to plan B."

Chapter 4

He had risen from the debilitating ashes of poverty to claim his place among the annals of Nigerian medicine. A resolute man of fifty-nine, the Amadi patriarch, Dr. Chidi Amadi knew first-hand the value of a good education and hard work. He was the only son of a yam farmer. His father Udoye Amadi was a strapping man, who toiled day and night to eke out a living from the meager harvests of the unyielding land of the Udi region. His mother Nnenna did her part by planting vegetables for sale at the market, but their efforts were barely enough to sustain the small family. Chidi grew up wearing hand me down clothes that hung around his bony structure and made him the object of caricature amongst his more fortunate peers. Growing up, he had to pick up odd jobs now and then to augment the little money that trickled into his father's hands.

At thirteen, Chidi found a job as a shoemaker's apprentice. He would run home after school and eat his lunch, then run to the Obgete market where his employer had a shop. One day at the shop he overheard a well-dressed female customer remark to her companion that she needed a gardener. By this time, Chidi had turned fifteen, and was in secondary school. He was interested enough to run after the woman as she was leaving the store and offer his services.

"Young man, what do you know about being a gardener?" the woman asked superciliously. Chidi knew enough about gardening from his Agricultural Science courses at school and from helping his mother cultivate her cassava and vegetable farm to convince the woman. She hired him on the spot and offered him a laughable salary for a gardener. Chidi took the job without hesitation. He was grateful that he was making almost double what he was earning at the shoemaker's shop.

The new employer, Mrs. Nwabeze was exacting and extremely demanding. In addition to tending to the garden, Chidi also inherited the backbreaking work of handyman and pool boy at the cavernous mansion perched at the top of Udi hills where she lived with her husband. Chidi had never seen such opulence in his life. He never visualized that it was possible for anybody to live in such luxury. The smooth marble floor that ran through the entire house, the golden fixtures that adorned the house, the sprawling size of the estate and the beautiful landscaped garden were things that he never imagined were attainable.

His employer's husband was the honorable Justice Nwabeze, the Chief Magistrate of the high court in the East Central.

State region, with an office at the Enugu high court. He was a rotund man with a receding hairline who loved to parade around the house wearing the stifling magistrate robe and the stiff white wig, practicing his briefs. The maid and the gateman often laughed themselves silly imitating Chief Magistrate Nwabeze, but not Chidi. Chidi made a big decision right there at the house of Chief Magistrate and Mrs. Nwabeze. He was going to escape the stifling poverty that kept his parents' hands coarse and callused from constant farm work. His future children would never have to struggle like him. He had a game plan.

He set the first step of his game plan into motion when he passed his West African School Leaving Certificate exams with flying colors. His parents were elated, and his father told him that he could join the family business. But Chidi had bigger plans – he would go into the university. He would become a Chief Magistrate like Mr. Nwabeze, and he would pave the way for a better life for his future generation.

For Chidi Amadi, money was a big stumbling block. Despite all the money he had saved working at the shoe shop and from his job at the Nwabeze residence, he was still short of the money that it would take to put himself through University.

Through sheer tenacity, he landed a job as a Statistical Clerk at the Ministry of Works at the Secretariat in Enugu.

He kept his job at the home of Chief Magistrate and Mrs. Nwabeze, and every day at three on the dot, he would jump onto his rusty old bicycle and race across town and up the hill to the home of Chief Magistrate and Mrs. Nwabeze to begin his second shift as gardener.

For five long years, he saved frugally, putting away as much money as he could, wearing only a pair of shoes until he wore them out, while preparing for the Joint Admission and Matriculation Board exams that would qualify him for entry into a University.

His hard work eventually paid off. At the age of twenty-two he gained admission into the Ahmadu Bello University in Zaria with a full scholarship. He concentrated in Biology, his favorite subject and proceeded to blaze a brilliant academic path. In no time he won the respect and admiration of his professors, as well as his peers. Soon, a mentor materialized in the person of Dr. Mustapha Abubakar, the Dean of Students, who recognized the potential that burned in young Chidi Amadi. At lecture hall one day, he told him something that changed the course of his life.

"Young man," Dr. Abubakar said in his raspy, high-pitched voice, pulling him aside after a particularly challenging day in the lags. "The country needs a lot of young people like you,"

"I think that you should be a doctor, mark my words young man." Chidi took Dr. Abubakar's advice and the rest was medical history.

◆ ◆ ◆

The doctor picked up the chart, and nodded at the nurse, who was taking the patient's temperature.

"One hundred degrees Doctor," the nurse said, glancing anxiously at his drawn face. Nurse Uchendu had worked for Dr. Chidi Amadi for the past ten years. To Nurse Uchendu, there were two sides of Dr. Chidi Amadi — the pre- and the post Dr. Amadi. The pre- Dr. Amadi was a compassionate, easygoing man, who had a permanent twinkle in his eyes and lived and breathed for his wife and children. The post Dr. Amadi was this embittered, brittle humorless shell of the former man, a man that lived only for work and his patients. And it was all because of the car accident, a tragic mishap that claimed the life of his wife and snatched the very essence of the man.

The doctor picked up the patient's wrist and felt for her pulse, glancing at his watch.

"Pressure?" he asked nurse Uchendu, who stood over the patient, pumping the pressure cuff device around the woman's bony arms.

"One fifty over eighty."

The patient craned her neck towards the doctor. "Will I live Doc'?" she joked, pulling back her parched lips into something that held the semblance of a smile.

"Your blood test shows that you have a combination of malaria and a viral infection. You need complete bed rest and you must complete the medication combination that I am going to prescribe. Are you allergic to any medication?"

"Not that I know of Doc'," the patient said wearily, sagging back on the gurney. "What about antibiotics, Quinine?"

"Ah yes Doctor, the malaria medicine makes me itch."

Dr. Amadi nodded and wrote something on her chart. He tore off a prescription pad and wrote something on it.

"I will give you Fancidar Mrs. Aladi. It does not have the itching reaction that Chloroquine could have, and you only need three doses, but you must take all of it. Do you understand?"

"Yes Doctor, I will do as you say."

"Paging doctor Amadi. Dr. Amadi, you are needed in Pediatric Room 369," a female voice came over the intercom system. Dr. Amadi glanced at his watch and handed the paper to Mrs. Aladi.

"You have to drink plenty of fluid and get a lot of rest. As we live in a tropical country, you cannot eradicate mosquitoes, but you can take certain steps to prevent their bites."

"Right Doc."

"Plastic meshes keep most of them out. You can also let the ceiling fan stay on during the evening. It drives them away since they thrive only in moist and warm environments. And of course, you know about the coil and the light. Those work wonders too. I do not recommend the spray since their fumes can be toxic."

"Thanks Doctor, I will do as you say," Mrs. Aladi said.

"Nurse, please complete Mrs. Aladi's chart. I am needed in Pediatrics." "Right Doc," nurse Uchendu said, as

Doctor Amadi turned to the patient. "Stay well Mrs. Aladi," he told her.

"Thanks Doc," she sighed, sagging back into the gurney.

Doctor Amadi grabbed his stethoscope and rushed out of the room. In the hallway, a fair-skinned man of about forty, wearing the green hospital scrubs of an intern stood in his path.

"I need your help Dr. Amadi, can you spare a minute?" he asked, scratching his beard thoughtfully.

"I'm on my way to Pediatrics, but give it to me in a nutshell," Dr. Amadi said brusquely.

"I have a Geriatric in room 250 who OD'ed on his pressure medicine. I just need-----"

"Is he lucid?" Dr. Amadi cut in.

"Yes sir," the Intern said. "He seemed a bit confused, but he came in on his own, and he brought the pill bottle with him."

"Start the pumping procedure immediately … give him a shot of Nitro to arrest heart failure. I will send Dr. Emenike to assist you."

"Thanks doc," the intern responded, staring at Dr. Amadi's rapidly retreating back and shaking his head in wonder at the way that the man drove himself.

Dr. Amadi rushed down the long hallway, towards room 369. He paused briefly at the reception desk, which was near the entrance of room 369. A middle-aged woman sat behind the switchboard, trying to look alert, while nodding behind her tinted spectacles.

Dr. Amadi leaned towards her and rapped sharply on her desk. "Wake up Justina," he said sharply. Her eyes flew open and a look of panic crossed her tired face. She snatched the glasses from her face and rubbed wearily at her eyes with the back of her hand.

"I am sorry sir. It's just that I was up all night. The baby has colic."

"You have to think about the image of this clinic. This won't do," Dr. Amadi cut her off.

Justina wilted, and her red-rimmed eyes stared out of a face lined by weariness. "Sorry sir, I am truly sorry sir."

"Page Dr. Emenike immediately. Tell him to assist Dr. Lateef in room 250." "Right away sir," Justina said, jabbing at a button on the switchboard.

"And try a warm water bottle. It does wonders for colic. Remind me for the rest of the remedy for colic before I leave."

"Thanks Doc. This won't happen again," Justina murmured, and spoke clearly into the receiver.

"Paging doctor Emenike----."

Dr. Amadi shook his head as he hurried towards room 369. He just couldn't understand why some people would continue having kids like that, especially at her age, she was pushing fifty. Justina was nursing a five-month old baby boy- and that was her seventh child, her only son. She had arrived at the age when a woman should ease into the process of middle age with grace and none of the worries of motherhood, but the office grapevine identified her husband Sunday Aku as the culprit behind her prolific procreation. He wanted a son and Justina had been giving birth to nothing but girls. The story went that at each delivery, Sunday would stand outside the delivery room, waiting for word about the baby's sex.

As soon as the baby was pronounced a girl, he would leave the hospital, refusing to touch the baby or speak to Justina. When the sixth child turned out to be a girl, he moved out of the house and sent his relatives to ask her for a divorce. Justina sent her aging parents to him, and they persuaded him to return home to her.

When Justina took in again for the seventh time, Sunday moved out again, complaining bitterly to anybody who cared to listen that he was not going to raise a harem. Then the news came to him that his wife had delivered a bouncing baby boy, and Sunday returned jubilantly, and slaughtered a cow to celebrate his first son. Now Justina had seven small children and a full-time job to keep her busy. She was often late for work and her performance seemed to be getting worse by the day; but Dr. Amadi did not have the heart to let her go. She had been with him at the clinic from the inception when he was struggling to build up his clinic.

Dr. Amadi rushed into room 369 just as an infant was being wheeled in. The baby was coughing and wheezing spasmodically.

"What happened?" Dr. Amadi asked the distraught woman, who ran alongside the gurney, her tear streaked face wracked by agony, her eyes red-rimmed from crying.

"My pikin-o! Make you no let am die-o," she wailed plaintively in Pidgin English, holding her head in both her hands.

Dr. Amadi grabbed the child's chart and glanced at it.

"Your child is not going to die," he said calmly, examining the child with quick, efficient movements. "Your child had an asthma attack, but something seems to have triggered it. What happened?" he asked as he checked for the baby's vital signs.

"I go backyard to get pepper from garden for evening meal. I lefam for a minute, and the stupid girl- my house girl she open turpentine for house. She say she want remove paint. Who send am? My baby come breath am de choke," the woman complained tearfully.

"Prepare an IV stat!" Dr. Amadi barked at the nurse, who was attaching the pressure cuff on the child's arm.

"Right away doc," she responded.

"And follow up with one unit of albuterol."

"Yes Doc," the nurse said calmly. "Pulse rate is normal. The pressure is slightly elevated but coming down."

"Very good," Dr. Amadi said brusquely. "We need the oxygen tank."

"The oxygen tank," the nurse shouted to the assistant, who rushed over with the oxygen tank.

Dr. Amadi adjusted the tent over the child's nose, and she reacted by wheezing and coughing more violently than before.

Her mother reacted by jumping up and down in wild panic.

"Chineke!" she exclaimed and clamped her hand over her mouth. The tears brimmed again in her blood-shot eyes, and she shook like a leaf.

The nurse admonished her with a stern look "Your child will be okay... you are not helping her like this."

Dr. Amadi placed gentle hands on the child's shoulders and spoke to her soothingly, encouraging her to breathe more slowly. The child took in gulps of the medicated oxygen mist and soon her breathing normalized.

Her mother heaved an audible sigh of relief and made the sign of the cross "Thank God!" she breathed with a smile upon her face.

"Madam," Dr. Amadi said calmly. "Your child will be okay. She just needs follow up, but you have to wait outside now. We will take care of it. I will come outside to talk to you soon."

The woman stared at her child, who stared back at her with big moist frightened eyes, staring out of a tear-streaked face. Bending down close to the child, the woman whispered gently, wiping the tears that flowed down the child's face.

"*Nnenne, you go better. I go buy you new toys, you hear? Make you better, you hear?*" She kissed the child gently on the forehead and slowly backed out of the room.

As Dr. Amadi worked on the child, he thought about his own children. He knew that he was a bit too hard on them, but without their mother to guide them, he knew that he had to push them extra hard if they were to make a ripple in the scheme of a thing called life. From his own experience, he knew how quickly doors shut in one's face when they did not have credentials and the money.

When he was a struggling clerk, working at the Ministry of Works, as a statistical clerk, he knew how differently people treated him. Now that he had his own practice, people treated him with deference and respect, and pretty much did his bidding. Nobody gives you anything that you didn't work for, and he knew that from his own experience.

He knew that they all felt the tremendous pressure of trying to live up to what he knew that they referred to as his lofty expectations but there was no other way. They were all doing very well, but his youngest child Uchenna had far exceeded his expectations. True to the meaning of his name, Uchenna seemed to have been born with a book in his hands and excelled in all his subjects with no efforts at all. His older children were doing very well too, but he would not relent in encouraging them. Better to make them work harder than to rest on their laurels. Adora had won a graduate scholarship and Chike was doing fairly well in his law studies. As his oldest child, he had wanted Chike to follow in his career footstep, but Chike had different ideas, and there was no sense in arguing with him. At least he was making a good effort.

"Heart rate normalized," the nurse said, as everybody in the room breathed a collective sigh of relief.

"Phew!" Dr. Amadi sighed and glanced at his watch. Seven P.M. He had another thirty minutes to finish his rounds before heading to the University hospital where he served as the Chief Resident Surgeon. Another three hours and he could go home to Chike.

◆ ◆ ◆

The sounds of a car engine approached faintly from the distance, increasing steadily in volume until it roared right outside the driveway of the mansion at 14 Park Lane Drive.

Inside the house, Adora and Chike and Amaka were standing by the window, watching the twinkling lights of the city that stretched beyond the distant gate. Through the gloom of the gathering dusk, they saw flashes of chrome from the car parked by the driveway.

"Uchenna!" they yelled simultaneously, sprinting towards the front door.

They rushed outside where they found a red Prelude, parked in the driveway. Through the tinted glass window, Adora observed her little brother Uchenna hug the woman who sat behind the steering wheel, then reach behind his seat for his bag. He jumped out of the car and sprinted towards Chike.

Tall and lanky for his age, Uchenna was wearing navy blue and white school uniforms, and wheeled a heavy canvas backpack behind him. He dropped the backpack at Chike's feet and aimed a mock punch at him. Chike grabbed him in a bear hug and he squealed in delight, exclaiming, "Chike, what are you doing home at this time?"

"I Came to see my two most fave people in the world of course," Chike responded and grabbed Uchenna's bag, placing a protective arm on his little brother's shoulder as they walked towards the front door, trailed by Amaka. At the threshold, Uchenna paused and turned back to the car, waving at the woman behind the wheel.

"Thanks, Mrs. O," he said effusively, and she tapped on her horn.

"Tell Olu hey for me ma," Uchenna shouted as he turned towards the house, keeping step with his big brother Chike.

Adora walked into the warm gathering dusk, illuminated by two lamp poles in front of the house, and towards the side of the Prelude, where Mrs. Olajide sat behind the wheels. A compact dark-skinned woman in her early fifties, Mrs. Olajide scratched her graying temples and peered at Adora through the wire-framed glasses perched at the tip of her small nose.

"You must stay in touch with your father. He needs you," she began.

"I know," Adora responded, wondering for the umpteenth time if she was not making a mistake.

"Maybe I shouldn't go---," she began gingerly, but Mrs. Olajide cut her off. "Nonsense my child. You need the challenge. You can't afford not to go. I

went to Unilag and I can give you firsthand information that you will be getting a first-rate education. I know Nsukka has a top-notch faculty, but I really think that you need the life experience by going away to Lagos."

"You really think so?"

"Yes, Adora. The experience would be invaluable," Mrs. Olajide said as she put her car back into gear. She reached out and patted Adora's arm.

"Don't worry, you will be okay," she said gently.

"T--thanks ma," Adora faltered, feeling far from okay.

"Stay well my daughter, and may God guide you through your journey."

"Amen," Adora shouted over the sounds of the car engine, waving heartily as Mrs. Olajide drove off into the night.

She found them perched on the high stools of the washed oak bar, sipping juices and munching on homemade pastry. The room was now enveloped in the soft light of a table lamp, which cast a soft glow on the room, and threw shadows at the far end of the dining room wall.

Amaka dropped her napkin on her plate and looked at Adora. "Mm, this is simply scrumptious," she commented. "Want some?" she asked. Adora shook her head, frowning at the sweet confectionery.

"How about some lemon ginger ale?" Chike offered. "I mixed it myself."

'No thanks," Adora countered. "Why don't you let me fix you guys something more substantial than pastry?" Adora offered.

"No thanks," Chike shot back. "I'll take my chances on the sweets. Why? You took cooking lessons in my absence?" he teased.

Adora suppressed an urge to giggle.

"I see that you missed your calling," she threw back at him. "Why don't you try comedy?"

"Too grueling. Law is much easier," he chuckled, and the two girls joined in his laughter.

Adora cleared her throat in controlled amusement and hopped onto the stool next to Uchenna. "How was algebra with Bosede?" she interjected, above the noise of the thirty-inch monitor television that stood in the corner of the room.

Uchenna scowled at her.

"I was studying with Olu, not his sister okay?" "Somebody has a crush?" Amaka teased.

"Not true!" Uchenna protested, making a face. "I do not have a crush on anybody!" Chike rose from the stool and fingered the TV remote control. Listlessly, he dropped the gadget on the barstool, and began to pace the floor like a caged animal, causing Uchenna to give him a startled look with a questioning expression on his face.

"Hey! What's the matter?" he asked, his concern etched all over his face.

"Remember plan B!" Adora cut in.

"I flunked trigonometry miserably," Chike blurted out.

"Correction you scored a C, which in my book is not the end of the world," Adora interjected.

"But trig' is easy," said a wide-eyed Uchenna. "All you need to know is the formula to...."

"That, little bro," interjected Chike, "is where you come in."

"Me? What do you mean me?" Uchenna asked with wide-eyed wonder.

Chike glanced at Adora and Amaka, who had moved to the entertainment center across from the bar. Amaka pointed the remote control at the big screen television that dominated one corner of the room. The television came to life and she flipped the channels until she tuned in to an American broadcast. A trim and tone Braxton dominated the big screen, dressed in a black beaded skintight micro mini festooned with strategically placed cut-outs that left little of her well-endowed anatomy to the imagination, crooning a ballad about broken hearts to a thrilled audience. Her lush contralto voice rose to a lilting crescendo and the audience howled.

Tearing his eyes reluctantly from the sexy image on the huge screen, Chike faced his little brother.

"What I want you to do is to help me brush up," he said earnestly.

"Brush you up? You?" Uchenna asked, barely able to hide his surprise. "I am only in secondary school. You are in law school.

"Don't be so modest, Uchenna," Adora said. "You know very well that you can coach him in trig'," Adora interjected.

"If you really think so," Uchenna shrugged, trying very hard to infuse some confidence in his tone; a fact that was not lost on Chike.

"Yes, not only do I think so, but I know so, and the sooner we start, the better for me."

On the television screen, Toni's voice trembled and washed over the room through the enhanced surround sound of the stereo speakers. The audience roared and everybody in the room stared in awed silence.

Chike let out a long wolf whistle. "That girl has tremendous talent," he remarked.

Amaka made a face and Uchenna snickered behind his hand.

Toni blew the stage audience a kiss, and they threw flowers up the stage at her. Several male spectators rushed up the stage and an army of bodyguards formed a protective shield around her as the audience howled.

Uchenna flipped the channel to MTV, and the loud sound of electric guitar filled the room. A tall drag queen sauntered towards the camera, wearing a platinum blonde wig, and a skintight pair of black leather pants, simultaneously playing the electric guitar with his tongue, while making obscene gestures at the camera with his hands.

Adora winced in distaste, and quickly changed the channel. Uchenna and Chike exchanged glances and burst into laughter at the expression on her face. The sound of rap music filled the room. An ebony skinned man of about twenty-three dominated the screen wearing a red and white bandana across his head and a heavy gold chain around his neck. His chest and his forearms were bare and riddled with tattoos. Surrounded by a bevy of scantily clad, beautiful girls, who gyrated smoothly to the sounds of his voice, he rapped in rhythm to the pulsating sound of the accompanying musical instruments, punctuating the air with his fingers. He fell on his knees and one of the female dancers squatted close to his face and began to grind her hips towards his face in a seductive undulating motion. He grabbed her hips and brought her almost exposed crotch close to his face, sticking out his tongue in a lascivious manner.

Chike grabbed Uchenna and covered his eyes. "Young man, I don't believe that you should be looking at this."

"C'mon Chike, I've seen worse on television," he giggled.

"Young man, Chike is right you know," Amaka asserted, and Uchenna rolled his eyes.

"Alright, I'm going up to my room. I need to change anyway. I've got lots of ground to cover with my math test coming up next week and I think I'll get some --."

"Weren't you studying with Olu just moments ago?" Adora countered. "Don't you think that there's such a thing as too much of a good thing. Maybe you should tidy up your room--- you know what I mean."

"Aw, alright," he concurred. He picked up his bag and made his way towards the door that led to the staircase followed closely by Chike.

Chapter 5

"What! All the Amadi kids in one place? My eyes must be playing tricks on me!" A short, plump, woman of an indeterminate middle age hurried into the living room. She was wearing a purple and gold print bubo and a matching wrapper tightly wound around her portly waist in the traditional manner and carrying a weighed down black shopping bag with some effort, and a worn brown leather handbag slung over her left shoulder. She dropped the shopping bag on the mint-carpeted floor, next to the marble center table, and sighed, then dropped her worn brown leather handbag on the white marble center table as Chike leaped off his barstool and sprang towards her. He bent down and embraced her warmly.

"Kids? I'm a teenager, not a kid," Uchenna protested, standing up reluctantly to acknowledge her.

"Miss Clara, it is good to see you," Chike said warmly and stepped back to beam at her.

Clara's plump face broke into a wide grin. She stood on the carpeted floor with her sandal clad feet planted firmly apart, arms at akimbo on her plump bosom while she appraised Chike.

"You look a bit thin, have they been feeding you at all at that University of yours?" she asked with a worried look on her face.

"Miss Clara, you know that nobody in the world can rival your cooking. Why do you think I came home today?" Chike shot back, patting her stout shoulder.

"Eh Chike, you have not changed a bit," Clara cackled as her plump body shook with laughter. Her huge bosoms heaved up and down, and her brown eyes danced with merriment.

Despite the cool air pouring out of the vents in the room, Clara's face was glistening from beads of perspiration, which stood out on her upper lip and her forehead. She picked up the edge of her wrapper, and fanned her face with it, then she re-tied her wrapper, and stuck the edge of the wrapper firmly into a crease on the material at her waist. She pulled out a white handkerchief from her ample cleavage, dabbing gingerly at the sweat, and being careful not to smudge the pancake make-up on her face that had caked in places, settling into the fine lines and furrows that the ravages of time had deposited on her face.

Clara spread out her smudged handkerchief, and fanned herself briskly, as the sweat continued to pop out on her face and neck, and stream into the synthetic material of her bubo that stuck to her skin in places. Watching her, Adora wished that Clara would stop wearing those synthetic materials, which added to Clara's sweaty condition but Clara loved nothing better than a shiny satin blouse over her traditional wrappers.

Chike was the first to speak, as he took Clara's hand and led her the sofa.

"Miss Clara, please sit down and put your feet up," he said gallantly, and Clara smiled, and sank gratefully into the chair, heaving an audible sigh.

"Whew! It was hot out there," she said emphatically, and took a deep breath. "Hot?" Uchenna cut in. "Why it is almost seven o clock. It is the coolest time of the day and not a bit hot."

"Not when you've been out bargaining at the market," said Adora, who knew about Clara's bout with hot flashes. "Can I get you something cold to drink Miss Clara?" she asked.

"Hoo thank you my daughter," Clara sighed and continued to fan herself with her handkerchief.

"I'll get it, and I'll take the shopping bag to the kitchen while I'm at it," Uchenna offered, jumping up from his seat.

"Uchenna, that's my baby," Adora said, fishing in her skirt pocket till she pulled out a paper napkin, which was slightly wrinkled but clean. She handed it to Clara, who examined it, and satisfied that it was clean; she dabbed at her face with it and stuck it into her handbag, then continued to fan herself with her sodden handkerchief.

Presently, Uchenna returned with a tall glass of cold water and Clara gratefully reached for it.

"Ahh, thank you my son," She said as she downed it very quickly and set the glass on the marble center table.

"Phew, this is so much better." She leaned back into the sofa and closed her eyes. "Miss Clara," Chike began. "You look more beautiful every time I see you."

Clara's eyes popped open and twinkled with merriment. "I can see that you still have a mouth on you," she cackled. The cackle turned to a dry cough, and she drank the remainder of the water in the glass and cleared her throat.

"But, flattery will get you everywhere. Did you receive all the food packages that I've been sending through that rogue James?"

"Thanks Ms. Clara," Chike said, patting his stomach. "And speaking of which, where's your husband?" Chike asked, raising a quizzical eyebrow.

"Right outside, unloading the jeep," Clara replied.

"I'll go help him in a moment," Chike said, adding, "And yes, Miss Clara, now that I am home, I am simply looking forward to a whole week of nothing but your divine cooking."

"Keep the flattery coming, young man. Who knows, I may even decide to add all your favorites to the menu tonight."

"Wow, I can't wait," Chike responded. "I hope that my poor starved stomach can handle the jump from junk to first class dining."

"I can see that they have taught you well at that school of yours," Clara joked, reaching over to pat him playfully on the cheek. She shook her head and took a hard look at him, clucking her tongue and shaking her head in amazement.

"Facial hair—goodness, it seemed just like yesterday when I was chasing you and your sister from the frog pond and from climbing trees at the back. Now here you are growing like an iroko tree every day."

"Definitely not from eating that mush they try to pass off as food at the cafeteria. Frankly, those people need to learn a thing or two from you about cooking," Chike shot back.

Clara roared with laughter and held her sides with her hands. The tears trickled down her plump cheeks, and she dabbed at them with her handkerchief, smudging the caking pancake on her face.

"Oh, you Amadi kids! You really know how to make an old lady feel good," she said between peals of mirth, as her mammoth body shook, and her huge bosoms heaved.

Uchenna stood up and stood next to his big brother.

"Ms. Clara, you are certainly not an old lady, not in my own opinion, right Chike?" "Of course not. Our Ms. Clara is full of youth and vivacity," Chike quipped.

"Our Ms. Clara is full of vigor and vitality," Uchenna shot back.

"Now Mr. Vigor and vitality, I think that there's a roomful of junk that needs your attention," Adora stated with a hint of sarcasm. "How do you know?" Uchenna began, but Adora glared at him."

Okay, okay," he muttered, heading towards the staircase.

"I'll go outside to help your husband. He is outside, isn't he Miss Clara?" Chike inquired.

"Right where I left him, I hope," Clara said, as she gathered her bag and headed towards the kitchen.

As Chike exited through the back door, Adora walked to the west window, just as Chike was approaching Clara's husband James Umeh, a tall, heavyset man in a light blue caftan pant outfit, who was leaning against the white Range Rover Jeep, wiping the windscreen window. He waved at Chike, who shook his hands and began to unload grocery bags from the trunk of the jeep, which was parked by the back door that led off to the kitchen. The man's face was in the shadows, but Adora could see that James had been adding a lot of weight lately.

Clara bustled around the spacious, white-tiled kitchen, chopping vegetables, washing meat, sautéing onions, and kneading dough on the chopping board with a wooden rolling pin.

Adora stood awkwardly by the sink, watching her frenzied activities, amazed as usual about the speed and dexterity coming from one so stout. She had tried to help, but Clara shooed her away with her usual rebuff, "not in my kitchen young lady, too many hands spoil the cook."

As usual, Adora had tidied the trail of utensils and spills that Clara left in her wake knowing that Clara would not stop to clean until she had accomplished her culinary mission. Clara was like a whirlwind in the kitchen and only stopped to assess the damage after the last fowl was stuck in the oven.

Before long, the kitchen was suffused with the most delectable intermingled aroma and almost as if on cue, Chike walked into the kitchen, sniffing the air appreciatively, trailed by Uchenna.

He headed directly to the oven and poked in his head.

"Mmm cake--- Ms. Clara, you see what I mean," he said as Uchenna shot him a look.

"You know better Chike, you know Ms. Clara," Uchenna warned.

"That's right young man," Clara chided.

"No inteference with my cooking. Dinner's not ready."

"Mmm, okay," Chike mumbled as he straightened up and grabbed a handful of roasted peanuts from the earthenware jar on the counter. He popped a few into his mouth and Uchenna glanced at him and burst out laughing.

"I'm with you all the way big bro. My stomach is growling too," he chuckled as he crossed the vast expanse of the kitchen to the gleaming white Formica counter, where a hand painted ceramic bowl stood, filled with an assortment of nuts. He grabbed a handful of roasted cashew nuts, and stuffed them in his pocket.

Chike laughed and glanced at Clara.

"You see the dilemma of dinner tonight; by the time that we get the chance to sample your masterpiece, we may be too full of junk to eat."

Clara shook her head and ignored Chike, who headed towards the exit.

"I'm going to the clinic to pick up dad," he announced, jingling a bunch of keys around in his pocket.

"I'll like to come--," Uchenna began. "But on the other hand, I think I'll stay and complete my geometry project on the Pythagorean theory."

"Hey, suit yourself," Chike said, chuckling under his breath. "Bye," Uchenna retorted.

"Hey, be safe," Adora added, waving gaily at him.

"Safe? I invented safe," Chike chuckled, and strode jauntily towards the garage, jingling the car keys in his pocket.

As the door closed behind Chike, Uchenna strolled to the window facing kitchen counter at the far end of the kitchen. He selected a plump cashew fruit from an ornate crystal fruit bowl that sat on the kitchen counter and rinsed it under the lukewarm sprays of the tap. As he whirred away from the sink, he ran into the path of Clara, who was headed towards the sink, carrying a bowl of freshly plucked hen. Her eyes widened and Uchenna spun adroitly, narrowly missing her by mere inches.

"Young man, you see why I don't like a crowd in my kitchen. Kitchen is for cooking and the dining room is for eating," Clara said sternly, as she turned on the faucet, and began to wash the whole chicken with strong, vigorous movements.

Uchenna muttered an apology and Clara nodded, and then burst into a litany of songs as she worked on stuffing the chicken.

Adora eyed the cashew fruit in Uchenna's hand and her stomach began to rumble. She picked out a golden cashew and washed it under the faucet. Feeling a bit guilty, she bit into the succulent, fleshy fruit and sucked at the squirting juices that gushed into her mouth in spurts.

"Mmm," she said absently, as she dabbed at the corner of her mouth with a paper napkin.

"Good huh?" Uchenna asked as he took a bite out of his fruit. The juices spurted from the fruit and rolled down the corner of his mouth, dribbling slowly towards his chin. Adora handed him a paper napkin, and he dabbed at the corner of his mouth.

"Careful now," she cautioned. "You know how difficult it is to remove those stubborn cashew stains from fabrics."

"Thanks," Uchenna grinned, dabbing at the juice that was making a wet path towards his shirt.

Adora stiffened her mouth to stifle the smile tugging at the corners of her mouth. For all his academic brilliance, Uchenna was still a typical thirteen years old, prone to the youthful nonchalance of his peers. Right now, he dropped the partially eaten golden fruit on the kitchen table and dried his hand with the napkin. "No messes in my kitchen," Clara cautioned. She snatched the half-eaten fruit and returned the sheen to the Formica table with a few swipes of her napkin. Uchenna scowled and turned to Adora.

"Dinner's almost ready?" he asked, rubbing his stomach.

"Almost, but you need to clean up your room and shower before dinner," Adora said.

"Clean up my room?"

"You didn't clean your room. And don't ask me how I know."

Uchenna balled up the damp paper towel in his hand, aimed it at the open wastebasket, and made a perfect slam-dunk.

"Yes!" he exclaimed with an expression of pure delight on his face.

"Yeah yeah," Adora countered sarcastically. "Now be a sweetie and go do as I say."

With flashing eyes and the indignant self- righteous anger of his wounded thirteen-year-old pride, Uchenna whirred around to face her.

"Sweetie? That's so sissy. I am thirteen, not three! I already did clean my room; how can you tell whether or not I did a good job when you didn't even see it? And please don't call me sweetie," he added for emphasis, screwing up his face at her. "It's a sissy word, meant for babies and girls. And I'm neither!"

Adora stared as her normally laid back brother as the words poured out of him. She took a step towards him and patted his cheek gently.

"Sweetie, that means that I love you and you know that. Yes, you are a big boy, and I know that. And you did not exactly clean your room and you know that. Someday, you are going to get married and you'll understand. I wouldn't want your future wife complaining to me about little brothers and big slobs," she said.

Uchenna's face lit up and the dimples on his cheeks deepened. "Okay, okay, you got me there. I didn't really clean up that well."

Clara looked up from the pots bubbling on the stove top and chuckled. Uchenna scowled at her, his eyes flashing.

"Hey, what's so funny---," he began, but Adora gave him a sharp look and he beat a hasty retreat towards the living room, mumbling as he went.

Clara glanced at the beautiful girl that she had helped to raise, standing in front of the kitchen sink, drying the dishes that sat on the draining board. She had watched Adora make the transition from a beautiful, gurgling baby that everyone loved to spoil, to a gawky, awkward tomboy that loved to get into fights, play pranks and climb trees with her brothers. Now she had grown into a fine young woman and was stepping very nicely into her mother's shoes. Adora had grown so dazzling, just like her late mother, and had inherited her mother's mass of thick, jet-black hair that cascaded down her slender neck in waves, and framed her beautiful oval face, contrasting nicely with her flawless, translucent skin, which was the color of gleaming warm copper. Her deep- set lucid brown eyes, framed by a fan of curly eyelashes, and accentuated by perfectly arched eyebrows held a strange combination of innocence and mystique.

With her fine boned facial structure, high cheekbones, and straight, finely chiseled nose- a trait that she inherited from her handsome father- combined with her full, perfectly shaped lips, Adora was making the first transition into beautiful womanhood.

As she moved around the room, with her lithe graceful figure, conditioned by years playing tennis, Adora glanced occasionally at Clara, and smiled her beautiful smile, the same dazzling smile that made her late mother Christina the toast of the town.

The sudden loss of her mother had forced her to grow up fast, Clara thought. She was practically taking over the role of mother to her brothers; and she was doing a fine job, raising her little brother Uchenna while her father toiled away all day at the clinic.

"Too bad madam did not live to see her daughter today," Clara mused, glancing at the beautiful girl that she had grown to love like the product of her own womb.

"What did you say?" Adora asked, breaking into Clara's reverie.

"Nothing my dear," Clara said, as she set down the last dish on the table. "I'm just glad that I'm a part of this household."

"Me too," Adora stated warmly. "I'm glad that you helped to raise me."

"Madam would have been so proud of you," Clara stated simply.

"You can't mean that. I used to give you so much trouble," Adora blurted. "Yeah, that was part of growing up," Clara mumbled.

"You really think so?" Adora asked uncomfortably, feeling a sudden pang of guilt about the past, but relieved that Clara understood. She searched futilely for the right words to convey her feelings, and failing at that, she swallowed a lump in her throat, and hugged the plump, middle-aged woman who had taken care of her from the cradle, straining her arms to accommodate her ample form. Clara returned the hug with such fervor that Adora felt the breath being squeezed out of her.

"Ohhh," she breathed, and Clara quickly released her.

"Sorry my dear," she said apologetically. "I totally forgot the kind of power that my arms pack."

"Thanks, Miss Clara, but I am afraid that I don't deserve that compliment at all. You forgot about my mischievous ways? I don't know how you managed to put up with me in those days. It is a miracle that you didn't leave."

"Leave?" Clara dropped the knife she was wielding, and it landed on the counter with a clatter. The corners of her mouth turned up, and she guffawed. She laughed so hard that her plump throat quivered, and her huge bosom jiggled. She dabbed gently at the tears that trickled down the corner of her eyes with the corner of her wrapper and retied the wrapper firmly around her corpulent waist.

"Oh, you silly girl," she said between fits of laughter.

"I was once a child myself, and believe me, I was no better. Again, this family is like my family. Can a person leave their own family?"

Strangely enough Clara's kind words, instead of making her feel better had the opposite effect on her. Guilt reared at her like a charging bull.

"I'm so sorry Miss Clara----," she sputtered.

"Don't be silly young lady," Clara admonished her. "Working with this family has been a very rewarding experience for me, and you know that you are all my kids."

"Oh, Miss Clara," Adora exclaimed, throwing her slender arms around the older woman's thick neck, and hugging her hard.

"Hey watch out for those killer arms," Clara quipped glibly.

Chapter 6

For Clara Umeh, the number three held a significance that seemed to complete the complicated puzzle that she called life. It was the number of years that she was married to her first husband Kanene Nwanganga, the man who had the distinct privilege of being the biggest stumbling block in her life. It was also the number of years that it took her to meet her current husband James Umeh, the man that she was sure that she had known in some previous life. As if to complete the circle, three was also the number of kids that her kind and generous employer Dr. Chidi Amadi had brought into the world with his beautiful late wife Christina. Those kids were a source of joy and contentment to her, and she couldn't have loved them any better if they were the products of her own womb.

Clara had joined the Amadi household at their Park Lane residence in Enugu, twenty-five years earlier; even before the first Amadi child was born, at a time when Dr. Chidi Amadi was struggling to establish his new practice. For Clara, that was the year that her life took a downward spiral into a vortex of misfortune, starting from the death of her parents in a tragic bus accident, and culminating in the death of her first husband Kanene Nwanganga.

Kanene was a lackluster man, who made a lackluster living tapping palm wine, the milky white wine of libation, from the top of the palm trees that grew in the palm grove behind the land, which his father before him, also a Palm Wine Tapper had left him. Kanene was a firm believer in tasting the product for quality assurance, and often drank up all his profits even before they came in. To augment the meager income that filtered through when her husband was not drinking it up, Clara acquired a stall at the Oguiyi market in Enugu, where she sold the palm nuts and kernels that she harvested from the family palm grove, and sometimes bottles of palm wine, bottled fresh the night before.

The raw pain of losing both her parents in one day was still fresh and bitter, a constant source of grief, complicating the fact that she was now heavy with child for a man who had been nothing but a source of pain and regret for her.

Clara had finished a trying workday, suffering from bouts of nausea and dizziness, and was on her way home when she heard a rumor in the taxi that she shared with several other passengers. It was another trader, a gargantuan man of mammoth girt, who flagged down the car and sat next to her taking up most of the space and, leaving her almost claustrophobic, squeezed between him and an old woman, who nodded off and roused herself occasionally. Apparently, the giant passenger and the taxi driver knew each other, for they launched into a prolonged rite of greetings and exchange of pleasantry amidst the giant man's alcohol laced breath. Clara was only able to pick up snippets of their conversation, as her tired body was longing for the solace of her bed.

"-- good to see you again oga driver. Are the children well?"

"They are well Cletus ----my middle one has just graduated from King's College. He is ready for -----." The driver stopped mid-sentence and pulled up at the curb to discharge the front passenger. Another passenger replaced her, a buxom woman of a medium brown complexion who pulled out a small mirror from her purse, and applied a coat of lipstick in a garish strawberry shade that seemed out of place with her rich brown complexion.

Clara fanned ineffectually at her face with her folded handkerchief, seeking relief from the oppressive midday sun that heated the metal roof and body of the taxi, sapping her of all her energy until she felt like a limp wet wrapper with all the water wrung out.

The giant next to Clara, the one that the driver had called Cletus leaned close to the driver, his alcohol laced breath increasing Clara's nausea.

"Brother Okeke, it be like you never hear o," he began in Pidgin English.

The taxi driver was driving with one hand, picking at his teeth with a chewing stick, which dangled from the corner of his mouth.

"*Hear wetin Cletus?*" he asked as he swerved the car sharply, barely missing the rear of an early model station wagon, whose driver stuck his head out of the window and let out a stream of expletives in his direction. The taxi driver laughed out loud and the old woman sitting on the other side of Clara roused herself momentarily and reminded him not to forget her stop. She peered at Clara's protruding stomach with open interest and mumbled something to herself. Soon her head dropped on her sagging chest, and she resumed her soft snoring.

"Ehe, before we were so rudely interrupted, what were you saying?" the driver addressed Cletus, who increased the volume of his voice, relishing the audience of the driver and the new passenger in the front, a rail-thin woman whose colorful gele scarf, wrapped artfully around her head took up much of the space around her, and blocked Clara's view of the road ahead. She listened with open interest and craned her neck towards the speaker in the back.

"*I hear say the palm wine tapper for Onitsha road done die o. Them say him fall off palm tree*," the giant Cletus continued in Pidgin English.

"Eh? Cletus, na true?" the driver screamed, and the chewing stick fell out of his mouth. He caught it and placed it on the dashboard just as a truck ahead of them screeched to a halt.

The taxi driver stepped on his brakes and the car jerked to a halt, rocking Clara's torso forward. "Careful Oga Driver," she warned, clutching her tummy and the driver grunted something unintelligible.

The giant to Clara's right shifted in his seat and picked up the thread of his

conversation.

"Like I say Kenene done join his ancestors. I hear say him wife pregnant."

The giant glanced at Clara's mammoth tummy and it hit her like a punch on the face that the palm wine tapper that they were referring to, who had plunged to his death was her husband Kanene. And that was just the beginning.

After burying Kanene, Clara discovered that she was in heavy debt. The money that she had put away so carefully from her business went towards paying the hefty bill for Kanene's funeral and assuaging the endless traffic of debtors who came to collect on his debts. The miniscule remainder was barely enough to subsist on.

As the weeks progressed towards the day that she was beginning to view with a combination of anticipation and dread, she began to pinch every penny, wondering how she was going to care for a new baby when she was speeding toward the road to destitution.

Her bouts of morning sickness worsened each day, leaving her feeling weak and dizzy; totally devoid of energy. Unable to get up some days, she gave up her stall at the Oguiyi market and lay in bed in a near comatose state each morning, clutching at her thick belly and waiting for each wave of nausea to pass before she could crawl out of bed.

Clara discontinued her prenatal appointments and rationed her food frugally, sometimes going to bed feeling sharp pangs of hunger gnawing at her bowels. When she started to experience a strange bloating around her limbs, and her face, she rationalized that it was just a normal part of pregnancy weight gain. Then the baby's frenzied kicking ceased, and she believed that the baby had reached the stage that she had heard about near the eighth month, when fetuses stopped moving around so much due to their growth.

A sharp pain in her abdomen jarred her awake from a dreamless slumber one afternoon, accompanied by a blinding headache. A discomforting nausea began from the pit of her bowels and rose in waves towards her throat, almost suffocating her. With difficulty, she rolled out of bed and fell on her knees, praying fervently for the most fragmentary vestige of strength. The prayer filled her with renewed resolve, and she struggled to her feet and tied her wrapper more securely around her bulging waistline.

Stumbling blindly into the street, she ran smack into her neighbor, Mrs. Nwokoli, a fruit trader, who was just returning home, as usual for her afternoon meal.

"What is the matter Clara?" Mrs. Nwokoli shouted, rushing to her side. "Pain —so much pain," Clara panted through parched lips.

"Come, lean on me," Mrs. Nwokoli commanded.

She guided Clara to the street corner, and a gaggle of neighbors rushed towards them. Their voices faded in and out of her consciousness, and she heard them through a pain filled haze.

"What is the matter with Clara?"

"Poor girl----and she just lost her husband."

"Clara, are you okay?"

"Pain---oh the pain," Clara cried through clenched teeth. "Maybe the baby is coming," someone suggested.

"No! Didn't she say she was in her seventh or eighth month?"

"Chibuzo, CHIBUZO! Get a chair for Clara." This came from a tall slim woman wearing a pale-yellow caftan set.

"Yes ma," Chibuzo, a skinny girl of about thirteen replied. She raced off to the front of the house next door, where two wooden chairs were arranged around a small table with a half-played game of Ludo™. She snatched one of the chairs and raced back to Clara, now supported by the tall woman and a man in a dashiki.

Clara's pain gave way to a black dizziness; the voices faded in and out of her consciousness as she struggled to focus on the present.

"My dear, sit down, and breathe deep. It will help with the pain," the tall woman commanded. Her voice came as though from a distance.

Vaguely, through waves of nausea and dizziness, she became aware of a car driving up to the spot where she sat.

"The taxi is here," a strangely disembodied voice said. "Come my dear."

A pair of hands guided her into the back seat of the car and she collapsed on the sagging seat of the vehicle, her lolling head cradled by gentle hands.

"Take care of her, Stella," another voice said.

At the entrance of a large building, something Health Alliance – Clara couldn't make out the entire words - a nurse and an orderly rushed in, placed Clara on a gurney, and wheeled her inside a room where they drew her blood and attached an IV line to her vein. Slowly, she felt some life returning to her body.

A young man in hospital scrubs walked into the room, and glanced at Clara's chart, then examined her with quick, efficient movements. He was tall and brown- skinned with very attractive features. His expression was unreadable, but Clara saw deep sympathy in his eyes.

"My baby is my baby alright?" she began. The young man shook his head very sadly.

"I'm really sorry Mr. Nwanganga. From our assessment, she was lost about two days ago."

Clara screamed, feeling a gut-wrenching pain that began at the core of her heart and spread to the very essence of her being.

"Mrs. Nwanganga. I am sorry. If you had come to us about a month ago, who knows-- but we cannot speculate. Right now, we need to focus on your own health.

We shall administer a medication to induce labor. This is safer for your future reproductive health than cutting you up. But I'm afraid there is no heartbeat on the baby."

For two days, Clara lay supine on the hospital bed, curled tightly into a fetal position and refusing to take anything orally. The doctor continued to come, checking her vital signs and giving instruction to the nurses about her care.

On the morning of the second day, the administrative nurse paid her a visit. She told her that she would have to pay her hospital bill in full for them to continue treating her. Clara's heart dropped.

"But I don't have the money right now. I'll find a way to pay you later," she wailed.

"We cannot help that," the nurse responded coldly. "We need the payment right now, or at least a deposit or we have to discharge you."

"Oh my God, what am I going to do? I'm still not feeling well at all," Clara wailed.

The nurse turned towards the door, nearly colliding with the young doctor, who had taken such good care of her.

"Good morning doc," she said and smiled brightly at him. "Morning nurse." He nodded curtly and turned to Clara. "And how are we doing this morning Mrs. Nwanganga?"

"I don't know what to do. I do not have the money to pay the hospital bills." "You have to pay the bills, or you can't stay," the nurse stated bluntly.

"Nurse Uzo," the doctor said calmly. "Can you excuse us?"

The nurse gave Clara a scorching look and left the room.

"I understand that you recently lost your husband," the doctor said.

"Two months ago —he left me without a single red Kobo. I have barely been able to survive, and I have nowhere really to go."

"What about your family?"

Clara dissolved in a flurry of fresh tears as her mind relived that awful day when she received the news of her parents' death

The young doctor turned away from her and she prayed silently to God for a way out of her predicament. When the doctor turned to her, she could have sworn that she saw a tear glistening in his eyes, but it could have been the reflection of the overhead fluorescent light. What he said next took her off her guard.

"I have a preposition for you madam. Can you come and work for me?" "Work for you?" she whispered softly, offering a silent prayer of thanks to God. "You would really hire me?"

"What kind of work can you do?"

"Oh I can cook and clean, and I am very good with my hands. Thank you, Jesus,!"

"Well, then we are in business. I am looking for a housekeeper, somebody to help my wife out around the house. She is very busy with her boutique right now, and the house is a bit too big for her to handle alone-----." His words trailed off and his

handsome face shone with love as he spoke of his wife.

Clara could not suppress a pang of sadness as her mind wandered to her late husband Kanene, who only left her a mountain of debts and a legacy of pain.

"We can't afford to pay a lot now, but I promise you, if you stick with us, in a couple of years, you will make about double of what I am offering you now," the doctor's calm voice broke through her thoughts.

Clara was happy to take the job. She believed in divine intervention, and the ability of God to use people when things seemed impossible. The monthly salary that she received from Dr. Amadi was more money than she had seen in her entire life. She also had a comfortable place to stay, and good food to eat.

Dr. Amadi was true to his words. Aided by good fortune and hard work, his clinic grew and his wife Christina 's boutique expanded into a chain. Clara began to receive the highest salary that she ever heard of for a maid and the good doctor hired more household staff, making Clara the head of household.

Then James Umeh walked into her life, three years to the day that she lost her last husband. James was everything that her late husband Kanene was not, and when, three months later, he asked her to be his wife, Clara had no doubt what her answer would be.

Chapter 7

dora stood hesitantly for a moment outside Uchenna's room, listening to the muted sounds of activity coming from somewhere downstairs. Then she knocked softly and entered his room. She could make out his silhouette in the semi-darkened room, sitting on the edge of his bed with his head in his hands. The television set was flickering with the audio turned off, throwing eerie shadows on the wall. Adora flipped on the light switch, and the overhead bulb flooded the room with warm light, bringing Uchenna's face into sharp focus. There was an acute sadness in his face. It brought a lump to Adora's throat, and for a moment, she considered changing her mind altogether

Uchenna sighted her and immediately faced her with a forced smile, which did not fool Adora one bit. She managed a thin smile of her own and walked to the edge of the bed.

"Can you keep this?" she began in a whisper, not trusting her own voice. She reached around the back of her neck and unclasped the treasured 18k gold herringbone necklace with the diamond-encrusted crucifix that her father had gifted her for her sweet sixteenth birthday. She took Uchenna's hand gently and dropped the gem in his open palm.

Uchenna's eyes widened like saucers and he shook his head vehemently.

"No – I – I couldn't possibly take this---," he sputtered, pushing the gold chain towards Adora.

"Oh, go on," she said firmly, closing his hand over the glittering gem.

"But d-daddy gave this to you," he muttered, almost unintelligibly, still shaking his head, and thrusting the chain at her.

"That's okay. Daddy will understand," she said, hooking the chain around his neck.

It hung a little lower on him than it did on her rounded chest. "But you do love this chain so much. You never take it off."

"That's why I am giving it to you. So you'll never take it off," she said gingerly. Uchenna ran his fingers over the chain around his neck gingerly. The eighteen-karat jewelry rippled around his neck, giving off fiery glints of golden lights in the lamplight. Uchenna shook his head hesitantly, and the diamond chips threw off sparks of light with every motion of his body. "I don't know what to say...." he began.

"I will miss you a lot," she interjected, moving away from further talk about the gold chain.

"Me too," he said, and flung his arms around her, and hugged her tight, quite forgetting the macho, grownup airs that he often put on. Adora clasped him in a tight embrace, unable to verbalize her jumbled emotions.

Uchenna was the first to break up the awkward moment and he skittered away and stood by the window. Adora followed him.

"I want you to take care of daddy – promise me that?"

Uchenna nodded mutely, and Adora continued gently. "P, promise to write me all the time."

"I promise to write. I would call you every day, but I don't want to run up daddy's phone bill."

"I understand," she said, patting him gently on the shoulder. "The mails will suffice--."

"Hey! I just had a thought. Aunt Agatha has email, and Daddy has E-mail set up on his computer at work. I'll send you E mails from there."

"That's right. I'll send you auntie's E-mail address the moment I get there. I'll set up an account for you."

"An account? "Adora queried, puzzled.

"An E-mail account. I can set one up for you. I'll tell you the username and the password once I set it up."

"Sounds good to me," Adora declared. "And remember to keep up the good work at school. That really makes dad happy."

You're such a good boy and I'm proud of you," she added.

Uchenna's head bobbed up and he straightened up his wiry body, assuming a macho stance.

"Boy? I'm thirteen after all — a teenager," he declared pompously. Adora gave him a startled look and nodded thoughtfully.

"Yes you're right. You are a teenager," she chuckled, glancing around the room and noticing for the first time since she walked in that his room was neatly organized.

She smiled fondly at Uchenna and stood up to leave. Uchenna gave her a shy smile.

"Listen, I—err, I'm really sorry I yelled at you earlier. I guess I was a bit angry --- I mean the fact that you are leaving. I'll miss you a lot."

"I'll be back before you know it. Besides, you fought for me to go."

"I know, I know," Uchenna said with a sheepish grin. "I did fight for you because I know that you wanted to go, but now that the dream has become a reality, I don't know if I can face hanging around this big old house without you."

"Oh yes you can. You are a big boy remember?"

That's right," Uchenna said quickly, straightening up his back.

The muffled sound of a car on the driveway interrupted them, and Adora tiptoed to Uchenna's window just in time to see their father and Chike stepping out of the gray Porsche in the soft dusk. Their faces were in the shadows, but their body language showed that they were engaged in a verbal battle, which would no doubt spill over to the house.

She threaded her way down the staircase, holding on to the ornately carved mahogany balustrade, her footfalls soundless on the thickly carpeted stairs. As she turned the second landing, she could see her father and her brother standing at the entrance hall, facing each other. Their hushed voices barely reached her ears, but she could tell by the disapproving expression on her father's face and Chike's wild gesticulation that they were holding a heated conversation. The intensity of their expressions told her that their conversation was about something serious. As she drew closer to them, snatches of that conversation drifted up to her ears.

"--promise to do better--make it up." Chike was saying in a conciliatory tone of voice.

Her father's deeper, more resonant tones were now more audible as she made her way closer to them.

"You have no choice if you want to graduate from law school with honors," he was saying. "I expect nothing less," he said in a muted voice, edged with a sharpness that showed he meant business.

As Adora reached the living room where they were standing, they stood out sharply in her line of vision. Dusk had completely enveloped the house, and someone had turned on a table lamp in the far corner of the room, which threw soft, muted shadows on the soft white walls giving the room a soothing atmosphere that belied the tension that hung palpably in the air. Overhead, the ceiling fan continued to whir silently, circulating the frigid air of the window air conditioner, which seemed to compete with their father's chilly attitude.

Dr. Amadi was standing ramrod straight despite his harsh, backbreaking schedule. His back was to Adora, and Chike was facing him and, as Adora reached them, he sensed her presence despite her silent footfalls, and turned around slowly to face her. His classically handsome face looked fatigued, etched with tired lines that made him look older, very stern and foreboding.

His back was now to Chike who was making funny faces and imitating his father's stern stance for her benefit. Adora suppressed an overwhelming urge to giggle at Chike's antics and bit her lower lip fiercely.

"Just like Chike to make a stab at humor at the most inappropriate time," she thought furiously. She must remember to get him later.

She ignored Chike and glanced at her father, her face a study of agitation.

Her father looked exhausted, laden with the weight of the frustration, the bewilderment and sorrow that he dragged around in taciturn stubbornness since that fateful day. Adora's heart rushed out in sympathy towards her father's suffering and she wished fervently that she had it within her power to ease his pain. She knew that his backbreaking schedule contributed greatly to his dilemma-he hardly made it home for dinner lately, and was out again at the crack of dawn, sometimes doing a double shift at the University Teaching Hospital whenever they needed his expertise. Although he owned his own practice and could dictate his own schedule, he continuously ran himself ragged in a desperate bid to fill the gaping void that seemed to have no end in his lie.

It was clear that her father was wielding his work as a shield which he used to keep at bay the excruciating pain that his beloved wife's death almost a decade earlier had left in his heart. Adora understood all that- she carried her own share of pain- pain that lay at her heart like a leaden weight, stubbornly refusing to budge or relinquish its strangle hold.

Sometimes, she found herself questioning God, and why in all his love and infinite wisdom, he would let such a thing happen to such a wonderful human being as her mother. But she always derived comfort in prayer, the only exercise that could dispel the melancholy clouds that hovered around her

Her father seemed to have given up altogether on his faith, only making half- hearted attempts at attending service on those occasional Sundays when he did not have to work.

Adora stood there looking at her father, who returned her gaze with a direct penetrating gaze that slightly disconcerted her, as if challenging her to dare change him.

"Da--Daddy, you look -- tired," she began hesitantly, clearing her throat gingerly. "I don't feel a bit tired," he snapped offhandedly, dropping his leather briefcase, which he had been holding stiffly by his side all that time. It landed with a dull thud on the marble foyer table, and Adora cringed quietly at what she saw reflected in his eyes. She cringed because it was a direct reflection of what she carried around. A burden that clearly the passage of time had not lessened.

"Daddy, you need to slow down a bit. You really need to stop," she said, thinking about his endless work schedule.

The air conditioner thermostat turned off with a barely audible click, but the ceiling fan continued to circulate the stale air-conditioned air around the room, somehow magnifying the eerie silence that seemed to dominate the room.

In the distance a dog barked suddenly- a sharp yapping sound that sliced cleanly through the heavy silence that had settled upon the room. The neighbor's dog must be antsy again, Adora thought absently to herself.

"Stop? Stop what?' Dr. Amadi asked vaguely, fiddling idly with the stethoscope that dangled from his neck. He seemed to notice it for the first time, and with an impatient motion, he yanked it off his neck and tossed it next to his briefcase on the marble console top. It landed on the hard surface with a dull thump.

"You work too hard daddy, you need to slow down, take a vacation. You have your staff who can take over,"

Adora pointed out wearily, letting out a tired little sigh that dragged out of her throat with a rasping sound.

It was so difficult to get through to her father these days.

"I'm not afraid of work. You need to work harder. Going to that University in Lagos seems more like a vacation than work," he countered, glowering fiercely at

her. "In my days at Ahmadu Bello, I had to work through Medical school. Scholarship money can only do so much. Now that's what I call work. You kids have it so easy, and all I ask is for a little more effort. It doesn't take too much to rise to the top of the class like Uchenna you know?"

He tossed an annoyed look in the direction of Chike, who had the presence of mind to rearrange his face into a serious visage before his father caught him. Adora shook her fist at him, her mouth pinched into a thin line of disapproval.

The air conditioner thermostat clicked on with a barely audible click, and the room temperature took a subtle dip. Adora shivered visibly, in reaction to the sudden chill that settled upon the air- or was it the chilly tone of her father's voice that really sent chills down her spine? She wasn't quite sure.

"All I was trying to say, Daddy, is that you are human, not a machine. You work too hard. How about a vacation?"

"Vacation?" Dr. Amadi smiled thinly at his young daughter.

He placed his briefcase on the console table and snapped the locks open. Deliberately, with studied slowness, he picked up a sheaf of paper from his open briefcase and studied it with deep concentration. Another frown furrowed his brows, and he tossed the paper impatiently on the marble console top. The silence was so thick; you could slice it with a knife.

Dr. Amadi finally lifted his gaze to meet Adora's, and gave her a grave, piercing look. He picked up the paper on the table and pushed it in her direction.

"That, my dear, is what happens when you have vacations on your mind. A 'C' in trig." He glanced at Chike, who shifted uncomfortably from one foot to another. He returned his attention to Adora, giving her a penetrating gaze.

"This is precisely what I've been trying to teach all of you. Nobody ever becomes a success in life by accident. Success comes only through old-fashioned hard work. You have to face all the challenges of life squarely and that's what I do. My patients need me, and I have to be there for them."

The words came out of his mouth in clipped, measured tones and fell on Adora's ears like the sound of gravel falling on a concrete surface.

Chike gave her a stern look. His eyes begged her to let go, but Adora was determined to get through to her father this time. She was not going to stand there and let him join their mother in the grave through his own doing.

She took a deep breath and looked straight at him.

"Daddy, you have a full staff of qualified doctors at the clinic. You can take a breather, I'm quite sure ------,"

Dr. Amadi interrupted Adora with an impatient wave of his hand, which effectively silenced her.

"Aha," he said quickly, cutting off any further protest from his daughter.

"If I didn't work so hard I wouldn't have acquired all the staff. The clinic is my sole responsibility. It is how I can feed and clothe you kids. You must remember that nobody ever made it in life by dumping their responsibilities onto others."

Adora sank into the sofa, feeling like a limp wet rag and scowled at her father.

"You never used to stay away this much when Mom was here with us."

The words tumbled out of her mouth suddenly, almost against her own volition. She regretted them as soon as they left her mouth and wished that she could take them back. He reacted with a slumping of his shoulders and flinched, almost as if she had physically punched him. He flinched visibly, and sagged, like a deflated balloon.

Adora could sense the conflict churning through him. She stared at him helplessly and wished desperately that she could wave a magic wand that could wipe out his pain - the pain that he had been carrying around for years, and the pain that she had just inflicted upon him through her careless words. Perhaps that magic wand could also help to ease her pain.

He picked up his briefcase from the console table and crammed the papers that lay on the table into it, jammed the stethoscope into it, and closed it with an audible sound that emphasized the tension that hung palpably in the air.

"I have a lot of reports to write," he mumbled quietly, and walked slowly towards his study.

Adora stared in dismay at her father's retreating figure, and then turned to Chike, who was leaning against the corner of the ivory wall unit that sparkled with crystal glasses and polished artifacts. His arms were folded, across his chest, and one long leg was crossed over the other. There was a hint of laughter in his eyes, and the expression on his face clearly said, "You should have known better."

He winked at her, and she stuck her tongue out at him, and flounced off in the direction of the kitchen. Her ears made out the barely perceptible chuckle that came from him as he made his way upstairs.

Chapter 8

She was only eleven years old the day that the course of her life spun out of control. The sequence of events that engendered that change was firmly, indelibly imprinted in the memory bank of her mind, and like the reels of a horror movie, they would often replay in her mind, plunging her into the deepest abyss of melancholy despair.

She would always remember her mother Christina as a serene, sweet-tempered woman of great regal beauty, whose beautiful life was suspended in a single fleeting moment.

It was a beautiful June day, one of those days when the earth sent her sweet essence to the world with beauty and sunshine, which streamed in golden rays and bathed everything with memorable loveliness. The air was clean and crisp, and the skies remained clear and sunny.

Adora was sitting on her desk in class, trying to listen to the monotonous droning voice of her history teacher Mrs. Udo, while staring outside at the cluster of flaming frangipani and hibiscus bushes that lined school grounds, inhaling and drowning in their heady fragrance. Mrs. Udo glanced in her direction and rapped on the desk sharply.

"Adora Amadi, stop daydreaming this very moment," she said loudly, followed by the sounds of laughter from class, which echoed around her. Adora snapped her head away from the window and cringed in shame as the kids banged on their desks and sing sang, "Daydreamer, daydreamer."

"Stop it right away," Mrs. Udo's voice rang out and the class went quiet.

"Don't mind them at all," her friend Ijeoma whispered from the desk behind and Adora nodded mutely.

The school bell rang suddenly, and Adora sighed with relief. She glanced at her friend Lily, who was packing her books into her bag said a hurried goodbye. She darted past the throng of school children pouring out of their classes and ran towards Chike's class. She found him packing his books into his school bag.

"C'mon, Chike," she squealed, as Chike caught sight of her and rushed past his friends towards her.

"Yeah coming," he replied, swinging playfully at her. She snatched his bag and took off running towards the school gate, with Chike in hot pursuit.

A rail-thin woman stepped in her path. It was Mrs. Madukwe, the school matron. She regarded Adora with a stern expression on her thin, bird-like face.

"Watch yourself young lady," she warned. There is to be no running like a wild animal on the school premises. Young ladies do not act this way."

"Yes Madam," Adora replied demurely, handing Chike's bag to him.

"See, you shouldn't run," Chike said, as soon as they were out of earshot of Mrs. Madukwe.

"Says who?" Adora challenged.

"Says Mrs. Madukwe. She said so and you know that is so."

"Let's walk home," Adora said.

"No, let's wait for Mr. James. He's coming to pick us up."

"Yeah, that's true," Adora sighed, as they stood by the gate, watching as a line of students crowded around the gate, waiting for their parents or driver to pick them up.

Their mother's BMW pulled up by the gate and Adora squealed in delight. The gatekeeper let them through and she flew into her mother's arms.

"Mommy, you came. I though you would be at work."

"That can wait," her mother said, as she helped her two children into the back seat of her car. "Today is for the three of us."

"What can we do today?" Adora queried."

"I know," Chike said. "How about the zoo."

"I have an even better idea. A picnic," their mother said.

"Yay!" Adora and Chike piped in simultaneously.

"What about the food? We'll go home to get the food?" Chike asked.

"I have everything we need in the trunk," her mom responded, leaning towards the back seat to smooth out a plait that was out of place on Adora's head

"What about daddy?" Adora asked.

"Daddy's still at work. I'm sure he won't mind."

"I'm sure he won't," Chike stated. "What about Uchenna?"

"He's home with the nanny. He won't mind a bit either."

At the park, they spread a fuzzy pink blanket on a grassy knoll and nibbled on a sumptuous feast of broiled suya beef kebabs, fruits, and mixed tropical nuts, washed down with freshly squeezed pineapple juice.

Adora and Chike enjoyed a game of Ludo while their mother Christina lay back on the blanket with a book, relaxing to the strains of jazz that wafted from the portable cd player that she had brought along for the trip.

The sudden rumblings of distant thunder interrupted their revelry- a sharp clap preceded by a white flash of lightning. The sky, which only a few moments before was clear blue and dotted with fluffy white clouds, turned a foreboding gray. The sun, which had been flirting with the flighty clouds and showing off its bright splendor, now made a hasty retreat from the ominous thunderclouds. In a flash, the raindrops turned into a torrent that thoroughly drenched their clothing and dampened their spirits.

Christina quickly gathered her children and the remnants of the picnic and

bundled them into the back of her white BMW sports coup for the short drive home. By the time car engine revved into life, solid sheets of water pelted the windscreen in blinding torrents and obscured a clear view of the road. The windshield almost seemed to buckle under the unusual weight of the water that pounded down relentlessly on it.

Christina switched on the windshield wiper to high speed. The windshield wiper was a blur, going 'swish, swish, swish, swish' as it struggled to dispel the heavy flood of water that obstructed a clear view of the road ahead. The rhythmic swooshing of the windshield wiper that accompanied the drumming sound of the solid sheet of water that pounded the roof of the car held a certain comfort for Adora. In its rhythmic swooshing, and the patter of the rain against the roof of the car, she seemed to hear a song that seemed to quell her rising trepidation.

Christina drove extra carefully, keeping a sharp eye on the road ahead, and clutching the steering wheel so tightly that her skin stretched tautly over her knuckles, which stood out in clear relief.

They drove through a puddle, and the car rocked slightly, swayed by the sheer force of the torrent. A brown tinged spray of muddy water sprang out from under the car and arced behind them with a loud splash.

Adora, who had been enjoying herself thoroughly now pouted her lips petulantly and tried to wish the rain away with a childish song.

"Rain, rain go away. Come again another day. Little children want to play," she chanted in a sing-song voice.

"Aw, that's so sissy," Chike taunted. Adora frowned and tried to catch her mother's attention.

"Mom, I'm scared. Let's park and wait," she said, feeling caged in by the foggy enclosure of the car. The dank smell of wet car seat leather tickled her nostrils, and a drop of rainwater squeezed its way through a small gap in the window, and splashed on her bare arm, prompting her to roll up the window tighter. She shivered visibly and stared miserably out the foggy window at the scenery, which, so sunny and busy, when they were coming, was now a bleak, dreary, and desolate contrast.

"Ooh, who's scared of a little rain?" Chike said in a mocking voice. "Not me," she said shakily in her bravest voice.

"I am not scared of rain," she reasserted, squaring her jaws and sticking them straight ahead.

Chike laughed and nudged her on the ribs with his elbow.

"Stop it! Mom tell him to stop!" she said, squirming around uncomfortably in her seat.

"That's enough, children," Christina said sharply, squinting through her glasses at the barely visible road, was blurred by the sheer volume of water that pelted the windshield.

In another fifteen minutes, they should be home. She hated to drive in this kind of weather condition, but she did not see the sense in parking the car and perhaps getting hit from behind by another car since it was very hard to see properly in this weather condition.

Better to keep going. They were almost home, and a warm atmosphere awaited them as soon as they got home.

It happened so fast that even under the best driving condition, it would have still ended disastrously.

As the little sports car was negotiating a sharp curve on the crest of a hill, a gigantic, lumbering truck appeared from nowhere and veered directly onto their path.

Christina instinctively swerved to the right, but it was no use. The huge vehicle

plowed directly into them with a sickening crunch of broken glass and twisting metal.

The impact of the crash sent the little car careening off the road. The BMW flipped violently in the air like a toy car, and landed on its side by the road incline, before righting itself with a sickening sound of crunching metal and shattered glass.

In a terrifying eternity wrapped up in one single quivering moment, Christina's luminescent light flickered as her lifeblood oozed out of the internal bleeding and stole her breath forever. The initial impact of the collision snapped her torso forward, and the seat belt ironically served as a catalyst that severed her spinal cord. As her head hit the steering wheel, her neck was

broken by the violent impact. She died instantly.

Screams ricocheted through the car, and Adora realized that the sounds were coming from her own parched throat. Something struck her on the head, and she was instantly plunged into darkness.

She woke up on a narrow bed in a strange, austere room that had a strong antiseptic smell. A strange form was bent over her, holding her wrist. Adora could not make out the being's features, because her eyes refused to focus. Everything seemed strangely out of focus.

She stared hard at the figure and could detect that the mouth was moving, but she could not make out the words because all sounds were blocked by a roaring sound--like the magnified rushing of winds in her ears. Everything had a strange, dreamlike quality. Her brain felt like mush and refused to focus on any lucid thoughts. A sharp pain sliced through the left side of her head, and she closed her eyes tightly shut.

She fought desperately to focus, to sort out the jumbled sequence of events that led to her being in that room, but her thoughts clanged around in her brain like unmatched pieces of a jigsaw puzzle that refused to be pieced together. Although her brain refused to function with any semblance of logic, she could not shake off the ominous cloud of foreboding that hung over her, like a specter from hell.

Then she remembered what her mother always told her. "Pray, when you are confused." Slowly, her brain began to focus, and she fought to grasp at the vague recollections that were slowly beginning to dawn on her. Slowly, her vision cleared, and the figure that was hovering over her approached with a wicked looking hypodermic needle.

It was a nurse in a starched white uniform, and something about the hypodermic needle seemed to jog her memory.

Suddenly her mind clicked into high gear and the events of the day flashed through her mind like the reels of a horror film playing in fast forward. Something snapped inside her, and she sat bolt upright. Her blood ran cold, and her entire body began to tremble like the leaves of a palm tree on a windy day. The nurse grabbed her by the shoulders and placed her head back upon the pillow.

"Calm down my dear," she said soothingly, placing a cool hand on Adora's forehead.

"You have been in an accident, and you need this to calm you down," she continued in her crisp voice. She drew closer to Adora with the wicked looking needle and reached towards her arm.

Adora sprang out of the bed like a wound-up coil and made for the open doorway. She glanced back at the nurse whose mouth had formed a surprised "O" and tore out of the room like a banshee. Her feet carried her through a long maze of corridors.

Although she heard the nurse calling her, she did not stop but ran blindly through the maze of corridors until she reached the waiting room.

She found her father pacing the floor furiously. His eyes were bloodshot, and his formally youthful face suddenly looked like a seventy years old mask of grief. Chike was hovering close by him, his head in his hands. He had a tiny dressing on his temple, which was the only visible attestation to the horror that he shared with Adora. She was vaguely aware of the presence of other people; assorted relatives and friends, but she did not focus on any of them.

All her attention was focused on her father. One look at his defeated expression and her entire world went crashing around her like a fragile house of cards.

"Where's...what happened to----Mom?" she shouted in a strangely disembodied voice that sounded unfamiliar to her like it was coming from a distance. She rushed into her father's arms, and clung tightly onto him, feeling the choking sobs that wracked his entire body.

Dr. Amadi struggled to maintain a tight rein on his emotion, although his face and demeanor betrayed every bit of the turmoil that was churning within him.

"What happened to mom?" Adora repeated, looking up at her father's tortured face. He shook his head helplessly, and she started to shout.

"But-----you are a doctor daddy, do something."

Her father held her tighter, soaking her hair with the hot tears that were streaming down his eyes.

"Where's my mommy," Adora screamed, tearing away from her father's grasp.

"I have to see her...I know that she will be okay if only I can speak to her.

She sprang away irrationally from the waiting room and ran blindly towards the general direction of the operating room. She was stopped by a firm grip on her arm, and she looked into the kind face of a doctor in surgical scrubs. He smiled compassionately at her and led her towards a chair.

"Please sit down, miss," he said in a conciliatory tone of voice and released his grip on her arm. She wobbled momentarily, her knees buckled underneath her, and her bottom hit the plastic surface of the chair.

A long, blood-curdling scream pierced the air- an agonized mournful wail that seemed to penetrate the very portals of hell. Adora realized that the scream was coming from her dry, parched throat.

She kept on screaming until her throat felt raw and swollen.

Strong hands held her arms, and she felt something cool and wet swab at her bare arm.

Vaguely, she smelt the acrid odor of rubbing alcohol, then felt the hot, stinging pain as the sharp point of a hypodermic needle bit into her skin. The sound of rushing winds filled her ears, and suddenly everything went pitch black.

She was drifting, drifting weightlessly, in slow motion down a cavernous, dark bottomless chasm that echoed with sounds.

Faintly, her eyes made out grotesque, nightmarish gargoyles which reached out from the sides of the chasm and tried to grab her with their ugly, slimy tentacles which stretched and strained ever so close to her, their soul-less, disembodied voices echoing all around her laughing mockingly at her distress.

"No!" she screamed as panic gripped the pit of her bowels and wrenched at the

very core of her being. She struggled futilely against forces that she could not fathom or even comprehend. All she knew was that she was enveloped with the strongest sense of foreboding, of impending doom and ultimate disaster.

"No!" she screamed again, falling deeper into the dark enveloping void.

Chapter 9

A strident staccato sound by her bedside snatched her from the fuzzy clouds of her deep slumber, quickly evaporating the memory of a dream that brought her mother so close she could almost touch her. She thrashed around in her bed, crying out her mother's name. Tears rolled down her eyes and she opened her eyes a crack and peered through bleary, sleep-encrusted eyes at the source of the persistent sound, the square-faced electronic alarm clock by her bedside, noting with annoyance that it was already 7:30 am. Ignoring the clanging alarm, she stretched and yawned lazily, snuggling deeper into the gauzy cotton coverlets that she had carelessly thrown off during the night, trying to snatch at the increasingly elusive cobwebs of sleep. The annoying sound persisted, and she reached groggily towards the clanging sound until her hand made contact with the electronic device, causing it to skid off the top of the night table and clatter all the way down, landing softly on the thickly padded rug with a soft thud. Adora sighed and crawled deeper into the thick cotton coverlet on her bed. She grabbed her fluffy pillow to muffle the annoying clanging, which persisted from the floor, forcing her to drag herself out of bed for her morning devotional.

She sat on her bed and read a passage from the book of Romans about God's sovereign love, meditating and ruminating on God's love and his supreme sacrifice through his son Jesus Christ; she thought about her mother, and the Bible passage stood out clearly in her mind. "---for all things work together for good, for those who love God and for those who are called according to his purpose." She bowed her head and said a silent prayer for her father, for herself and for her two brothers, asking for God's supreme guidance as they struggled to grapple with the gaping chasm that their mother's death had left in all of their lives.

The house was early morning quiet when she slipped into the bathroom that adjoined her bedroom. Through the white shaded window, the sun made a lazy appearance, the rays dancing off the edges of the slices of the louvered windowpanes. A solitary bird perched at the tree branch that waved lazily from the corner of the house and twittered chattily, forcing Adora to smile wryly to herself as stepped under the sprays of a cool shower, feeling the soothing tepid liquid sliding down her warm skin, cooling her body warm from the tropical heat that was already beginning to seep through her open bathroom window.

Her dressing room was now bare with the exception of a few lone outfits that hung forlornly on their hangers in neat rows. She dressed quickly in the mustard colored pant set that she had selected the night before, and glanced at the mirror, at the poised, stunning woman that stared back at her. That person seemed alien to the conflicted confused person inside her, buckling to the ogre of uncertainty that kept rearing at her.

The kitchen looked as inviting as it smelled, with the early morning sunlight streaming in through the open louver windows. Chike was sitting on a tall stool across from the kitchen counter munching on leftover meat pie from last night's dinner and perusing the contents of an open textbook in front of him. Clara, wearing a bubo set in a subtle shade of green was bustling around in front of the gleaming white stove, preparing breakfast while Uchenna stood over the kitchen table, placing dishes on place mats. Over his striped cotton pajamas, Uchenna had thrown on his favorite robe, a white linen frock that Adora had made for him in her University design class. It had lost the sparkling clarity of the original color and was now an indeterminate shade between gray and egg white, but Uchenna refused to part with it. "It's just so comfy," he always said.

As Adora stepped across the threshold, an uneasy silence fell across the room, and they all froze in their tracks; their eyes riveted on her slender form. Clara was the first to break up the tense atmosphere. She gave Adora an uneasy smile, her wooden spatula poised in the air.

"Oh, Adora you look so radiant. I like that brown suit on you. Come sit down so that you can eat breakfast."

"I don't feel very much like breakfast," Adora shrugged.

"Breakfast is the most important meal of the day. You should eat," Uchenna said, reaching for a mini meat pie from Chike's plate.

"You should ask first," Chike said, slapping Uchenna playfully on the hand. Chike turned to Adora. "Uchenna's right you know, you should eat."

Adora's stomach was doing flip-flops, and not inclined towards breakfast. All the insecurities that had been nagging at her for the past weeks rose like bile in her stomach. Right now, her future seemed uncertain; she was set to leave her familiar surroundings and step into another world. Going into the Master's degree program at the age of twenty was quite a feat by any standard, a feat that had not created a dent in her father's exacting expectations. Would she ever attain the elusive goals that her father expected, or would she fail? And what did life hold in store for her?

Chike pulled out the stool next to him and she sat there, facing him with a forced smile on her frozen face.

"You're studying really hard for your make-up test," she remarked in a voice that she hoped sounded gay, although she was feeling far from gay.

"Yep," he replied in a gruff voice, averting his eyes.

"Why don't you join me?" she turned to Uchenna, indicating the breakfast table.

"I, I ate already," Uchenna replied hesitantly as he rose slowly from his stool.

"I have to go get dressed now," he announced, followed by Chike, who glanced nervously at Adora.

"Yep, same here," he said. "I have to get ready too."

Adora stared morosely at her breakfast, a vivid concoction of egg omelets, laced with colorful chunks of tomatoes, red onions, and fresh spring onions, sitting beside a stack of Clara's famous banana fritters. The food smelled heavenly, but somehow, they tasted like plain egg whites today as she tried to force a few bites down her throat. The effort made her feel like gagging and she gave up completely and lowered her fork silently, standing up abruptly with a sigh.

Clara looked up at her in alarm. She was still tinkering with the stove, wiping down the pristine white surface with short quick movements. "Why, you didn't eat at all," she accused.

"Thank you for breakfast Miss Clara. I had enough."

"You're going to turn out fine you know," Clara said gently, as she busied herself peeling a bulbous red onion by the counter, slicing through the juicy tuber with quick, deft slicing motions. She sniffed and nodded mutely, dabbing at the corner of her eye with the corner of her green bubo.

In a sudden onslaught of uncontrolled emotion, Adora rushed to Clara's side, and gave her a tight embrace. Clara returned the embrace, her plump arms smothering Adora, who burrowed deeper into the folds of Clara's embrace, feeling the motherly love that flowed from her.

"Ms. Clara, God bless you. I have to go to daddy now," Adora said suddenly, glancing at her watch.

"God will grant you a safe trip. He will take care of you."

"Thank you, Clara, I will come back before you know it."

Clara sniffled silently, and turned away, as Adora rushed out to say goodbye to her father.

She found him in his study, sitting on the brown leather reclining chair behind

the expanse of the massive oak table, staring at, but not quite reading a copy of the Daily Vanguard spread out in front of him. Adora noticed that his eyes were red-rimmed and slightly moist. The permanent furrows that had crept up on his forehead appeared to have deepened today.

Adora stood hesitantly before him, searching for the right words to break the tense atmosphere.

"Morning daddy," she said in a voice that she hoped sounded bright, trying to swallow the lumps that kept forming in her throat.

Dr. Amadi turned to his daughter and his eyes clearly reflected the pain that his heart must endure. Standing before him in her smartly tailored linen suit, his daughter had never looked as close to her late mother as she did today. He shuddered as she came very close to him and knelt in front of him. He cleared his throat and patted her arm cursorily, motioning for her to rise.

"You don't want to miss your flight my dear. Now go, and don't forget any of the things I told you.'

"Yes daddy," she said softly, reaching out to hug him.

He hugged her stiffly and walked out the side door that led to the indoor garage.

Adora stood there, watching her father's stooped retreating back, her dismay etched all over her beautiful face. His abrupt dismissal hurt her to the core, but somehow, she understood; she father kept all his feelings bottled up since her mother died. But how long would he keep himself from feeling, from enjoying the joys of life? She started to run after him but her eyes went to the wall clock by his oak bookshelf and she changed her mind. She didn't want to miss her flight.

She looked longingly around the room, inhaling deeply, smelling the scent of leather that characterized this room, her father's favorite haunt, etching every single detail of this opulent room in her memory. This exercise brought an early wave of homesickness, and she ran out of the study, with

tears streaming down her eyes, almost colliding with Chike, who gathered her in his arms and gave her shoulders a squeeze.

"Remember Adora, always a trooper to the end," he said soothingly.

"A trooper to the end," she echoed, smiling through her tears, as she silently returned the embrace.

They walked to the front door where her father's Range Rover jeep stood, its chrome bouncing off bright rays of the morning sun. James stood by the trunk, loading her suitcases into the car trunk. He smiled pensively at her and held the passenger door open for her. Adora smiled uncertainly at him, and he grabbed her hand, and shook it vigorously.

"No forget us, you hear," he said in Pidgin English.

"I won't forget any of you, and thank you so much, she said, as she climbed into the passenger side next to Chike, who already had the engine of the jeep running.

They drove in silence, through the twisting lanes of Ekulu, and into the traffic clogged Uwani area. Uchenna sat stifflly at the rear, staring morosely out the window at the cluster of one and two-story homes that raced past them.

Chike glanced in the rear-view mirror at Uchenna. "Hey! Your face won't crack if you smile," he said half-heartedly, attempting to break the tense atmosphere.

"What?" Uchenna asked, startled. "Your face is too long. Shorten it."

Nobody laughed at Chike's jokes and an uneasy silence settled in the confines of the car for the rest of the drive.

They arrived at the Enugu airport terminal, and Chike maneuvered the

jeep into an empty spot in the dusty parking lot. Her brothers carried the heavier part of her luggage set and she trudged silently besides them, clutching on to her brown suede handbag, and wheeling the tiny valise that matched her luggage. Chike checked in her luggage and they stood awkwardly, blending with the people that milled around the terminal, waiting for her flight announcement.

Too soon, the dreaded announcement cackled over the loudspeaker, and Adora stood up and straightened her pants over her hips. Amid a flurry of hugs, promises, and tears, she stumbled out of the terminal, her vision blurred by the tears that she was suppressing for the benefit of Uchenna. She stood on line with the other passengers waiting to board their flight, finally allowing the floodgate of tears to erupt.

"A trooper to the end," she reminded herself as she dabbed self- consciously at the corner of her eyes with the edge of her kerchief.

Swallowing deep gulps of air to dispel the butterflies that fluttered around in her stomach, she kept her shoulders straight, and marched down the tarmac and up the gangway to the small passenger airplane. At the top of the stairs, oblivious to the people on line behind her, she turned and waved at her brothers, who were still standing behind the plate glass walls of the terminal, peering at the "Air One" passenger plane. The man on line behind her glanced at his watch and cleared his throat noisily, clutching at his frayed leather overnight bag. Glancing nervously at the sweating red-faced European man Adora smiled apologetically and stepped into the narrow aisle of the airplane.

"May I see your boarding pass please?" A soft female voice said from behind her, startling her. She blinked as she tried to regain her composure and looked up at the smiling face of a pretty flight attendant in a smartly tailored navy-blue suit uniform that hugged her petite curves. Numbly Adora fumbled around in her suede handbag until she found the stub and held it out stiffly at the attendant.

"This way please," the flight attendant said cheerily, leading Adora down the narrow aisle until they located her seat, which was by the window.

A mammoth sized woman, resplendent in a light green caftan sat on the isle

seat, snoring softly through her slightly open mouth, next to a dark-skinned girl of about twenty-three, whose legs seemed to go on forever in a skimpy white mini dress and matching sandals. The girl was attempting to read a paperback novel, and as Adora leaned towards them, she lifted her eyes from her book, glanced at the sleeping woman, and shrugged, almost apologetically. Adora cleared her throat softly, startling the sleeping woman, whose eyes flew open. She looked dazed for a moment, and then made room for Adora, who squeezed past her ample form and the long legs of the young girl in the middle seat. Adora nodded at the tall girl and settled into her window seat. The girl in the middle seat nodded acknowledgement, and her eyes wandered to the sleeping woman next to her, who rested her head on the plush headrest and resumed her soft snoring, her mouth gaping open.

Adora settled on her seat by the window and stared out the tiny airplane window at the busy terminal. It was bustling with people, but it looked lonely without her brothers. Her eyes searched frantically among the throng of people, until she finally located them standing a distance from the crowds, staring forlornly at the plane. She tore her eyes away from them, knowing that they could not see her through the plane window from that distance.

With a soft, barely audible sigh, she settled into her seat, flipping through the pages of a paperback that she had brought along with her for the flight, making a futile attempt to absorb its contents. Failing at that, she closed the pages with a loud thwack, startling the sleeping woman next to her, who stirred and murmured something unintelligible. She scratched her ample cleavage, causing the synthetic material of her caftan to rustle noisily, and settled down on her seat again to resume her soft snoring.

Once the plane was air bound, Adora ordered a ginger ale from a flight attendant, who passed by, rolling her trolley down the aisle.

"I'll have a ginger ale too," the tall girl in the middle seat said, glancing briefly at the reposed form of the woman in the aisle seat next to her, who was now scratching her plump double chin and murmuring something in her sleep.

"Can you believe this?" the tall girl whispered, rolling her eyes and giggling softly. She stuck out her hand and introduced herself.

Her name was Monica Udeh, and she was twenty-three. Monica had just completed her OND degree at Imo State University in Owerri and was going to Lagos to study theater arts at Yaba College of Technology.

"But I also want to try my hand at modeling, and I think that you should too," she concluded.

"Oh no, my dad would kill me," Adora exclaimed.

"Are you serious?" Monica queried.

"Yeah, seriously. My dad would definitely have a fit if I even so much as try. But I can see why you would want to do that," Adora concluded, glancing at Monica.

Even from her seated position, Monica was tall. Her micro mini dress hugged her svelte form, accentuating her slender arms and impossibly long lean legs. With her smooth coffee mocha complexion and her beautifully sculpted face accentuated by a short, bobbed do, she could have been a live replica of a masterfully rendered ebony carving.

"No telling where you might run into your prince," she said with a giggle, as though she read Adora's mind.

With a fluid movement, she unbuckled her seat belt, and stood up, leaning over slightly to avoid bumping her head on the abutment of the airplane ceiling, while tugging ineffectually at her super short, tight dress to cover her exposed legs. "I have to use the bathroom," she said apologetically, squeezing past the sleeping woman on the aisle seat, who did not stir. Moments later, she returned, and leaned close to Adora.

"You would think that with her hefty load, she would be smart enough to sit by the window, and save people the headache," she whispered with a giggle.

"That's her assigned seat," Adora responded curtly, irritated by the girl's insensitivity.

"She could have asked to switch seats," Monica concluded, making a face.

They sat in awkward silence for a while, and Monica cleared her throat.

"Adora, that's your name, right? Where are you staying in Lagos?" she asked, as she tugged at the hem of her little white dress, which was riding steadily up her thigh.

"Victoria Island." Adora intoned.

"VI?" Monica exclaimed her voice rising in excitement. "I am staying in VI too. My cousin Regina and her husband Charles, they have a duplex close to the Marina. I'll be staying with them. Regina is my first cousin, but she is also like my second cousin and my cousin-in-law because her mother is my mother's cousin. Her father, my uncle is my father's brother, and her mother is my mother's second cousin. Isn't that funny? That's almost like incest, but it really isn't because her mother is only married to my uncle, who is not related to her."

"Oh my goodness," Adora chuckled in amusement as she listened to Monica's lengthy monologue.

The trip passed quickly, and soon, the landscape of Lagos appeared beneath them like toy figures on a map. The radio system cackled into life and the voice of the airline pilot came through.

"Ladies and gentlemen, this is your captain speaking. We are approaching the outskirts of Lagos at an altitude of five thousand feet. Please fasten your seat belts and prepare for landing. And thanks for flying Air One."

As the passengers obeyed, the metallic click of seat belts clicking into place filled the cavernous interior of the airplane. The sleeping woman continued to snore, and Monica nudged her gently. She woke up with a startled expression on her face and peered at the two girls curiously. Adora pointed at the seat belt sign and realization dawned on her face as she yanked at her seat belts and struggled to wrap them around her copious girth. Once she had succeeded in locking the seatbelt device, she closed her eyes and resumed her soft snoring as the barely detectable sound of the disengaging airplane landing gear reached Adora's ears. Moments later, the plane touched down on the tarmac and rolled swiftly down the runway for a smooth landing. The sleeping woman stirred, opened her bleary eyes a crack, and closed it again. She yawned, stretched, scratched her neck and mumbled something unintelligible. Adora and Monica exchanged glances and giggled as they sat up and squeezed past her.

They filed out of the airplane, and headed towards the crowded, noisy terminal.

The muggy midafternoon air hung still and breezeless, making Adora's tank top underneath her sleeveless jacket to feel like a restraining band around her torso.

"Man, it's way too hot," Monica complained, as she whipped off her short white jacket, revealing her bare toned brown arms.

"Your jacket looks altogether too hot. I think you should take it off," she instructed Adora.

"I think I'll keep it on," Adora protested, thinking about the lacy camisole that she wore underneath the jacket. Her skin felt hot and sticky, and she unbuttoned the jacket a few notches, feeling self-conscious about the cream- colored lace that peeked underneath her jacket.

"You shouldn't have worn it then, it's too hot for Lagos weather," Monica said wryly, wrinkling her nose at Adora.

"You are right Monica, I didn't think of it because Enugu is so cool and breezy because of the hills," Adora responded.

Standing beside their coordinated luggage sets in their smart outfits, the girls made a striking pair, and soon a throng of men besieged them, trying to catch their attention. Motorists honked their horns and two men pushing a trolley filled with bread whistled at them, gesticulating wildly at them.

"Stupid guys," Monica said through clenched teeth.

"They have nothing better to do," Adora said as they kept a sharp eye on their luggage while scanning the road for a taxi. A muscular young man in a sleeveless multi-colored dashiki appeared before them, pushing a trolley. A chewing stick dangled from the corner of his lips, and he pulled it out of his mouth and shoved it into the pocket of his khaki pants.

"Where to?" he asked, hefting their luggage pieces onto the trolley, without obtaining their permission.

"We're going to the taxi terminal; we need to catch a cab," the girls said, almost simultaneously. He regarded them through hooded eyes and smiled, flashing pearly white teeth.

"Where and where?"

"Same place, VI," Monica said.

"Oh, so you need to share a cab then? Follow me," he instructed. He wheeled the trolley to the busy taxi depot and started to negotiate with the girls.

"If you pay me a thousand Naira extra, I will find you a cab."

"No thanks," Adora stated firmly, and pushed a crumpled bill into his sweaty palm. He shrugged and pushed his trolley towards the terminal, zeroing in on another customer.

"He has some stupid nerves," Monica hissed. The going rate for skycaps should be five hundred and fifty Naira.

A battered taxicab rattled to a screeching halt in front of them, and the

driver, a short, stocky man in his late thirties stepped out of the cab and approached them. He was wearing a faded tee shirt that showed perspiration stains under the armpit. His shorts were loose and ill-fitting and hung limply around his skinny legs.

"*Ekaro-o*," he greeted in Yoruba.

The girls stared at him blankly, and his face broke into a smile.

"Oh, Omo Ibo. Ehe, you speak Ibo," he declared. *"My mama be omo Ibo but I never speak am ooo,"* he continued in Pidgin English, the unofficial language of both the educated and the uneducated that served as a bridge to the language barrier that existed in Lagos, Nigeria's city of cultural convergence.

"Where you dey go fine girls, make I take you," he said in a loud voice, which mixed with the sound of traffic and the mid-afternoon bustle of Lagos. Adora understood him because Pidgin English was a derivative of the English language, but she shrank away from him in dismay. Something about him made her very uncomfortable.

"I want take you, where you want go," he said, and emphasized that by pointing at his battered cab, making a driving motion with his hands.

The girls shook their heads firmly, and the man waved at another man, who was standing by the taxi parked in front of them. The man walked rapidly to them and whispered something to the first man. He was tall and rangy, and his shifty, blood-shot eyes darted this way and that and gave him the look of a cornered rat.

His dingy, ill-fitting clothes looked like they had seen better days and hung limply on his bony body. He exuded a pungent combination of sweat and cheap cologne and Adora wrinkled her nose as he stood over her, his sweaty armpit almost flush with her face.

"We don't need your services, neither of you," Adora said shakily, trying to infuse some authority into her tremulous voice. She fanned herself with her paperback novel and backed away from the odious man. His stocky friend motioned to him and they exchanged furtive glances. The cornered rat grabbed Monica by the hand and scooped up her luggage pieces with the other hand, while his friend grabbed Adora and her luggage pieces and rushed them towards the taxi. It happened so fast that none of the girls had the chance to react.

"Hey! What do you think you are doing?" Adora recovered fast and began to fight but he dragged her along easily, while she tried to dig her heels into the ground.

"You don't have to be afraid girls," the cornered rat said. "We will take care of you."

Adora tried to scream as the men dragged them along but discovered that her voice did not travel far in the noisy environment.

Monica kicked the cornered rat, who had her in his firm grasp, and he laughed low in his throat and kept dragging her. Adora dug her feet deeper into the graveled road, but he pulled her easily like a rag doll.

Adora flashed back to her aunt, who had offered to pick her up from the airport, but she had refused, claiming that she wanted to be more independent and test her wings. "What a time to be independent," she thought as she fought desperately to calm the rising panic that engulfed her entire being. Her heart pounded as she clawed at the stocky man's hand with her manicured nails and dug her heels into his shin; but he flicked her off and did not break his stride as he dragged her closer to the battered cab.

They reached the waiting taxi, and the stocky man handed Monica to the cornered rat, and he held onto the struggling girls, while the stocky man piled their luggage into the trunk of the taxi. Adora's eyes were stinging with tears as she continued to scream at the top of her voice, but nobody seemed to hear.

"Stop it right there," a deep voice came from behind them, and Adora cried with relief as a policeman rushed towards them and the touts clambered into the cab and drove off with their luggage in their trunk. A patrol car cut them off and they came to a screeching halt. Another officer stepped out of the patrol car and rounded up the thieves and handcuffed them while his partner pulled the girls' luggage pieces from the trunk of the taxi.

"Oh, thank you so much," the two girls said simultaneously. The cop scratched his chin and pulled the girls to the side of the street.

"Thank you again officers," Adora repeated.

"Yes, you girls should be more careful," he said, eying their expensive luggage pieces.

"We didn't expect this to happen," Adora said defensively, but he cut her off.

"You have made my work more difficult," he said sorely. "How?" Monica asked.

"I was on my way home, and now I have to help my partner book those men. That is extra work. My shift is almost over.

"Oh, we are so sorry," Adora said sympathetically. "But we weren't expecting anything like this."

"Sorry is not enough," the officer said gruffly. "You have to compensate me."

"Compensate you how?" Adora asked in shock.

"You know what to do, you were not born yesterday," he responded tersely. "You can't be serious," Monica screamed in anger. "Are you crazy?"

"I will tell you who is crazy," the officer said dryly. He glanced at Adora's designer luggage set and his eyes lit up.

"Those look expensive madam. Can you show me receipts for them?"

"What?" Adora said in a voice tight with anger. How can you expect me to carry around the receipt of my luggage?"

"You must be out of your mind," Monica hissed.

"You dare not speak to me like that," he said to Monica in a voice that rang of steel. "You will see who is crazy. I am taking you girls in to the station and you can explain where you got all the expensive things that you are carrying." He picked up his radio and spoke into it.

"I have two suspects here at the airport car depot. Stolen property, resisting arrest, menacing a police officer. Can you send back up now?"

Adora stood aghast as the man replaced the radio in his pocket.

"Ten thousand Naira. No negotiating. Or you go to jail."

Chapter 10

Adora opened her mouth again, but the protest died on her lips as a gleaming white Bentley convertible purred to a smooth stop in front of the startled trio. The driver's side door swung open and a man stepped out of the car and walked towards them. Dressed nattily in a beige colored silk suit of a tropical weight that seemed crafted entirely by hand, he looked like he had stepped out of a Nollywood movie screen. Monica's mouth flew open and Adora's breath caught in her throat. The corrupt officer that was harassing them dropped Adora's bag on the ground and gaped stupidly at the handsome stranger.

Towering above six feet, the stranger had a rugged, athletic build that suggested a physical, athletic lifestyle. His complexion was a perfect balance of coffee and buttered chocolate with a glowing sun kissed quality that offset his handsome features, which were a sculptor's dream come true. He had high cheekbones, a sculpted straight nose, and the softest, most sensual lips that Adora had ever seen on any man, accentuated by a fine, cultivated mustache that she had the most irresistible urge to stroke. His dark, wavy hair, cropped close to his scalp, gleamed in the midday sun, and his dark, riveting eyes had an arresting quality that seemed to pierce through the portals of her very soul.

His handmade silk suit lent him an easy elegance, offset by lambskin suede shoes, which looked hand crafted by skilled artisans for his feet. This handsome, well-groomed stranger overlooked no detail, and carried himself with an air of confidence that complemented his perfect grooming. He approached them and smiled disarmingly at the girls

"What seems to be the problem here?" he asked in a smooth, velvety voice that sent a strange shiver up and down Adora's spine. His cultured diction had a cosmopolitan flair that made it difficult to trace what part of the world he grew up in but seemed to indicate that he had traveled widely.

The handsome stranger focused his attention on the policeman, towering over him, his disdain mirrored on his handsome face. The officer's hand went to his rifle, but he thought better of it.

"No interfering with police business," he said brusquely.

"I see you menacing these young ladies. What is their offense?"

"Stolen property," the policeman said in a voice that lacked confidence this time. "They have no receipt for their bags.

"Can you cite the ordinance that states that one must carry their receipts all the time," the handsome stranger queried.

"Ehm, err, uh," the officer stuttered. "They should prove that it wasn't stolen."

"What is your name officer?" the stranger asked. You should have your badge visible at all times.

"I was about to close, sir," he said weakly.

"Then you have no business harassing these young ladies. I will call the police commissioner right now if you do not get away from here." He reached into his chest pocket and pulled out a cell phone.

"I am sorry sir----errrr, I didn't mean any harm. I was just doing my job," he stuttered. "I 'm leaving right away," he huffed, and rushed away, towards the patrol car, where his partner had just finished loading the offenders. He slid behind the passenger front seat of the patrol car and they drove away in haste.

Relief flooded through Adora's body, making her weak in the knees, and leaving her to wonder if it was really the feeling of relief that left her weak kneed or the effect of the perfectly handsome stranger. She expelled the air trapped in her lungs and straightened her jacket, fussing with the lapel.

Monica practically swooned under the handsome stranger's spell and began to gush.

"Oh thank you so much Mister," she exclaimed, fluttering her eyelashes in a most beguiling manner.

"I am glad to be of assistance," he said with a slight bow and Monica glowed. "May I take you beautiful ladies to your destination?" he offered gallantly in his deep, caressing voice.

Adora tried to respond, but no words came out of her gaping mouth. Feeling like a total idiot, she swallowed hard to alleviate her parched throat. "W, we were waiting for a cab. T, thanks for offering, but I am sure that we'll locate one very soon," she managed, feeling like an utter idiot.

Monica was still gaping, and Adora nudged her surreptitiously on the elbow.

The handsome stranger smiled his perfect smile, revealing perfectly shaped white teeth.

"Let me introduce myself," he offered. "My name is Randall Okere, but you can call me Randy, all my friends do." He pulled out a gold-filigreed card from his breast pocket and handed it to the girls. It read — Randal Ikenna Okere. Aviation, Transportation, Air something---, Adora could not make out the rest as Monica palmed the card and slipped it into her jacket pocket, then offered Randy her long slender hands.

"Mm Randy, I'm Monica Umeh," she cooed, flashing him a brilliant smile.

"Well Monica, it is my pleasure," Randy said in his heart stopping voice. He took her outstretched hand, raised her fingers towards his lips, and smiled into her eyes.

Adora felt a strange, unreasonable stab of jealousy, and admonished herself

immediately. Randy was a perfect stranger after all, and she had no right to feel anything like this. The sooner she got through with the formalities of introductions, the sooner she could get away from those heart melting eyes, now riveted in her direction. Adora lowered her eyes shyly and studied her shoes to avoid the scrutiny of those piercing dark eyes.

Monica's voice yanked her back to reality.

"Randy, hmm, I like the sound of that," Monica was saying.

"And this is my friend Adora Amadi," she added coyly, finally releasing his hand.

"Adora," Randy said, looking directly at her. Her name dripped from his mouth like melted honey.

"Pleased to meet you," Adora mumbled, reaching for his hand.

"The pleasure is all mine," he said, taking her hand and staring deep into her eyes.

Something very strange happened the moment their eyes locked, like a palpable current of electricity, which started from her fingertips, and ran through her body, creating an exhilarating rush that set her heart fluttering in her chest. Her heart thumped wildly, like the wings of a trapped bird flapping against the restraining rails of a cage. Her almond amber eyes searched the velvety charcoal depths of Randy's own, and detected a hint of fire that flickered in the unreadable depths of his deep brown, almost black eyes that sent her pulse racing, and left her throat feeling dry, almost parched. She dropped his hands abruptly, like they were hot coals and lowered her gaze to the ground and kept her eyes averted. She could still feel his hot gaze on her, and her heart beat quickened.

The exchange was so brief, so fleeting that Monica missed it, and Adora began to wonder if she had imagined it.

"Now that the formalities are done with, may I take you ladies to your destination?" Randy offered, with genuine concern on his face.

"Sounds very nice, but how?" Monica queried, glancing at the sleek two seater convertible sitting by the side of the road, and then at their pile of luggage. It was a beautiful car, fit for a king, but strictly made for two, and could not possibly accommodate the girls and their luggage.

"That should not be a problem," Randy said, smiling his perfect smile. He reached into the Bentley and retrieved a gleaming silver phone.

"Forgive me for not explaining properly, but I have an office very close to the airport. If you ladies can give me a moment, I will call for a more suitable car."

He activated the phone and started to punch numbers on the keypad. "Oh wow!! You would do that? Really thanks Randy. It would--," Monica began, but Adora cut her off.

"We're grateful for your kind offer, but we'll manage," she said curtly. "Believe me, it is no imposition at all," Randy said in his melted chocolate voice.

"We'll make out okay," Adora said firmly. Randy smiled again, and a dimple appeared on his left cheek.

"Then at least let me help you find a taxi, just wait right here," he said.

Randy stepped out of the curb and raised his hand. A taxi rolled to a stop in front of him and he reached into the breast pocket of his silk sports jacket.

"Wow, so fast," Monica said. "Thank you, Randy," Adora said.

"Don't mention," Randy said and retrieved a wallet of embossed alligator skin from his breast pocket.

"How much to VI?" he asked the taxi driver. He pulled out a monogrammed gold and silver money clip from his wallet.

"No, no," Adora protested.

"Really, Randy, it's okay," Monica added.

"I'll give you a hand with this," Randy addressed the driver, as he hefted pieces of the girls' luggage into the trunk. The taxi driver stepped out of the cab and picked up the rest, loading them into the trunk. He glanced at the plate number of the taxi and took a quick picture of it with his phone.

"Just making extra sure," he chuckled, "and sorry about your experience earlier."

"Can you imagine," Monica spat out "The same people that are supposed to protect you are the worse thieves."

"Thanks again for helping us Randy," Adora said, feeling unreasonably nervous in this stranger's presence.

"It was my pleasure Dora," he said and Adora felt a strange chill run through her body.

As Randy helped Adora into the car, their eyes met briefly, and she lowered hers, fussing with her handbag as Monica held his hand too long, and thanked him profusely.

"Glad to be of assistance," he stated as the driver taxi started the ignition of the car.

Randy climbed back into his Bentley, and honked once, waved and then drove off into the traffic.

Adora felt a slight twinge to regret stemming from the knowledge that she would probably never set eyes on the handsome stranger again. Monica was nudging her and garbling in excitement.

"Hmm, what?" Adora said absently, snapping back to reality.

"Oh Adora!" Monica exclaimed excitedly. "Pinch me and tell me that I was not dreaming. Can you believe that?""

Adora smiled vaguely, and despite her wildly beating heart, she blinked at Monica. "Believe what?" she said deliberately.

"Randy silly, wasn't he something else?" Monica said eagerly. "He was very nice," Adora murmured.

"Very nice?" Monica sniffed. "C'mon admit it Adora, he was a dish."

"He was okay," Adora said stubbornly, knowing deep inside that she found

him more than okay. "Okay? You need glasses?"

Adora smiled and stared through the dusty window, at the busy streets that flew past them. They were zipping through a fly-over bridge, and the city lay vast underneath them, stretching further than the eyes could see.

"Randy--hmm, what a name. Don't you think that fits?" Monica said. "As far as names go, I think it is a regular name," Adora responded. "I wonder who he is?" Adora found herself saying.

"The card," Monica exclaimed, fumbling with her jacket pocket and her purse. "Oh no!" she exclaimed. "I lost it."

"Lost what?"

"The card that he gave me." Monica stated tersely. "Oh," Adora said.

"Well I guess that we'll never find out now who he is. Such a shame because we didn't give him a chance," Monica said with a sigh.

"Chance to do what? Adora asked absently.

"Drop us off silly. Who knows---?" She let her words trail off, nudging Adora by the elbow.

"No way," Adora said.

"I didn't see any ring on his wedding finger. You just never know," Monica responded.

Adora glared at her fiercely and she giggled girlishly, making Adora to scowl at her.

"Monica! You know better than that. He may be nice, but a stranger is a stranger, and you just can't go about accepting rides like that. Lagos is a big city. Besides, you can't judge people by their looks." she said firmly, trying with difficulty to believe her own spiel while she fought against the secret twinge of regret about what would never be. With a little sigh, she pushed her focus on the streets rushing past them.

The streets of Lagos were full of life - loudspeakers blasting a music from the many storefronts that lined the streets, and the loud noises mingling with the strident blare of cars, trailers, and bus horns. Above the clamor of traffic, voices rose and fell, with the blend of various languages that reflected the cultural diversity of Lagos. The sights were just as colorful and varied — sky-high buildings juxtaposed next to low-slung bungalows and split-level homes; solid brick duplexes and residential buildings nestled between imposing office buildings and commercial facades; and storefronts jostling for space with restaurant facades. Now, a stretch of gleaming car dealership storefront windows, showcasing long lines of shiny new cars emblazoned with "for sale" signs, competing with outdoor dealerships cluttered with lines of used cars.

Here, a large schoolyard, brimming with excited children in school uniform, and there, a stately old mansion, dressed up in white marble facades and encircled with tall imposing fences to keep out prying eyes, right next to a storefront brimming with an array of goods for sale.

Soon the traffic wended its way to the outskirts of Surulere, and traffic came to a grinding halt; the streets erupted into a discordant cacophony of blaring horns, mixed with the clamorous sounds of Juju music that blasted from the loudspeakers of the storefronts that lined the streets.

A battered Molue bus rattled by, its overworked engine spewing choking black smoke through the exhaust pipes. Ignoring all rules of traffic and sanity, the bus tried to maneuver through a break in the traffic, resulting in more confusion. The girls stared in dismay as the driver discharged a set of passengers illegally, adding to the general traffic pandemonium.

As traffic picked up, a brown-skinned man, wearing a faded khaki safari pantsuit darted through the traffic towards the bus, as the bus driver brought the vehicle to a screeching halt, causing the Audi sedan behind it to veer abruptly to the right. The smoke from the bus's exhaust continued to pour in through all gaps in the taxi, and Adora glanced at Monica's window, which was halfway down, letting in grayish wisps of smoke.

"Please wind up your glass," she told Monica, coughing and waving delicately at the wispy puffs of smoke that swirled around them.

"Omigosh, there is no handle to the winding mechanism," Monica exclaimed, as the taxi driver chuckled, and handed her the missing winder.

"Here, use this Miss," he said tartly.

"This is ridiculous," Monica hissed, as she attached the handle to the winder, and wound up the window against the wispy black smoke, which was still drifting in through the rapidly ascending glass.

"This is Lagos," the taxi driver said, as he stretched out his hand, and she handed the

metal handle back to him.

On the street, hawkers seized advantage of the slowed traffic condition, and approached the long lines of vehicles, displaying sundry wares, ranging from newspapers and magazines to cosmetic products, perfumes, sunglasses and hair combs. They darted through the slow-moving traffic, sweating in the mid-afternoon sun and chasing the cars in their efforts to make a sale. People darted in front of cars, crossing the streets with no regards to the rules of traffic or the overhead crossing bridges that had been designated for that purpose. Impatient motorists honked their horns and panhandlers approached the long line of cars that snaked down the expressway, begging for handouts, bursting into songs, or words of praises for their intended targets.

A small child of about twelve approached the taxi on Monica's side, thrusting a dented pan, jingling with coins towards Monica. She was a beautiful child, with liquid brown eyes staring out of a dirt-streaked face.

"Poor thing," Monica sighed. She dug into her wallet and extracted a handful of coins. Adora leaned over Monica and deposited a fistful of Naira bills into the child's pan.

"God bless you, pretty Miss," the child said with a wan smile, and headed to the next car.

"Poor thing," Adora said, staring at the child's retreating back. "I wish I could take her home."

"Then you might as well take the rest of them home, maybe their parents too," Monica countered.

"It's just so sad and hopeless," Adora commented.

"Well, that is society--- one of the grim realities of several developing societies."

"Actually, it's the same the world over. I've seen it in London and New York city," Adora stated.

"That is life," Monica intoned.

"True, but that doesn't make it feel any better," Adora said wistfully.

Finally, the taxi crawled past Surulere, and approached Ikeja, the busiest section of Lagos. Here, the streets were filled with gaily-dressed people wearing vividly hued native attire- asheoke, damask, lace and jacquard outfits in vivid and iridescent colors of the rainbow. A handful of people in business suits, clutching briefcases in their hands marched through the portals of office buildings that they passed with signs like P. Olamide and Sons Ltd, Akinlade Holding PLC, Amanze Trading Inc.

"Wow! So many people," Monica enthused.

"Well, you know what they say," Adora replied. "What's that?" Monica asked.

"Well, they say that the streets of Lagos are so highly populated that

sometimes the spirits of dead people manifest themselves in human forms and stroll amongst the living.

"Oh, I heard that before. In fact my cousin Regina's neighbor saw one of those," Monica stated.

"What?" Adora asked in surprise.

"Yes. She had a neighbor, mama Adebayo who died during labor." "Such a shame, poor thing," Adora said.

"Well, the day that she died, Regina's neighbor saw her at the market; she had just gotten off work, and she had to buy fresh meat from the abattoir. She saw mama Adebayo at the shoe department, buying shoes for her son. Regina's neighbor was surprised to see her because she was supposed to be at the hospital giving birth. So she approached her and said, "Mama Ade, what are you doing at the market? What about the baby?"

"And she told her that she had to run to the market for a little errand. I needed to buy something for the new baby, she had said. But do me a favor. Will you keep this for my little boy? I will be away for a while and I do not trust my husband because he is right as we speak on top of his girlfriend, and I do not want him to spend my hard-earned money on his tart."

"Is this really true?" Adora asked.

"Every single word. One day you will meet my cousin. You can ask her." "Wow!" Adora exclaimed.

A woman approached the car, carrying a tray piled high with artfully peeled oranges.

"Buy my delicious oranges," she said in a sing song voice.

"No thanks," the girls chorused, as the traffic moved slowly past the woman, and she darted towards the next car.

"Anyway," continued Monica. "Mama Adebayo handed Regina's neighbor a bank passbook.

"I will be in the hospital for a while," she said. "Please take money from this account

and make sure my son is well cared for."

"You're joking right?"

"No really, it's quite true," Monica responded, and continued.

"Mama Adebayo handed Regina's neighbor the pass book. She also handed her a bundle of brand-new shoes and clothing for her son. Regina found out later that day that mama Adebayo had passed away that morning."

"Wow!" Adora commented.

"Wow look at that," Monica exclaimed. A group of people had gathered

around the front of a compound, where two men were dancing and twirling, towering head and shoulders above the three-story building.

"Stilt walkers," Adora said.

At the front of a large mercantile bank, people streamed out with briefcases and the girls played a little game, trying to piece out the lives of the people that rushed past them.

"Those are probably co-workers going to lunch together," Adora said. "Over there, those love birds, holding hands. Maybe they're newlyweds, so much in love," Monica said.

"Maybe they're lovers, married to others, perhaps stealing a few furtive moments with each other," Adora said.

A group of women marched by, clutching tightly to their children's hands. A middle-aged woman walked into a restaurant, carrying an infant boy on her back with a sling made out of a long strip of wrapper. An errant toddler broke free from his mother's restraining hand and dashed towards the slow-moving traffic. His mother chased him hotly and caught him moments later. She marched him to a nearby flower hedge and stripped a young sapling from the hedge. The whip came down on the boy's back and he yelped in pain. Monica wrinkled up her nose. "Kids are such brats," she commented.

"They require a lot of patience," Adora responded.

"I don't think I want one of those," Monica stated tersely. They are too much trouble.

"I think you will change your mind one day, "Adora responded with a laugh. "I think babies are so cute."

"Buy my sweet mangoes," a fruit vendor cried out in a singsong voice as she walked past them, a colorful plastic tray piled high with a pyramid of ripe mangoes perched on her head. She walked with ease and grace without holding on to the tray and stopped besides a white Lexus in front of them as the woman in the front passenger seat leaned over picked out three mangoes and paid her. She walked towards the taxi and Adora bought four for her aunt.

"I wonder," Monica said, staring at the woman as she disappeared among the throng of people. "I wonder how those people manage to keep those trays of fruit balanced on their heads and walk so effortlessly."

"Practice," Adora said.

"I keep thinking that the fruits will tumble out of the tray any moment."

"It's all in the neck. They have really strong necks."

As the taxi turned a corner, they caught glimpse of school children in school uniforms milling around behind the gates of a school compound, in perfect line formation. Their exuberant voices rang out, almost drowning out the strident sounds of traffic.

They neared the outskirts of Ikeja, and as the traffic condition cleared considerably, the taxi increased speed, zipping past the imposing edifice of the National Theater of Arts.

"I can never get over the beauty and the unique architectural style of this structure," Monica sighed.

"I love that sculpture in the courtyard---so graceful," Adora agreed.

You are approaching VI, the driver said suddenly, as the blue lagoon snaked past them and the outskirts of

Victoria Island stretched out before them. Here the heavy traffic thinned out and the boisterousness of mainland Lagos gave way to an upscale neighborhood with wider streets and quieter lanes, lined with tall, willowy palm trees that swayed gracefully in the tropical afternoon breeze. The tall high- rise buildings of mainland Lagos and the bustling enterprise that characterized Ikeja and Surulere gave way to a more laid-back atmosphere, with shops, boutiques, beauty salons, and restaurants storefronts flaunting signs like 'Ladies of distinction beauty palace' and 'Nneka's fine cuisine.'

The detached houses in this upscale neighborhood were gated and larger, with shelters for the guards that watched the houses.

"Just like Ekulu," Adora thought idly.

Here and there, one could glimpse the grandeur of the stately homes through gaps in the well-manicured hedges spilling with colorful tropical flowers which decorated the tall fences that surrounded the homes. Lush, verdant lawn and shrubbery were evident all around the sprawling estate that vied for attention with their magnificent architectural styles. Here and there, through gaps in the fences, the girls could glimpse signs of life- a lone gardener pushing a lawn mower, trimming a hedge; children shouting in sing-song voices playing in a backyard playground, a couple sitting in a bench under the shade of a mango tree, a large Olympic sized swimming pool whose surface glistened in the sun.

Chapter 11

At last, they turned into Victoria Lane, and soon Aunt Agatha's high-walled estate rose into view.

Adora stepped out of the cab and walked to the front of the tall, imposing gate. She jabbed at the buzzer button with her middle finger, and within moments a burly, ebony skinned man in his middle thirties emerged from behind the gatehouse. He peered suspiciously at her through the grills of the gate and scowled at her.

"Yah?" he barked gruffly. His eyes flicked up and down her lithe form. "M, my aunt Agatha is 'xpecting me. I believe she lives here, " Adora stuttered, stepping back from the gate, visibly shaken by the man's gruff demeanor.

The look of suspicion lifted from the guard's stony face, replaced by a wide grin and a shift in his body language.

"Hey!" he said loudly. "You must be Adora then. Madam is certainly expecting you."

The gate man sprang into instant action, and rushed to his post in the gatehouse, where he picked up the intercom phone, speaking rapidly into it. When he replaced the receiver, he sprang out of the gatehouse, and flung the wide ornate gate wide- open. He waved vigorously as the taxi drove through the gateway, down a long, sweeping driveway, past a neatly manicured lawn bordered by neatly clipped hedges bursting with a profusion of colorful flowers. A stone cupid reposed at the end of the lawn, spouting clear sparkling water from a brass spigot set inside its mouth upon which reposed a stone cupid fountain that sprouted clear, sparkling water from a brass spigot set inside its open mouth.

Moments later, the house, a colonial style two-storied mansion rose into view, with massive ornately decorated pillars at the front door that supported a huge front porch. The front door opened and a tall slim woman wearing a long flowing aquamarine green blouse over a matching skirt stepped out, and hurried towards them. She wore her bronze-highlighted hair short, cropped close to her scalp.

"Auntie!" Adora screamed in excitement as the taxi slowed to a stop, and Adora jumped out of the vehicle, and ran towards her.

"Adora!" the woman exclaimed, grabbing Adora in a tight embrace. "Auntie Agatha, omigosh," Adora exclaimed in an excited voice. Aunt Agatha released her and held her at an arm's length.

"My goodness, it's so good to see you again. Look at you, you've grown into quite a fine young lady," she exclaimed, amidst a soft cloud of lavender soap and French perfume. Adora noticed that her eyes were slightly moist. Adora's eyes swept around the expanse of the compound, as far as the eyes could see, hoping to catch a glimpse of her four years old cousin. "Auntie, it's good to see you too, where's Melissa?"

"Melissa is in the house with Lola," Aunt Agatha responded, looking past Adora, and noticing for the first time Monica, who was sitting pertly behind the passenger seat of the taxi. In response to the question in her aunt's eyes, Adora motioned to Monica who stepped out of the cab. "This is Monica Umeh. We met today in the plane and she lives close by."

"Nice to meet you Monica," Aunt Agatha said, extending a delicate hand to Monica, who shook it vigorously.

Monica turned to Adora, with a puzzled expression on her face. "This is your aunt?"

"Yes---."

"It's just that I was expecting someone much older. Why, your aunt looks barely out of her twenties."

"I think I'm going to like your friend," Aunt Agatha joked with evident pleasure, turning to Adora.

"Auntie, she's right you know?" Adora said as she turned towards the taxi driver, who was unloading her luggage from the trunk and paid her own share of the fare. Monica stuck her head out of the car window. "Don't forget to call," she called out as the taxi engine revved into life.

A man brown skinned man of about thirty-five hurried out of the house, and turned towards Agatha with a slightly obsequious posture.

Aunt Agatha acknowledged him with a nod and grabbed Adora's hands.

"Biodun, this is my niece Adora," she told him. "I need you to take her luggage to her room."

"Yes madam," he responded, then turned to Adora with a broad smile. "Ekpele ma," he greeted her effusively, as he hefted her entire luggage effortlessly in his big arms, and bustled into the house with them.

Adora turned around, admiring the lush landscape that surrounded the white painted mansion. "Oh, auntie," she exclaimed in pleasure. "The grounds are so beautiful! It looks even better than I remember."

"We renovated a bit from the last time that you were here," Aunt Agatha replied with a smile. Paul had some landscaping done at the garden. You will see it later."

Adora glanced at her beautiful aunt, and noticed that she was staring at her. Adora lifted her eyebrows quizzically, and her aunt laughed at the expression of puzzlement on her face.

"Nne," Aunt Agatha began, addressing her with the Ibo language correlate of the endearment 'sweetheart' a word that means 'mother' in direct English translation.

"It's just that I can't believe how much you have grown from the last time that I saw you. You remind me a lot of the way that your mum Christina used to look when she was your age. She was just a knock out, and you have turned out just as beautiful."

"I don't think that I deserve that high compliment," Adora said modestly. "Then you need to really look in the mirror. You are beautiful my darling."

Adora glanced at her aunt, and thought, how strange, since she was thinking along the same lines. There was a picture of her mother that stayed hidden in a drawer in her father's study, where he kept most of her pictures to keep from dredging up painful memories of her. In the picture, her mother was wearing a flowing white dress, shading her eyes from the sun with her left hand, and smiling into the camera. There was an air of vulnerability about her in the picture that struck a chord in Adora's heart, and her aunt, as she stood there in her flowing green skirt, shading her eyes from the sun, reminded Adora of her mother in that picture.

Aunt Agatha was a strikingly beautiful woman of forty-five, who could easily pass for a woman in her late twenties. Tall and willowy, she was blessed with a slim, graceful figure that belied the fact that she already had two kids. Her features were extremely attractive, wide almond eyes, a small, pert nose, and smooth, flawless skin, which was the same radiant copper that Adora had inherited from her mother. She wore her hair extremely short, cropped close to her scalp, adding to her youthful appearance. A pair of rose- tinted wire rimmed glasses perched on her nose, giving her a sage look. But the uncanny resemblance that she had with her late sister was intensified by the fact that she even spoke with the same clear, dulcet tones that Adora remembered about her mother.

Aunt Agatha placed a comforting hand on Adora's shoulders, and she shivered. "My dear, you must be tired after your trip," she said. "Please come inside and rest a bit before dinner."

"Thanks auntie," Adora sighed, and followed her aunt's lithe form through the front door, past the white walled foyer, and into the spacious, marble floored living room.

The room was an oasis of airiness, with white painted walls magnified by floor

to ceiling mirror panels on the entire length and breadth of the west wall, and lush potted palm trees, placed close to the huge windows, where they could catch the sunlight. The floor was an expanse of gleaming mint colored marble, accented by a thick pile hand-knotted Persian rug in mint and white, which lay on the middle of the floor under a white marble center table. To the west of the room, huge domed windows looked out to the blue expanse of the swimming pool, and the endless rolling green lawn, bordered by colorful, well-tended hedges. The wide widows were accented with whispery light transparent white curtains, which fluttered in the slight draft that came from the air conditioner vents, diffusing the bright afternoon sunlight that was streaming into the room. The whole effect lent the room an ethereal elegance.

Aunt Agatha led Adora to a white leather couch with a matching ottoman, and gestured towards it with her slim hands, making the gold bracelets on her wrist to jingle musically.

"Nne, why don't you sit down and put up your feet for a while. Lunch will be served shortly."

Adora obeyed her aunt and sank gratefully into the soft leather confines of the sofa, stretching out her tired legs on the white leather ottoman. Inhaling deeply, she sighed softly, as the faint smell of leather from the sofa, intermingled with the unmistakable aroma of coconut rice wafted in from the direction of the kitchen. Closing her eyes, she luxuriated in the cool comfort of the centrally controlled air that floated around the room as she felt the fatigue of the day gently slip away.

She heard a soft jingle beside her, accompanied by the sweet perfume that hung around her aunt, and she opened her eyes, as her aunt sank gracefully onto the plush seat of the sectional next to her.

"Nne, I have really missed you. How was your trip?"

"Fantastic," Adora replied, leaning deeper into the reclining chair and examining the tip of her perfectly manicured nail. She had done it in a shimmering shade of shell pink for the trip.

"The service was good, and I can honestly say that it was one of the most flawless landings that I ever experienced. Thanks for recommending Air One."

"You can say that I have a vested interest. You see Paul has a big account with them. But the truth is, they are one of the best in the country."

"I totally agree, I would fly them again," Adora responded, looking around the opulent room.

Her gaze rested on the silver-framed picture of her aunt with her husband and two daughters, resting on the gleaming baby grand piano by the staircase.

"How is Nneka adjusting without you and uncle Paul?" Adora began.

"She's doing well at her school in England. Matter of fact, I spoke to her yesterday. We call her every weekend."

"She must miss you a lot. She's so young," Adora stated.

"Well, it is one of the sacrifices we make. Her boarding school is one of the best there is and we did not want to disrupt her schooling when we came back. As you know, we had always planned to return home and once Paul's CPA firm took off and the University of Lagos offered me the professorship, we both decided to let her continue schooling in England. She'll be eleven this year and Paul's sister Colette keeps a close eye on her. She's having a ton of fun and told me that she's looking forward to the holidays when she can come home and spend time with her little Melissa."

"Oh, how sweet," Adora exclaimed, watching her aunt, who picked up a remote control that lay on the side table and pointed it at the washed oak entertainment center containing a large screen TV, a compact disc stereo system, and a DVD player. The large screen of the TV came to life, accompanied by the mellifluous sounds of acoustic jazz.

A picture of Nneka dominated the TV screen, standing with a group of girls her age, all in parochial uniform, smiling into the camera. There were other pictures that followed, showing various aspects of Nneka in her day-to-day activities in England, all reflecting a pretty, vivacious, well-adjusted girl.

A scrabbling sound caught Adora's attention, a small sound, like the sound of tiny feet scrapping against the smooth marble floor. Adora cocked her ears towards the sound, which came from the direction of the arched doorway that led off to the white marble staircase. The sound came again, closer this time, from the gleaming ebony carving of a female dancer, which reposed on a tall white pedestal close to the staircase. Adora looked up in alarm, then smiled as she realized what it was.

"Where is Melissa?" she said loudly as she turned down the music with the remote, cocking her ears towards the sound, and listening for the patter of little feet.

She winked surreptitiously at her aunt, who turned her head in the direction of the sound. "I think Melissa is in the kitchen pretending to help Lola cook," Aunt Agatha responded, leaning closer to Adora.

"Probably hiding out somewhere in this very room," she whispered in conspiratorial tones to Adora.

"Melissa?" she called, raising her voice. There was the same patter of little feet from the direction of the wet bar, accompanied by the sounds of suppressed giggling.

"Come on out Melissa, and greet Adora," Aunt Agatha said, raising her voice slightly.

A little girl of four, wearing a pink gingham checkered play dress scampered

out from behind a white lacquered latticework trellis, interwoven with green climbing vines, ferns, and climbing ivies that stood by a gleaming baby grand piano and darted across the expanse of the living room towards the back of the sectional where Adora and her aunt were sitting. She dived behind it, giggling childishly. Aunt Agatha stood up and walked around to the back of the couch. The little girl was a blur as she dived from her new hiding place, and hid behind the staircase.

"Come on out Melissa, and meet Adora your big cousin. She won't bite," Aunt Agatha cajoled.

Melissa stepped out from her hiding place and stepped hesitantly towards Adora.

"Hello Melissa," Adora said, reaching towards her. Melissa reacted instantly by diving towards her mother, hiding behind her, tugging at her skirt, and taking little peeks from behind the safe haven of her mother's form. Gently, her mother extricated her hand from her skirt, and nudged her gently towards Adora.

"C'mon Melissa! It's only me," Adora coaxed. "Remember me Adora?"

Melissa finally came out, and stood uncertainly before Adora, lowering her gaze to the floor and shifting uncomfortably from foot to foot. Her mother gave her a stern look.

"Melissa, be a good girl and say hello to Adora."

"Hello," Melissa said stiffly and backed away from Adora. Adora sank on her knees and reached towards Melissa, who bit her lower lip nervously and tugged on her newly plaited hair in a tense motion. The pink satin ribbon on one of her plaits came loose and she slipped it quickly into her pocket, glancing quickly to see if her mother noticed. She returned her attention to

Adora, staring with wide liquid brown eyes; then her gaze lowered shyly to the floor.

"Hey little princess, you have grown so pretty, look at you--- you are growing so fast. Come here and give your big cousin a hug," Adora said, squeezing her tightly and patting her hair gently.

"Y,yes," she muttered, keeping her eyes downcast, and holding on tightly to her mother's hand.

"Don't you remember me from last year when I came to visit with my little brother Uchenna?"

Melissa nodded mutely and kept close to her mother.

"You don't have to be afraid of me Melissa, I am your friend, and I think that we will get along very well," Adora said, gently coaxing her from her mother's side, and placing a reassuring hand on her shoulder. Melissa squirmed around uncomfortably, and wriggled free from Adora's grasp, then made a hasty retreat in the direction of the kitchen.

Adora stretched out her feet and laughed heartily at Melissa's antics. "I wonder why she is so shy today!" she exclaimed. "Last year, she was so friendly and talkative."

"I think that she is going through a phase right now," Aunt Agatha said. "Kids go through phases I guess," Adora agreed.

"She just started school, and I believe that she is rather bewildered with all the changes. Just give her time and you probably won't be able to get rid of her."

"That would be nice," Adora said pensively, smiling.

"Let me get you something cool to drink," Aunt Agatha offered, rising gracefully from the sofa, and walking briskly towards the kitchen. She returned a few moments later, carrying a tray overflowing with fresh fruits, tiny triangular shaped hors de oeuvres, and freshly baked shortbread.

She placed the tray on the marble table in front of Adora, who exclaimed in pleasure.

"Mmn nice!" she commented at the mouthwatering selection. She picked up a steaming wet nap and wiped her hands briskly.

A slight noise came from the direction of the kitchen entrance, and Adora replaced the towel on the tray and turned around.

"Melissa!" she exclaimed, lifting her eyes towards the sound. A young woman of about twenty-five came towards them, pushing a brass embellished glass trolley, which was loaded with various beverages, a crystal bowl filled with ice cubes and a pitcher of fruit juice. As the trolley rolled to a stop in the center of the living room, the girl picked up a silver tong, and scooped ice into two cut crystal highball glasses, placing them over coasters on the glass-topped marble center table in front of the two ladies.

"Welcome auntie," the girl greeted Adora, smiling broadly and assuming a slightly obsequious posture before walking towards the kitchen.

Aunt Agatha caught the puzzled expression on Adora's face, and chuckled.

"What's so funny?" Adora asked, looking slightly hurt.

"Oh, my dear," Aunt Agatha said, patting Adora's arm.

"This is just a cultural thing. Lola only called you Auntie to express her respect. She was not trying to call you ancient."

"I certainly hope I don't appear that old. Biodun also called me auntie, but I thought I imagined it," Adora breathed, feeling visibly relieved.

Aunt Agatha viewed Adora pensively through her rose-tinted wire-rimmed glasses.

"You see, in the Yoruba culture, respect is extremely important, and the term auntie doesn't necessarily denote kinship or age gap. It is a title that delineates social status and is bandied as an expression of respect. That's the culture talking."

Adora nibbled on a juicy slice of mango and paused for a moment to relish the refreshing taste.

"It's amazing the range of cultural differences that exist in this country of ours," she commented.

"That's what makes our country so unique," Aunt Agatha remarked. "One people, but different orientations.

With a population of over one hundred and fifty million, over fifty languages and dialects, we are indeed a cultural hodgepodge."

"Uh huh," Adora yawned as the weariness of the journey overtook her body.

"Aunt Agatha touched her gently on the shoulder.

"Nne, I think you should rest before dinner. I'll show you to your room.

◆ ◆ ◆

When the door closed behind her, Adora allowed her eyes to sweep across the room, a large room, sumptuously decorated in romantic shades of pink and white, obviously decorated with a young girl in mind.

The room was cool, inviting, and ultra-feminine- very much like her room in Enugu. The walls were wallpapered in a pale pink and white candy stripe design, bordered with pink and lilac colored sea shells, and interspersed with tiny pale rose flowers, scattered among the bold pink and white stripes.

The same patterns were repeated on huge, satin pillows, which occupied a window seat on one side of the room, matching the plush, pale rose hued wall to wall with carpeting, which sank and sprang under her feet.

She found all her luggage pieces neatly stacked in a corner of the closet and her clothes hanging neatly on plastic hangers She selected a sleeveless georgette dress of crinkled silk with tiny yellow butterfly patterns that did not require ironing. Slipping off her shoes, she tossed herself on the pink satin covered bed and closed her eyes, and flexed her feet, feeling the tension of the day slip away.

The soft pink material of the bedding caressed her skin, and she bounced herself gently on the firm mattress, giggling like a kid.

Closing her eyes, she inhaled deeply, reveling in the invigorating fragrance of the freshly cut flowers that had been artfully arranged in a multi-faceted crystal vase on the white lacquered night table.

Slowly, she eased out of her brown linen jacket and placed it on the pink cushioned vanity stool that stood in front of the mirrored white dresser table and lay back against the pillow in her lacy ivory colored camisole and her linen pants, luxuriating in the cool, evening breeze that blew in through the window, stirring up the sheer, pink window curtains, which fluttered slowly in the wind, lending the room an ethereal, dreamlike quality.

Lulled by the comforts of the room, her body gave way to the weariness of the day, and slowly, her eyes fluttered shut.

A sound awoke her, and she stretched lazily and rose from the bed, padding barefoot towards the sliding glass door that led off to the terrace, which overlooked the lush, colorful tropical garden. The gilded rails of the terrace were lined with luxuriantly green potted plants, which added to the ambience of the beautiful scenery.

Adora leaned over the balustrade, taking in the breathtaking beauty of the estate, which stretched infinitely, beautiful and endless, from the roof of the guest bungalow, sweeping towards the tennis courts beyond the shaded trees of the garden and the sweeping proportion of the swimming pool.

The sounds of laughter startled her, and she realized that it was coming from under the shades of a mango tree near the servants' quarters.

It was Lola and Melissa, playing hide and seek. Melissa skipped away from Lola, and darted under the overhanging branches of a gum tree and stood in clear view of Lola, covering her face with her hands.

Smiling, Adora stepped back into her room and opened the louver windows, letting in more air, despite which her skin felt hot and sticky.

In the adjoining, pink tiled bathroom, she peeled off her remaining clothing, hanging them on a towel rack near the window. She turned on the faucet, which coughed and sputtered, then belched air and a few sprays of discolored liquid.

With a little cry of amazement, Adora stepped back as the faucet released a streaming geyser of discolored water, which splashed off the side of the tub and splattered her bare thighs.

She frowned in distaste and dabbed at the spatter with a tissue, letting the water run for a while till the liquid ran crystal clear, wondering why that happened.

Then it hit her. The bathroom had not been used for a while, and although

everything sparkled and smelled of disinfectant, the faucet on the bathtub had not been turned on in a while. She stayed in the shower, letting the warm water massage her skin, while she lathered up her skin with the lavender scented bath soap that was sitting on the shower caddie.

Throwing a towel around her torso, she walked barefoot to the bedroom and slipped on a brown georgette dress which fluttered around her body, light as air in whispery soft swirls and closed her eyes, inhaling deeply, almost feeling giddy from the buoyant scent of fresh roses and freshly mowed grass, drifting in with the cool evening breeze from the garden.

The faint strains of piano music greeted her ears when she opened the bedroom door, a haunting sound that stirred something within her, bringing a lump to her throat. She ran back to the closet and pulled on a pair of brown leather tong sandals, then followed the sound.

It led her to the family room next to the living room, where she found her aunt seated behind a beautiful ebony baby grand piano, her slim fingers caressing the ivory keys. Melissa sat next to her, giggling and tapping at the keys of the piano at intervals.

A tall, dark skinned man, wearing an oxford blue work shirt sat on a blue sofa, perusing the pages of the Daily Observer newspaper, and tapping his feet to the rhythm of the music.

His head was sprinkled with a mix of salt and pepper, and the horn-rimmed glasses perched on the bridge of his nose lent him an air of intelligence.

He rose to his feet and grabbed Adora's delicate hands in his broad brown own, then clasped her shoulders effusively.

Adora smiled politely and returned his hug.

"Adora, it's really good to see you again my dear," he exclaimed. "Welcome to Lagos.".

He stepped back and lowered his six feet frame on the sofa, tickling a shrieking Melissa, who had scampered onto his laps.

They made a striking picture, father and daughter, both brown skinned and slim, although Paul had developed a slight paunch under his light blue dress shirt, which was rolled up at the sleeve.

"And how is the family back in Enugu?" he asked in a soft baritone voice that seemed to quietly fill the room.

Chapter 12

Adora awoke to the strident sound of the phone by her bedside. As she struggled to shake off the last cobwebs of sleep from her brain, she mumbled a hoarse hello into the mouthpiece.

"Hey wake up sleepy head!" a cheery female voice said to her from the other end of the phone.

"Who is this?" Adora mumbled, still trying to focus, and feeling slightly disoriented from waking up on a strange bed.

"This is Monica, remember?" the voice replied with a trace of impatience. "Monica? Oh yes. Hello!" Adora exclaimed, feeling slightly guilty that her brain did not click right away.

"I'm sorry Monica. I am just waking up," she responded groggily, yawning and stretching lazily on the soft pink sheets.

Sitting up in bed she rubbed her eyes and glanced at the clock by her night table, noting with slight annoyance that it was only 7:00 am.

"Guess what?" Monica said, her excitement coming through in her voice.

"What?" Adora said brightly, feeling more alert.

The sky was visible through the gauzy haze of the pink window curtains. It was a flame shade of orange from the rising sun and the beauty drew Adora from her bed. She walked barefoot to the window and drew the blinds, letting in the bright early morning sunlight.

"I'm listening," she said to Monica, who sighed impatiently, as though she expected a more enthusiastic response.

"I found out a lot of stuff about you know who, you know?" "Who?"

"You know, tall handsome chocolate dream," Monica sighed.

"What are you talking about?" Adora asked, not feeling particularly chatty, but trying to accommodate her new friend.

"C'mon Adora, wake up. I'm talking about Randy, the guy we met at the airport."

"Oh him? You mean the one whose card you lost yesterday?" Adora asked with a hint of sarcasm, trying to infuse nonchalance that she did not feel into her voice. The velvety caress of Randy's mesmerizing gaze lingered on her mind, especially the way that he had gazed into her soul, as though he could read their contents.

"Yes, Randy," Monica said with rising excitement. "I mentioned his name to my cousin Gina, and you won't believe this, but she works for the very same company that belongs to his family. His father is into oil and transportation. His mother is a leading fashion designer. You ever heard of Electra?"

"Who hasn't?" Adora said with a hint of sarcasm.

Electra was one of the leading fashion designers in the country whose collection was always on the cutting edge of fashion, often paving the way for other designers to follow. Everybody who was anybody yearned to be seen in her sumptuous creations at least once at social gatherings. Electra's pictures often appeared on the society pages of fashion magazines and newspapers across the country- a tall, slender beautiful woman, who seemed to have the world at her feet. Adora's late mother Christina had built her boutique around the beautiful designs of Electra and some of Electra's creations still hung neatly in her mother's closet exactly the same way that she had left them.

"Well check this out," Monica began dramatically. "Electra is Randy's mother."

"Electra is Randy's mother? Adora echoed in genuine surprise, accompanied by a twinge of sadness brought on by treasured memories of her own mother. "She looks kind of young to be Randy's mother," Adora said with rising interest. "Exactly my sentiments when I heard. Anyway, I love her clothes a lot," Monica said enthusiastically.

"Who doesn't? The woman is a genius," Adora chimed in.

Somewhere within the house, the sounds of morning activities drew Adora briefly from the conversation. In a room nearby, somebody turned on a television set. Faintly, from a room downstairs, the electronic hum of a vacuum cleaner drifted up to her ears, blending with the drone of the lawn mower drifting in through her open window. Soon the mower stopped, and sounds of the hedge clipper drifted in. "Clip, clap, clip, clap." From somewhere outside, the sound of laughter reached her ears, and she dragged her phone to the terrace.

Her breath caught in her throat, as she caught sight of the view, which was

spectacular in the soft light of dawn. The sky was a lovely shade of blue, and the clouds were fluffy cotton balls in a warm shade of orange, tinged with purple and pink, and seemed ready to burst into flames from the brilliance of the lazily rising sun.

The guesthouse, the garden with its interplay of riotous blooming colors and the western tip of the tennis lawn all beckoned to her, bathed in the soft orange glow of the rising sun.

"I said, do you remember Air One?' Monica began, snapping her out of her reverie.

"You mean the airplane that we flew into Lagos yesterday?" Adora asked, wondering where this was going.

"Well, you won't believe this bit of coincidence," Monica announced. Guess who owns Air One?"

"Don't tell me, Randy's family again," Adora interjected sad with a twist of irony.

The drip drip of water drew her attention to the bathroom and she saw that the bathtub faucet was dripping water. She turned it off and returned her attention to Monica's voice on the other end of the line.

"That's right Adora. They own Air One, and a shipping company---- the Eagle

Shipping Company. I know this because my cousin Regina works for Eagle Shipping. Anyway, she told me that she heard through her co-workers that Randy has an MBA from Oxford University in England and studied Aeronautical Engineering in the U.S. He is a licensed pilot, but it seems like he has a hand in every aspect of the family business. They say he is a shrewd negotiator and has quite a sharp business acumen." "Sounds nice, but what does that have to do with any of us?" Adora threw in. "Well, you need to hear this," Monica asserted.

Adora stifled a yawn and returned to the bedroom, and flopped on the bed still feeling a bit tired from having her sleep interrupted so early on a Sunday morning.

She made a great effort to contribute to the conversation, careful not to let her mounting irritation at Monica's aimless rambling show in her voice.

"Hey! Did you know that he is single as in unmarried, unattached, unfettered? Do you know what that means?" Monica announced suddenly.

"Exactly what does that mean?" Adora asked with a hint of sarcasm. "Well you figure it out missy. Tall, handsome, charming and the most eligible bachelor in town. C'mon, you do the math."

Adora was only half listening now. Apparently, Monica had thrown herself into a flurry of excitement over a guy she hardly knew because of his good looks, and social status. Monica could drool all she wanted. She was not going to swoon over Randy like a schoolgirl. Why then did her heart skip a beat at the mere mention of the handsome stranger's name, a total stranger that she only encountered for a few minutes?

Why was she experiencing this strange, thrill of excitement just from the memories of their first encounter, and the magnetic spell that the man seemed to have cast on her with that first caressing gaze that held her spellbound, and suspended on the crest of a cloud? And why was her heartbeat quickening, just from the memory of the way that his lips had caressed the back of her hand? She could almost feel the electrifying caress of his lips brushing against the back of her hand, magnifying the magical effect of his presence. Where was her iron reserve anyway?

Clearly, the man generated an electrifying excitement that sent her head reeling, but she was not going to allow herself to get swept up in that foolishness.

Suddenly, Adora realized to her dismay that in her own small way, she was allowing herself to be swept up like Monica in the exhilarating excitement that Randy seemed to generate, and she did not like it one bit. Determined to stamp out those feelings before they flamed into some full-fledged emotion, she made a quick mental decision. She would delete Randy from her mind, she had absolutely nothing to lose, did she?

"Did you sleep well last night? Did you sleep at all?" she joked.

"Who could sleep at all?" Monica retorted breathlessly. "I could only think about the party. I have to figure out what to wear."

"Party, what party?" Adora asked in a bland tone of voice, glancing at the clock on her bedside table.

The digital face indicated that it was already 7:30 am. She had been on the phone with Monica, talking about the same trifling issues for thirty minutes! She had to shower, get dressed, eat breakfast, and service began at 10:30 am. She was not going to miss church, especially on her first week in Lagos.

"I don't think that you've heard a word that I said," Monica said crossly. "You mentioned a party. What party?"

"Let me tell you Adora. Randy is going to turn twenty-nine next week. My cousin Gina informed me that Electra is going to surprise him with a major bash at the Sheraton. It is supposed to be the social event of the year." "That's nice," Adora said. "But what does that have to do with me or you for that matter?"

"Well guess what?" Monica began, with the air of one who was privy to the news of the century. "My cousin Regina is an invited guest to the party, and she is allowed to bring her own guests. You know what that means? Just arrived in Lagos, and already, I am hanging with VIP's—plus, you never know who else you could meet," she gushed breathlessly in a voice bubbling with excitement.

"Oh, how nice," Adora sneered, unable to keep the sarcasm from her voice. "Oh, isn't it exciting?" Monica enthused, oblivious to Adora's tone.

Apparently, nothing was going to dampen her enthusiasm.

"I do hope that you can attend too," Monica prattled. "It is supposed to be the social highlight of the year, the absolute. I heard that the guest list reads like a Who's Who. All the VIP's are supposed to be coming- Actors, Models, Senators, Politicians, top ranking military officers, even the president's wife is expected. Adora, I am so excited. I think that this is kismet. And who knows? I might get to meet Electra. And you know what that means don't you?"

Adora knew exactly what that meant. As an aspiring model, Monica knew that a show with Electra could make or break a model's career. Adora could see already that her friend did not intend to waste that opportunity. While she was aiming for the man, she also intended to shoot for his mother who could give her a leg up in her career aspirations.

"Oh, you must come too, tell me that you will. Oh, what will I wear? Oh yeah. I know exactly what I'm going to wear, but I'm not telling." "Excuse me. Did I hear you mention that I should attend?"

"Of course, you have to come."

"Absolutely not! I will not attend a party where I'm not really familiar with the hosts, besides, I wasn't invited exactly."

"Oh yes you are. Gina's invitation card allows four people. I know she wouldn't mind. And who says you have to be buddies with the hosts to attend a party? Haven't you ever crashed a party?"

"I think not," Adora said.

"Oh, such a pity," Monica said in a voice that suggested that Adora was missing out on a lot. "Anyway, what are you going to wear?"

"Wear? Why would I want to do that?"

"Wo girl, easy now. I know you have a beautiful body and all, but to go showing it all? Hm, hey, on the other hand, why not? Look at the Hollywood stars. They do it all the time----." Monica began with a chuckle.

"Slow down young lady, I never said I would attend," Adora corrected. "What do you mean Adora?" Monica asked, her voice betraying her surprise. "I would never turn down a golden opportunity like this. It is called networking. You place yourself in certain circles, you meet people from that circle, and presto, by association, you are a member of that circle. From there, you never know."

"Well, I don't know Monica," Adora replied hesitantly. "This is not a good time. School starts next week, and I don't need the distraction. Besides, I don't think that my aunt would approve."

"Your aunt?" Monica exclaimed, cackling in unrestrained mirth, an action that stung Adora, and prompted an indignant "Hey what's so funny?" "Giiirrl, are you for real or what?" Monica stated, resorting to a conciliatory tone, one that's often reserved for a very slow recalcitrant child.

"Oh, come off it," Adora snapped.

"Okay, Okay," Monica said in a more serious tone. "But you must be joking right? Why would you need your aunt's permission to attend a party? Hey! If you think that your aunt will constitute a problem, then I could cover up for you.

"Cover up? No dear. I do live under her roof, and I don't intend to lie to her. If I really had to go to the party, then I'd tell her."

"What are you, a prude or something?" Monica asked in a voice that barely masked her irritation.

"No Monica. I am not a prude. I have certain principles that's all."

"Well, suit yourself then Ms. Principles, but please promise me that you will think about it, and at least consider coming. You won't regret it," Monica cajoled.

"I'll try," Adora said in a voice that clearly stated that she would do no such thing.

"Oh puhleez! You are only twenty for goodness sake. You need to enjoy your youth before you wake up one day, and find yourself old, wrinkled and alone, and what's worse, you never experienced life. You need to live your life to the fullest girl." Adora bit off the retort at the tip of her tongue and simply listened. Adora would decide what was right for her, and that was that.

Thankfully, Monica's long-winded monologue ended and she promised to visit after church service. As soon as she dropped the phone, Adora went down on her knees, as she always did, and praised God for another new day. She read a brief Bible passage from the book of Isaiah that prophesied that Christ would die for us all and felt a fleeting sadness because of the suffering of Christ, mixed with a feeling of comfort from the knowledge that Christ's death was not in vain, but served a purpose as part of God's divine plan due to his infinite love for mankind.

She stepped out of the shower and changed into a flowing white caftan, feeling renewed and extremely at peace with herself, as she listened quietly to the sound of activities coming from the house; the muffled whirring of the blender from somewhere in the kitchen, followed by the sound of laughter.

The stereo came on from the living room, and the melodious voice of Mahalia Jackson accompanied by the soft strains of piano music floated up from the living room. Soon the aroma of freshly baked bread wafted up to her room.

She followed her nose and found her aunt in the dining room wearing a thin,

cotton shift, and sipping tea from a steaming porcelain teacup.

"Good morning auntie," she greeted cheerily. "Good morning dear. Did you sleep well?"

"Like a baby," she said, pulling out one of the high-backed, fabric upholstered chairs that were arranged around the gray marble dining table. "Where is everybody?"

"Paul went out for his regular morning walk. Melissa is still in bed."

Aunt Agatha poured tea into a white teacup, nestled on a saucer and handed it to Adora, who thanked her, added a cube of sugar, and stirred in a smidgen of creamy milk.

"I hope you'll come with us to church my dear."

"Of course, auntie," Adora said, glancing at the clock that hung on the wall next to the china cabinet. "It's almost eight you know, I think I'd better get started, and I'll check on Melissa."

"Good idea," Aunt Agatha agreed, falling in step with Adora.

"She told me last night that she remembers you. She said you look kind of different now, that you look all grown up and so pretty."

Adora chuckled as they stopped in front of Melissa's room and stood by the doorway, watching her aunt, as she walked down the long hallway to the master bedroom.

Melissa's room, located in the North wing of the second floor, two rooms from Adora's, was filled with an overwhelming array of toys, piled into an open white wooden toy chest that sat in a far corner of the room, next to a pine bookcase near the window, which was stacked with a collection of storybooks, dolls of various ethnic backgrounds and more toys. Melissa was sitting up in bed, playing with a collection of dolls propped up against her pillow. She tumbled out of bed and bounded towards Adora, flashing what Adora considered to be a million-dollar smile.

"Hi," she greeted brightly, stretching her arms towards Adora, who bent towards her, and hugged her very tightly. Melissa hugged her back, smelling faintly of lavender soap.

"Come, stay with me," Melissa said dragging her towards the bed.

Once they were seated, she regarded Adora pensively for a moment, then smiled her perfect little smile.

"I remember you now," she said in a voice that rang with excitement. "We went to your house last year when I was little. Your brother was always reading a book, can you teach me to read?"

"Of course, I can teach you to read."

"I am in *kindergarden* you know, soon I can read very well. My mom says so. When I went to your house with my mommy, *your **another*** brother was funny and made me laugh all the time, and your daddy was never home. I think that it will make me very sad if my daddy never came home. Oh, do you know who this is?" Melissa asked in the next breath. She pushed a doll towards Adora, who shook her head.

"No sweetheart, the right word is kindergarten, and not kindergarden, and what do you mean by my *another* brother?"

"Because you have two brothers. Your **another**, um, I meant, your other brother, he was soooo funny," Melissa enthused.

"Yes, you are right Melissa, my brother Chike is a bucket of fun," Adora agreed.

"Look," Melissa said pensively, and pointed at the doll that she had thrust into Adora's hands.

"Do you know who this is?" she repeated. "No," Adora responded. "Who is this?"

Melissa pushed the collection of dolls that cluttered her bed out of the way, and sat closer to Adora who was examining the pretty black doll that Melissa had handed to her.

"Well, her name is Nina, and she is my friend, and I have other dolls but Nina is my best doll friend. She is my *imagic* friend."

"You mean imaginary friend?" Adora corrected.

"No *imagic*, get it? Magic. I have a lot of dolls, but Nina is my very best friend. She listens to me when I am sad and she **protakes** me from the monster that lives under my bed."

"You mean protect you?" Adora interjected.

"Yes she **protakes** me. When my mommy puts me to bed, and when she leaves, the monster scares me and my mommy said that there is no monster but I know that there is, and then she said that if I hold Nina, she will make the monster go away, and it really works because Nina is magic, and I think the monster is scared of Nina because mommy told me that she is an African princess and she has magic and it keeps the monster away, so I am glad that she is my friend."

The words tumbled out of Melissa's mouth in an excited jumble.

Adora held out her hand and patted Melissa gently on the back, speaking in a most reassuring voice. "Melissa, your mom is right you know, there is no such thing as a monster."

Melissa rolled her eyes and expelled a short blast of air, while she shot Adora a look that one reserves for a very slow and recalcitrant child. She shook her head slowly, at the seeming lack of knowledge and ignorance displayed by the older girl on the subject of monsters.

"Oh yes there is," she said firmly. "My friend Ronke said so. Do you want to say hello to Nina?"

Melissa picked up the doll from her lap and thrust it into Adora's outstretched arms. Adora took the doll from Melissa, and cradled it gingerly in the crook of her arm, the way that Melissa demonstrated.

It was an elaborately crafted doll with realistic brown toned plastic skin and glassy brown eyes, framed by thick dark eyelashes that fanned over her cheeks when she was placed in a reclining position, and fluttered open when she was placed in a vertical position.

The doll had a cute button nose, well-proportioned lips, and round cheeks, with the hazy glow of an expertly airbrushed on earth tone blush. A gleaming mass of jet-black micro braids, cut in bangs, cascaded down her elegantly slim neck.

"Daddy bought Nina from Kenya," Melissa announced proudly.

Adora examined the plastic doll carefully, admiring the intricate attention that went into the craftsmanship, and the care with which its accessories had been selected and matched.

"She is pretty and so are you Melissa," Adora commented, handing the doll back to Melissa.

"Nina says thank you," Melissa replied with a bright smile. Moments later, her expression turned pensive, then metamorphosed into a dazzling smile that lit up her beautiful brown face. She leaned close to Adora and whispered conspiratorially.

"Nina said you are very pretty and guess what? I think you are pretty too. My mommy said so, and I heard daddy tell mommy so **yestoday** you know." "You mean yesterday?" Adora corrected.

"Uh, yesterday," Melissa repeated.

"Mommy said you're smart too. I think that my mommy is smart. She is a profession, and daddy said----"

"You mean, mommy is a professor," Adora corrected.

"Yeah, mommy is a professor." she said that word very slowly, and got it right this time.

She smiled and continued without missing a beat. My mommy is smart because she is a professor, and my daddy is smart too. He has a biig, big big office near the Marina." She emphasized the word by opening her arms very wide to demonstrate how big her father's office was.

"It has a biig, big window, and you can see the ocean from the window. My daddy says it is a biig, big ocean, and it is almost halfway around the world, and it is called the Atlantis--"

"You mean the Atlantic," Adora corrected.

"Oh yes, daddy says you can't go swimming very far there because you can drown, but sometimes, daddy gets a biig, big yacht, and we go sailing on the

yacht, and daddy said you can't drown then because it floats on the water and is fun and it goes like this." She rocked herself from side to side to demonstrate the listing motion of the yacht.

A soft scrabbling sound accompanied by the soft clearing of the throat, coming from the direction of the slightly ajar door interrupted Melissa's long-winded speech. Adora looked up at the slight form of Lola who was standing awkwardly by the doorway.

"Hey good morning Lola," she greeted brightly.

"Good morning auntie," Lola responded, smiling back at Adora. "I came to give Melissa her morning bath."

"I don't want to bath this morning, the water's too cold," Melissa stated, placing Nina gently by her pillow.

"No, it's not, the water is nice and warm," Lola insisted.

"Melissa, be a good girl and take your morning bath okay?" Adora cajoled. "Okay," Melissa said, hanging her head. She placed Nina carefully on her pillow and followed Lola to the adjoining bathroom.

"Guess what I have for you," Adora stated mysteriously, hiding a packet behind her back. Melissa was just returning from the bathroom, wrapped up in a fluffy white towel that reached below her knees and dripping water all over the pink carpet while Lola berated her. Her face lit up and she flung herself at Adora.

"Oh, let me see please," she squealed in delight, snatching the packet from Adora. It was a dress that she purchased for Melissa at the mall in Enugu. Melissa tore through the packet and held up the dress to her chest.

"Oh, it's so pretty," she declared.

"Can I wear it please, please," she pleaded, while Lola berated her, bending to retrieve the towel, which had slipped to the floor. She wrapped the towel firmly around Melissa's slight body and began to rummage in the closet but Adora stopped her.

"It's okay Lola, I'll take care of her. I have something for her to wear."

"Really, I can wear this?" Melissa squealed in delight.

"Really, you can."

"Oh, it is so beautiful," Melissa shrieked, holding the dress in front of her.

It was a lavender colored silk and organza frock with frilly bits of lace at the sleeves and the hem with an attached wide satin sash, tied into a bow at the waist and peppered with sprinklings of tiny sparkling rhinestones at the inset lace bodice. It was a perfect Sunday dress, and as Adora pulled it over Melissa's head and pulled up the zipper, Melissa pulled at the sash, trying clumsily to tie it. She grinned from ear to ear, twirling and pirouetting like a ballerina, oohing and aahing at her reflection in the sweeping mirror that ran the length and width of her closet doors.

"Oh, look at me, auntie, I love this dress," she said, flinging her tiny arms around Adora, who was kneeling at her side, and helping her to adjust the dress.

"Can I show this to my mom, oh can I, can I please?" she begged breathlessly.

"Of course, you can," Adora said. "But one more thing."

Adora took out a matching hat from the bag that she left on Melissa's bed and placed it gently over Melissa's head, which had been done up in curly ringlets. Together, they went to Melissa's closet, and selected a pair of cream-colored shoes and Melissa sat on the plush carpeted floor and pulled them on.

"Now, can I please?" she begged.

"Certainly," Adora said, taking her cousin's tiny hands in her own and leading her down the the hallway, towards the stairs.

As soon as her feet hit the last rung of the marble staircase, Melissa disengaged Adora's hold on her arms, and scampered off to find her mother, while Adora followed, calling futilely after her.

"Oh, mommy look, look what auntie bought me!" Melissa exclaimed, pirouetting before her mother like a perfect little ballerina, and giggling out of pure excitement. Her mother looked up from setting the table and beamed at her little girl. "Oh Melissa, you look like a dream, look at you. Did you thank Adora?" "Oh, mommy yes, I said thank you," Melissa said, hopping up and down on her feet. She rushed into Adora's arms and nestled on her lap as breakfast was served.

"Nne, you shouldn't have gone to all that trouble" Aunt Agatha commented, as she placed a silver fork on the folded white linen napkin by the place setting.

"Trouble? That was no trouble at all," Adora responded airily, waving off the compliment. "But aunty, you look fantastic."

"Wow! Thanks," Aunt Agatha responded with a slight smile.

Aunt Agatha's was wearing a long sheath gown, which was rendered in melon colored silk, embellished with hand laid gold embroidery at the edge of the boatneck neckline. The dress clung to her lithe form, accentuating her svelte figure. It came with a sweeping white cape of the same material, lined with the melon colored material of the gown, and embellished at the edges from the neckline to the hem with the same intricate hand laid embroidery of the gown. The look was completed by a pair of shoes of the same color and material, detailed with the gold embroideries of the outfit. In the outfit, her aunt looked like a queen, and Adora stared in wonder, stretching out her hand and feeling the sumptuous fabric of the outfit. "Oh, it is beautiful," she breathed, awestruck by the dazzling Sunday gown.

"You really think so?" Agatha asked, while helping Melissa onto a chair on the dining table.

"Yes," Adora breathed. "It's simply perfect."

"I can have that made for you darling. We can drive down to the Electra showroom next weekend for the fitting. She has a showroom right here in VI."

Adora felt a slight tremor at the mention of the name Electra. The woman

responsible for the breathtaking outfit that swirled around her aunt was also the woman behind the perfect male specimen that made her heart tremble at the mere mention of his name.

"Thanks auntie," she said, shaking her head. "Electra's couture line is well beyond the reach of my budget."

"Never mind that, my dear, I will pay for it if you want it."

"Wow! That's really nice, but I couldn't accept this," she said sagely. " Glamour can wait for now. Right now, I need to focus all my energy on my impending schoolwork. "

"You have a very good point my dear," Aunt Agatha agreed. "But I have to say that you impressed me. Most girls your age would have jumped at the chance to own a piece of Electra. But I can see that you have a good head on your shoulders and the right values, and you are quite goal oriented. No wonder you are in grad school at twenty-one."

Melissa wriggled free from Adora's grasp as she saw her father approach the dining

table and rushed into his arms. "Daddy, daddy look, look what auntie bought me," she cried in her high-pitched voice. She shot out of her chair, and rushed towards her father, who scooped up his little girl in his arms and kissed her fondly on the forehead. Melissa squirmed out of her his arms and tugged insistently at his sleeves in high excitement.

"Daddy look! Look what auntie bought me," she repeated, in renewed excitement.

"It's beautiful Melissa, did you thank her?" Paul asked, helping her back to

her seat.

"Oh yes I did daddy. You look nice daddy," Melissa added, eyeing her father's outfit.

"Do I Melissa?" Paul asked, as he pushed Melissa's chair gently towards the table.

"Oh, you do, both of you," Adora interjected, appraising his outfit.

It was a three-piece embroidered Agbada suit, a Nigerian caftan outfit generally worn by men, and popularized by the name "Alhaji one thousand," alluding to the fact that only the moneyed could afford them -so intricate and lavishly detailed were these outfits.

Like most agbada suits, Paul's version was showy, of the finest quality pure white linen, consisting of long baggy pants, a matching loosely constructed caftan, and a second voluminous caftan called a dashiki rendered with flowing sleeves. The neckline and the sleeves of the inner caftan was embellished with the most intricately designed gold embroidery, a design that was repeated on the edges of the dashiki, which was worn in such a way that it fell in neatly ordered folds over the inner caftan. The outfit, while perfect for the tropical climate, also conjured an air of affluence and style, and was a perfect complement to his wife's ultra-feminine outfit. They made quite a striking couple, and as they sat down to breakfast.

Adora noted wryly that in their lovely European clothes, she and Melissa ended up looking quite incongruous in juxtaposition to the older pair.

Chapter 13

Christ Episcopal Church, located in the Mende region of Maryland Lagos was one of the oldest churches in the city. Housed in a huge architectural structure of gothic proportions, Christ Episcopal Church was designed in a manner reminiscent of Roman cathedrals, with stained glass windows, high slung ceilings, and dark oak pews arranged in a semi-circle to face the dark oak pulpit on the altar. The recessed lighting and the strategically placed floral arrangements all combined to create an overall soothing and reverent effect worthy of a sanctuary of God.

"Welcome to Christ Episcopal." A smiling female usher led them to a pew close to the altar, and they filed in, and bowed their heads silently for a moment. The Sunday school service was just wrapping up, and a tall, thin man of about thirty-two strutted to the pulpit and took up the mike. His body language conveyed an air of cockiness, and in his contrived two-piece European suit, which seemed out of place for the climate, he was sweating profusely. He stood next to the pulpit in a relaxed stance, with one hand in his pant pocket. Clearing his voice slightly, he grabbed the mike off the pedestal and tapped the tip of the mike with the edge of his fingers. As he made the announcements, he paused every now and then to mop his sweaty brows with his handkerchief. Wrapping up his announcements, he introduced the choir group before stepping down, and disappearing behind a door off to the left of the pulpit.

The choir group filed in and took their place near the band, decked out in royal blue choir gowns. The first strains of heavenly organ music filled the air and the cavernous space of the church became inhabited by the beautifully harmonized voices of the choir. They belted out song after moving song, rendered in melodious voices so mellifluous and harmonious that Adora was held in the throes of rapture, and moved to tears. It was so easy to envision the gates of heaven opening up at any time, and the angels descending to bear her off to heaven on swift wings. The congregation joined in a vigorous accompaniment to the moving praise songs that ebbed and flowed into other praise songs, and Adora lifted up her voice and sang her praises to the creator with a joyful heart and a loving spirit.

A woman at the end of their pew, wearing a silver spangled gown lifted her voice high above the rest of the congregation, and belted out her own version of the praise song. Her voice rose and crested above the other voices around them, rising to a lilting crescendo as she allowed the wave of worship to sweep her away. Soon, the tempo of the songs became slow and reverential as the choir and the congregation shifted to worship songs. Adora felt herself caught up in the joy of the moment, as this was a far cry from the repetitious routine of the Ekulu Catholic Diocese that her family attended in Enugu, which was more conservative, and rooted in ceremonious monotony.

The choir concluded their routine, and the pastor stepped up to the podium. He was a middle-aged man of mammoth girt with a receding graying hairline, a thick mustache that was sprinkled with touches of gray, and a booming voice that echoed throughout the entire church. He conducted a lively sermon, regarding the congregation over the rim of tortoise shell spectacles that perched at the edge of his bulbous nose, making reference to several chapters of the Bible, and driving the captive congregation into a fevered pitch of religious ecstasy. He talked about faith and hope and love, and the love that Christ has for us all. When the service wrapped up, Adora was sorry to leave the church, but she was determined to let the message live forever in her heart.

Monica was waiting for them when they arrived at the house. She was perched on the edge of the settee in the living room, wearing a white tank top over a figure-hugging pair of white Capri length jeans. Her hair was done in a soft wrap style that framed her pretty oval face and bobbed around when she moved her head. She was flipping through the family album, which sat on her lap, talking to Aunt Agatha's maid, Hanatu when the family walked in. Hanatu greeted them and made a quick exit, and Monica stood up, and in her flat white slippers, she dwarfed the two women with her slender six-foot frame.

Aunt Agatha was the first to speak. "Monica, what a nice surprise," she said warmly, clasping the younger girl's hand. She turned to her husband, and introduced Monica, who seemed surprised by her unexpected presence.

"Paul, Monica is Adora's friend," she said by way of introduction.

"Nice to meet you sir," Monica said, shaking Paul's hand warmly.

"Great to meet you Monica," he responded and gave his wife a quick peck on the forehead.

"Honey, I have to go now," he said. I have that Okere account I'm working on. I have to meet the deadline."

"I understand," Aunt Agatha said as she threw off her cape and draped it on the edge of the sofa. "And what can I offer you my dear," she asked Monica. "Really nothing. I just ate, and I have to watch my weight very carefully," Monica objected, flashing a perfect smile that showed off her even, white teeth.

"Watch your weight?" Adora exclaimed in surprise.

Monica chuckled, and patted her pert hips. "Trust me, I have to stay on top of things," she said perkily.

Her eyes swept across the lofty living room and she nodded appreciatively, then she turned her attention to Aunt Agatha and began to gush.

"Madam, this place is beautiful. I need to compliment you on your decorating taste, which I can see is reflected in your taste for clothes. That outfit is positively spectacular. It looks like an Electra original," she said with a whistle.

Aunt Agatha dropped her satin handbag on the center table and smiled. "Why, thank you. You have a good eye for detail. I do have to go change. This is not exactly comfortable," she said, as she picked up her cloak and made her way to the staircase. Melissa scampered after her, clutching tightly to her mom, and almost tripping the two of them in her haste, an action that elicited a stern reprimand from her mother. "Careful now Melissa, or we will both fall," she said firmly, gathering her cloak with one hand, and grabbing firmly onto Melissa's hand with the other.

"Kids!" sighed Monica as soon as they disappeared from view, throwing up her hands and shaking her head slowly. "I don't understand them, and I guess that I never will."

"Remember that you were once a little girl yourself, and there is no telling what you were like then," Adora countered, standing in front of the entertainment system, and spinning the CD rack.

"I guess you're right," Monica giggled standing beside Adora and watching the incredible selection of compact disc music that spun before her line of vision.

"I've heard some incredibly funny stories about my silly antics as a little girl. I'll tell

you about it someday."

"I'm sure," Adora responded, and I could tell you a few of mine that could curl your hair."

Monica giggled and stood close by as Adora selected a jazz compact disc by Earl Klugh, and slid it into the compact disc player. The earthy jazz riffs of Earl Klugh's masterful guitar strings filled the room and the girls tapped their feet and nodded their heads to the jazzy sounds.

"Wow! That is absolutely soul stirring, I never heard this before," Monica enthused, closing her eyes, and swaying her body from side to side. Adora smiled at her reaction.

"Earl Klugh is a black American jazz musician who plays with a blues influence. You might say that he belongs with the jazz legends along with Miles Davis, Kenny G, and David Sanborn.

"Wow groovy!" Monica exclaimed, tapping her feet in time to the music. 'I always thought that jazz was so boring," she commented.

"Then you haven't listened to contemporary jazz musicians like Hugh Masekela, Jean Luc and the Fat Burger composition," Adora countered.

"Fat Burger!" Monica exclaimed with a loud laugh. "What kind of a name is that?"

Adora watched in controlled amusement as Monica threw herself on the sofa, and continued to laugh. "Really," she said, regaining some of her composure. "The fat burger--- that sounds like a bunch of fat people who like to eat a lot of burgers," she concluded.

"That's not funny Monica," Adora remonstrated. "Their name is their name and you have to admit that it is a catchy name."

"You are right," Monica agreed.

As the girls went through the family photo album, listening to the music selections, Adora regaled Monica about her incredibly positive experience at the Christ Episcopal Church in Maryland.

"In Owerri, my family and I attend the Cherubim and Seraphim church, where they wear white robes and can only enter God's sanctuary barefoot, but my cousin Regina and her husband Charles attend the Celestial church, which is quite similar in edicts and process. They both have prophets, and the church members are similarly garbed, and their prophets see visions and prophesy and go in the spirit, so I didn't find the sharp contrast that you found in your own experience."

"Talking about robes, that's a lovely outfit, where did you get those," Monica commented in the next breath, eyeing Adora's silk dress.

"London last year. I followed my dad to a medical conference."

"Cool!" Monica said. "You attend conferences with your dad?"

"No silly," Adora laughed. "Dad attended his conferences. I visited with relatives, and I did a lot of shopping and sightseeing."

"Anyway, I came to get you," Monica stated changing the subject. "Not for the party I hope," Adora joked.

"No silly, to see where I live."

"I know," Adora laughed. "I was just kidding; we'll go after lunch."

"Awesome!" Monica said enthusiastically.

Monica followed Adora upstairs to her room, and twirled around the spacious room, marveling at the feminine elegance of the furnishings and the size. "But it is much too girlish for me," she concluded.

"Actually, this room belongs to my cousin Nneka, who lives in England. She is in boarding school over there."

"England! That's a little too young ---don't you think?" Monica commented.

"She is well taken care of," Adora began. "And Paul's sister, who lives in England often goes to visit her at the school. She also comes home during the holidays."

"And where will you stay when she comes home?" Monica queried. "Share a room with a little girl? Now that's not for me."

"You have a point Monica," Adora agreed. "I do plan to go home during the holidays, besides, there's plenty of room for me here if I decide to stay," Adora replied.

"I'll say," Monica agreed. "This place is huge."

She threw herself on the bed and giggled in childish delight as the mattress bounced gently up and down. Adora watched her in controlled amusement and smiled.

"Talking about kids, now tell me that this is not the little girl in you?" she joked. Monica stopped bouncing and followed her to her closet.

"Wow, that's a lot of space," she commented.

She ran to the terrace and flopped herself in a white chaise. Adora remained in her closet and selected a loose-fitting cotton poplin shirt in white, and a long black denim skirt and slid her feet into a pair of low-heeled mules. "Are you decent now?" Monica called out as she re-entered the walk-in space, and assessed everything in the room.

"Nice clothes, and when did you have the chance to put them all away so neatly already?" She ran her hands along the clothes, lined up neatly in the closet.

"Actually, I didn't," Adora responded.

"Didn't what? You mean arrange the clothes?" "No, Mina did."

"Mina?"

"Mina is my aunt's head of household. I think she did this when I went to church today. I heard my aunt giving her instructions in the morning."

"I see that---hmm, lucky you, I have to put away my own clothes, and believe me, they're still sitting in the suitcase. I don't plan to touch anything till at least next week-end."

"Oh," Adora said.

"Yep!" Monica said as she flicked through the row of clothes hanging neatly on rods in the walk-in closet, and examined them with a critical eye. She fingered the clothes and turned to Adora.

"Your clothes are of very good quality, but they are all so proper. You don't have a single funky thing in here. Girl, you need to live a little, and strut your stuff in something bold and revealing sometimes."

Adora only smiled as she led the way out of the room in her long black skirt and big cotton shirt.

They followed the hum of voices to the patio where lunch was being served. A picnic table was draped with a lively lime green checkered tablecloth, replete with a selection of light, savory seafood dishes. There were tureens of lobster and prawns, crabs, periwinkles, stewed fish, and pepper shrimp. A steaming porcelain platter, heaped with steamed rice garnished with fresh leaf curry herbs was laid on the table, next to a silver tureen covered with a salad of lettuce, carrots, tomatoes, pickled onions, marinated mushrooms, and fresh green baby peas. The mingled aroma of the various foods on the table lent a delightfully savory aroma to the air, along with the mouthwatering essence of the appetizing looking seafood feast making Adora to sniff the air appreciatively.

"Wow, that's a lot of food auntie," she exclaimed with wide-eyed wonder. Paul stood up and pulled out chairs for the two girls.

"We eat like this every Sunday as a celebration of life and as a way of thanking God for everything that he has blessed us with," his wife said with a twinkle in her eyes.

Adora recalled similar Sunday feasts with her family, almost a lifetime away, distant memories that she tried to shove into the deepest recess of her memory. She felt the prickling of tears on her eyelids, but she valiantly fought it back, and forced a smile upon her trembling lips. She bent her head as Paul said grace, and offered a silent prayer for the memory of her mother.

"Hey! What are we waiting for?" Paul said.

He doled out filets of salmon, and lobster meat for his daughter and his wife and waited as Adora piled her plate with rice, prawns, and shrimps, topping it off with the salad.

"Mmm, my mouth is watering already, she said, and popped a jumbo shrimp, dripping with herb sauce into her mouth. The food was delicious, and she heaped a second helping of everything onto her plate. Monica picked at a

small plate of salad, and watched goggle eyed as Adora ate every morsel on her plate with relish.

"Where does it go?" she asked Adora. "You and your aunt. How could you eat all that, and manage to keep those beautiful figures?"

"This is all seafood and fresh vegetables," Aunt Agatha laughed lightly. Monica tapped the tip of her fingernail on her drinking glass.

"Frankly, if I ate like that," she continued. " In a few weeks, somebody would have to roll me around because I would definitely turn into a ball of blubber."

They all laughed at Monica's piquant imagery, but Adora didn't. She grasped Monica's shoulder and shook her head.

"Give me a break Monica. I would like to see that happen from this," she gestured at the remaining food on the table.

"You don't know how lucky you are. You have good genes," Monica said to Aunt Agatha.

"My dear, you need to eat more, you need balanced nutrition."

"Eating more would help me to look like you?" Monica asked, and Aunt Agatha gave her a look of concern.

"It's dangerous to starve yourself like that. This food is light and nourishing. You won't gain weight from such healthy fare."

"I really need to watch everything that goes into my mouth. If I eat what I want, I might as well slap it directly on my hips and tummy," Monica insisted.

"My dear," Aunt Agatha said, looking levelly at Monica. "You are a beautiful girl, and you do not have anything to worry about, but if it means that much to you, I studied nutrition in College. I can help you chart a healthy, balanced diet. But if you want my opinion, you don't need to go on any sort of diet, don't you think so love?" she addressed her husband, who had pushed away his empty plate, and was perusing a page of the daily newspaper.

"Honestly honey! Reading at the table," she reprimanded him.

Paul folded up the paper, and dropped it on the floor by his side.

Melissa giggled and her mother glanced at her. She was picking at her food, filling her tummy with glasses of freshly squeezed orange juice. "Finish your food Melissa," aunt Agatha urged.

"But mom, I'm not hungry------," she began to protest.

"You heard your mother young lady," Paul said firmly. "Finish your food."

Melissa's lips trembled into a pout, and she pushed her food around the plate with her fork and reached for another glass of juice.

"Promise honey, you'll get to drink all the juice that you want, but you have to finish your food."

"Okay mommy," Melissa said, as she took little bites from her shrimp stew. Monica nibbled at a piece of lettuce and drank a tall glass of water. She pushed her plate aside and stood up.

"Hey! Why don't we go over to my place now?" Monica suggested. The girls were upstairs in Adora's room, looking through Adora's picture collection.

"I need to tell my aunt."

"Oh yeah, I almost forgot. You can't make a move without telling her," Monica said in a voice that barely concealed her sarcasm.

"Whatever," Adora retorted, as she set off in search of her aunt. She found her in the gazebo with her husband and Melissa, setting up a game of scrabbles.

"Do you girls need a ride?" Paul asked.

"No thanks," Monica said. "It is not that far, Lake Crescent. We'll take a taxi."

"But that would……." Aunt Agatha began.

"It doesn't cost that much," Monica interjected.

"You're right.....Lake Crescent. It's not that far," Paul agreed.

"Guess what?" Monica said as soon as they were out of earshot. "What?" Adora asked, anticipating that Monica had something under her sleeves. She had the air of the cat that had swallowed the cream and seemed very pleased with whatever information that she had to divulge.

"My cousin Gina and her husband got an invitation to Randy's party, and they can

bring along two guests. Isn't that exciting?" she gushed like a schoolgirl.

"That's not news---if I remember clearly, you already said that. You need to stop obsessing about------"

Just then, a light spray of water arced towards them and Adora ducked down quickly, noticing that the water was coming from the sprinkler system, which was sending a steady stream of water arcing high in the air, drenching a perimeter of greenery.

"Watch out Monica!" Adora warned, as another geyser curved towards them. Adora ducked quickly, but Monica stopped in her tracks, and frowned in

dismay as the stream of water caught her, lightly dampening her bouncy hair. "Ooh," she squealed, running her hand vigorously through her bangs, sending a fine mist of water cascading from her hair. Her hair instantly lost its bounce, and lay in a limp mess on her head, framing her oval face with wisps of damp curlicues.

"Oh, I must look awful," she complained.

"Really, it is not that bad, I think that it does have a charming quality about it," Adora said with sincerity.

"Easy for you to say, your hair is perfect," Monica said, glancing enviously at the thick mane of shoulder length hair that cascaded down Adora's neck, forming a perfect frame for her beautiful face.

"You have nice hair Monica."

"Thanks to my hairdresser, I have hair."

"You mean they're not real?" Adora asked in amazement.

"As real as my real fake nails," Monica said, flashing her perfectly manicured acrylic nails.

"Wow! Couldn't tell."

"I do have hair. Just that I get bored with the same old style, so I had Jennifer weave in those for me, and cut them to style. They're really wash and go.

See." Monica flipped her hair back and forth and ran her fingers through them. The bounce returned to her hair, as did much of the style.

"That's really good," Adora said. "If my hair got wet like that, it would look like a limp rag by now."

They reached the cupid fountain, and Monica ran her hand through the arcing spray of water that splashed out from the spigot.

"Ah, that feels cool and refreshing," she commented. "The extra invitations were

tentative yesterday, but now they are definite," she said, as she picked up the thread of their last conversation.

"Excuse me?" Adora said blankly. Monica gave her a funny look and she laughed heartily.

"Oh, you mean the party?" Adora queried. "My aunt and her husband were discussing it this morning over breakfast. They've been invited too."

"Oh, you bad girl," Monica admonished Adora. "And you never even mentioned it until I brought up the subject."

They approached the front gate and Suleman smiled amiably at the girls, swinging the gates open and waving them through.

"How come you didn't mention it to me?" Monica started as they tried to flag down a passing taxi, which sped past them.

"His loss," Monica said sourly. "Mention what?" Adora asked.

"That your aunt has connection to the Okere enclave?" Monica queried.

"Because I didn't consider it that important," Adora responded, wondering why her stomach was doing flip-flops if she did not consider it that important to see Randy again.

"Not important?" Monica sniffed disdainfully. "You must be out of your mind girl.

We're talking about the social event of the year – most luminaries of the society will be there. It is the place to be seen, and you tell me you don't find it that important. And remember Randy? Wouldn't you like to see him again? I know I would," she said with rising excitement.

"It's not my cup of tea." Ador stated tersely.

"And you really expect me to believe that? You need to wake up girrl," Monica shot back.

They flagged a dilapidated taxi, the only one that they could find at that hour and Monica gave her gave her cousin's address to the driver, a young man in his early twenties, wearing a black tee shirt over khakis' and a faded khaki cap set jauntily atop his head. The tip of a toothpick was jutting out from the corner of his mouth, and he pulled it out of his mouth. "Drop or charter?" he asked.

"Charter," both girls chimed simultaneously, opting for the costlier but more convenient choice.

"I don't blame you ladies, at all," he said, the toothpick bobbing up and down in his mouth. "You have to pay for your comfort."

"Comfort indeed," Adora said cynically, smiling at the irony of the driver's words, considering the state of his car.

"Well think of the alternative," Monica responded.

"Good point," Adora responded, thinking with distaste about the other alternative where passengers are often sandwiched between sweating strangers while the driver made a circuitous trip through the neighborhood dropping off and picking up passengers along the way until their own destination was reached. This was a normal practice in Lagos and much of other parts of the country because of the overpopulation.

The taxi swung into the approach of Lake Crescent and Adora looked around in excitement. The streets in that part of Victoria Island were narrower, and the houses were mostly semi-detached and closer to the street, comprised mainly of bungalows, split level duplexes and blocks of tall buildings, subdivided into flats. Here and there, Adora caught fleeting glimpses of building facades from beyond the foliage covered scrolled gates that protected the privacy of the residents from prying eyes. The taxi dropped them in front of a white painted split-level duplex fronted by a white picket security fence. There was no gatehouse here, and no gatekeeper to monitor the visitors.

"Five hundred Naira," the taxi driver said. The toothpick in the corner of his mouth bobbed up and down.

"Five hundred?" the girls chimed simultaneously.

"Lagos is 'xpensive," the driver said succinctly.

The girls split the fare, and the driver counted out the money quickly, then put his car into gear, and rattled noisily down the deserted street.

A gentle breeze blew in from the coast, slightly ruffling Adora's thick hair, and furling through her white blouse.

"That feels good," Monica remarked.

"Yep, nice and cool, took the words right out of my mouth," Adora responded.

Monica unlatched the gate and they stepped through. The tiny front lawn was green and immaculately kept. The hedges were neatly trimmed and bursting with brightly colored tropical flowers. The doorbell chimed softly under Monica's thumb, and presently the door swung open to reveal a plump, diminutive woman who seemed to be in her late twenties. She was wearing a loose-fitting, cotton smock in an understated shade of purple, which could not conceal the obvious swell to her stomach.

Her face lit up when she saw them, a warm, friendly smile that highlighted the special glow that came with pregnancy. Monica, in her talkative manner had apprised Adora of her condition, and Adora knew that Gina was in her seventh month. "Hello, you must be Adora," she greeted effusively. "I have heard so much about you, and it is a pleasure to finally meet you. My name is Regina, but you can call me Gina."

But we only met yesterday, so how could she have so much to say? Adora was on the verge of asking Gina, but she refrained herself. Monica's penchant for long-winded speeches, and exaggerations said enough.

Gina led them through a beige carpeted foyer, and into an L shaped living room, which was partially separated from the dining area by a beige and black silk screen

edged with gleaming black lacquered wood. The living room contained a beige colored sectional with huge black silk pillows arranged strategically to contrast with the stark color scheme reflected in the living room. A giant teddy bear of a man wearing a plain black tee shirt and baggy blue jeans reclined on the sofa, amongst huge black throw pillows. The teddy bear was stuffing fistfuls of peanuts into his mouth from a bowl on his lap. He had a luxuriant growth of hair on his face, trimmed into a clipped beard and mustache. He wore a very low-cut afro which right now looked like it could use a quick pick of the comb through it. His black cotton tee fit too snugly around the middle, which stretched the fabric, as though to accommodate a pregnancy, Adora thought.

On the black coffee table in front of the bear sat a half-finished bottle of Gulder™ beer, and a smoldering tobacco pipe from which emanated the most comforting aroma. The teddy bear's eyes seemed permanently affixed to the television screen, which featured a pre-recorded soccer game in progress. He was waving his arms, shouting and cheering on his favorite team. "Go, Green Eagle, yes Okocha, go," he chanted.

Gina shook her head, sighed wearily, and snuffed out the glowing embers on the mouth of the pipe. She dumped the gray black ashes into a towel, which was sitting on the coffee table and hissed angrily. The teddy bear's eyes did not flicker from the television screen.

"Charles, I thought I told you about smoking inside the house, especially in my condition. The doctor said---,"

"But love," the teddy bear interrupted her in a gentle voice that belied his gruff

exterior. You were outside on the patio when I was smoking, and the light is gone

now."

"It's a goooooooooal," the television sports commentator announced on the television, amidst a roar of cheers and applause from the stadium audience.

Charles shot out of the couch and lifted his hands in the air. "Yes! green eagle, yes, yes, yes," he shouted, jumping up and down gleefully. His rotund stomach bobbed up and down in a most comical manner, and Adora contained an overwhelming urge to laugh hysterically.

He sat down again, and swigged beer from the Gulder bottle. His eyes never left the television screen, and he seemed oblivious to the fact that the others were still in the room with him.

His wife stood in front of the set, blocking his view of the television screen. He made a slight motion with his hand, as though to flick her from the front of the screen.

"Charles, how rude," she said crossly. We have a visitor, and you are watching soccer. I want you to meet Monica's friend Adora." Gina squeezed her lips into a thin line of displeasure at her husband's seeming lack of manners. Charles tore his eyes from the television screen long enough to grunt a mechanical sounding hello without obviously giving much thought to why he was saying it.

"Charles, where are your manners?" his wife admonished him, fiercely. She snatched the remote control from the coffee table and flipped off the television set. She flung the remote at him, and it sailed through the air, missing him by mere inches. It landed on the edge of the couch with a dull "thunk" and slid noiselessly to the carpeted floor.

Charles blinked in surprise, and started to protest before realizing - it seemed for the first time since the girls' arrival that he had company.

"Honey!.." he began as he reached for the remote lying next to his feet. He squelched his protest, and snapped on the television with the remote.

"All you do is watch soccer," Gina berated him.

He lumbered to his feet and stretched himself to his full height of six feet three.

He seemed to take on a life of his own, and filled up the room, completely dwarfing everybody, even Monica; and his pregnant wife Gina, even with her mammoth belly looked miniscule next to him. At a mere five foot three, the disparity in height between the pair was so incongruous it seemed almost comical. Adora's eye wandered to the entertainment unit, at a framed picture of a slimmer Regina, during her pre- pregnancy days, looking svelte in a black halter dress. Another picture showed Gina in a long white wedding dress, almost looking like a doll in Charles's arms.

On the television, the stadium spectators erupted into an uproarious roar and Charles's hands shot straight up. "Yea!" he shouted jubilantly. "Charles, you still haven't said hello to Adora!" Regina said sharply. "Pleased to meet you," Charles mumbled, almost unintelligibly, and stuck out his hand without looking at Adora. Adora took his outstretched paw and

shook it. He muttered something unintelligible and heaved his mammoth bulk back on the sofa. His eyes never left the screen the entire time, and he could have shaken his wife's hands for all the notice that he paid.

Gina was seething, and watching her, Adora found herself envisioning a

cartoon character who actually had smoke blowing out of its ears when they were angry. It was with apparent effort that she kept a tight lid on her anger. Instead, she threw her hands up in the air in exasperation, expelled a blast of air, and rolled her eyes at her husband. Her actions were lost on Charles who was right now bouncing up and down in his seat, his fists tightly clenched, urging Omokachi to go for it.

Gina inhaled deeply, and led the girls to the patio, which was shaded from the hot sun with a striped green awning, muttering quite volubly. "Men!" she gritted out through clenched teeth. "Who can figure them out? They court you like a prince. They marry you and transform into frogs," she complained loudly.

"Charles could never do enough to please me before we were married. Now he could never do enough to please himself. Smoking his stinking pipe in the house when I'm expecting, can't even remember his manners, and could somebody please tell me why men become so boorish once a game is on?" Her litany of complaint went on and on, and the girls nodded sympathetically.

Adora understood, especially since her father was a doctor. Women at any

stage of pregnancy often rode an emotional roller coaster due to the hormonal changes in their bodies, and could be set off by the slightest provocation. Charles' boorish behavior in the face of his soccer game was enough to make anyone see red, and in Gina's precarious condition, her emotional reaction was all too normal.

"It's okay Gina, I understand," Adora said sympathetically, keeping pace with Gina, who was pacing the floor rapidly in spite of her mammoth tummy. Her movement was so swift that Adora feared that she might just go into labor. At her stage of pregnancy, it was possible for her to go into premature labor from stress. Beads of perspiration stood out on her brows and her upper lip, and her breathing came in labored puffs.

Adora glanced anxiously at Monica, who took the hint, and joined her pregnant cousin. "Gina, you need to sit down," she said firmly, indicating a sturdy patio chair. Gina ignored her and kept pacing.

Monica drew herself up to her full height and glared at her.

"Do you forget that you have a baby growing inside here?" she queried heatedly, patting Gina's big stomach. "Can't you see that men will be men? You have to calm down for that baby!"

"Monica is right you know," Adora added.

"I am sure that your husband meant no harm. You know how men are with sports. My daddy is hardly ever home, but when he's home, don't mess with the TV when a tennis game is on. Men speak a universal language when it comes to spectator sports. Don't risk your baby's precious health over this. Just sit down and breathe slowly.

You will feel better."

Gina thought about this for a second, and finally calmed down. She heaved herself onto a green trellis patterned lawn chair and stretched out on it, her mammoth belly sticking straight out like a beacon in front of her. All

the fight seemed to have gone out of her, and she fanned herself with a magazine.

"That's much better my dear," Adora said and Gina managed a smile. She closed her eyes and soon, the tension eased and her plump face relaxed, and brightened up.

"You're right. I think I overreacted," she said with a wry little smile. "And my Charles isn't really that bad." She turned to Adora with a smile that made her look younger.

"I hear you are here to start your Master's program," she began.

"Uh huh," Adora said, picking up a magazine on the patio table, which featured the picture of a beautiful television actress, Nikki Essin on the cover, and began to fan Gina with it."

"Gina's face relaxed, and she smiled even brighter than before. "Thanks, Adora. I'm totally impressed," she commented.

"I fan you all the time, and you aren't ever impressed," Monica cut in.

Regina's face broke into a bigger smile, and her big stomach began to bob up and down.

"I was talking about Adora's academic record. Graduate school at twenty-one is quite impressive.

"I knew that Gina, just wanted to make you laugh," Monica said.

"Thanks Gina, but I don't think that my age should have any bearing on it at all. I just started school a bit early that's all."

"And don't forget about the pushy father," Monica began. "I wish my parents were pushier. Maybe I would be starting grad school too.

"Monica, you don't know half the story," Adora sighed. "You don't want to be in my shoes with my dad."

"Yeah right," Monica scoffed.

Give me a rich dad who takes me overseas on a whim and you won't hear me complain."

The oppressive heat of the afternoon had given way to a cool breeze, which blew in from the Atlantic, whistling through the swaying palm trees and the spreading branches of the jacaranda tree that partly shaded the backyard porch.

"You must be thirsty, what can I get you" Monica asked Adora, as they sat on the verandah, keeping Gina company as she napped intermittently on a chaise in the balcony.

"Oh no, don't worry," Adora responded.

"Don't be silly," Monica said. She disappeared into the house and returned quickly, carrying a jug of ice-filled lemonade and three glasses on a tray, which she set down on the glass-topped picnic table. She poured a glass of lemonade for everybody, and they sat in the warm orange glow of the setting sun, sipping the lemonade.

It had a tart, sweet taste that woke up Adora's taste bud, and the melting ice slid down her throat, cooling her parched throat. "Mmm, this is really good, tastes homemade," Adora said, shivering slightly, and hugging her shoulders.

"It's really easy," Gina said. The secret is in the lemon. You have to use just the right balance of lemon and sugar. I'll show you how if you want."

"I'll love to learn," Adora said gratefully.

"I wouldn't waste my sweat if I were you," Monica said sardonically.

"Why would you say a thing like that?" Gina queried, with a surprised look on her face.

"You are looking at a pampered princess, who never had to lift a finger. She has a

legion of house-help at her disposal---why her clothes were already unpacked and hanging neatly in her closet by the time that she came back from church today, and I bet she had the same thing at her parent's estate in Enugu."

"You are quite wrong," Adora responded. "I do have to help a lot of times." "Yeah, yeah," Monica giggled, bending towards Regina, who was reclined on the lounge chaise, fanning her face with the magazine, while her stomach rose and fell with her breathing. Monica bent towards her cousin; her angular face wreathed with concern. She picked up a napkin from the table, and also fanned Gina with it.

"Thanks." Gina opened her eyes and smiled her half-moon shaped smile. "Any time," Monica said with her angular laugh.

Adora could not help noticing the sharp physical contrast between Monica and Gina. Where Monica was tall and angular, Gina was plump and diminutive. Gina's smooth caramel colored skin – made almost luminescent from pregnancy also contrasted sharply with Monica's warm mahogany skin tones. In an uncharacteristic show of tactlessness, Adora blurted out her thoughts.

"You guys look so different from each other," she said to Monica, who was still fanning Gina with the napkin.

Gina lay back on the chaise, and laughed so heartily that her belly bobbed up and down and the tears rolled down her eyes.

"If I had a Naira for every time people said that, I would be a millionaire. You see, we're maternal cousins, as well as paternal cousins. Monica took after her grandfather who was extremely tall, dark, and thin.

"Mom and dad too------," Monica started.

"Yeah," Gina interjected. "Both her parents are extremely tall people, but my

own parents are rather short. I come from her mother's side of the family," Gina said with an earthy laugh. Adora joined in the laughter, feeling very comfortable in the presence of her newfound friends.

"Your husband is so tall, how did you guys meet?" she blurted tactlessly, voicing the question that had been burning on her mind. Gina laughed out loud again.

"My dear, you have so many questions. I hope you have the time."

◆ ◆ ◆

"Well, girls, I have to make dinner now," Gina announced, struggling to rise from her chaise. The girls sprang instantly to their feet, and stood at each side of Gina, helping her to her feet.

"I can't imagine ever getting pregnant," Monica said disdainfully, wrinkling her pert nose. "I can't imagine dealing with the stress, and I don't even want to think about the havoc it would wreak on my figure."

"C'mon Monica, you must be joking," Adora said with an air of unbelief. "Never mind her," Gina said coolly, leading the way to the kitchen. "Someday she will understand."

"Until then, I have to be me," Monica retorted.

The gleaming, white tiled kitchen was a well-appointed, modern one, filled with all the latest kitchen gadgetry. Gina was obviously proud of her kitchen. She kept it spotlessly clean, with nothing out of place. She apparently felt at home in her kitchen and despite her burgeoning stomach, she was a blur of activities, deicing carrots, chopping onions, slicing mushrooms, chopping herbs- alternating between the chopping board and the food processor which sat atop the gleaming white surface of the granite countertop. Effortlessly, she maneuvered her way around the octagonal kitchen, steaming fish and vegetables, boiling rice, frying potatoes, steaming vegetables, and stirring the contents of the steaming pot, which bubbled merrily on the stove.

"Why won't you let us help" Adora said for the umpteenth time, as she sat by helplessly on one of the high-backed bar stools that was arranged in front of the counter by the fridge, watching the dizzying whir of activities that emanated from one so encumbered by a bulky stomach.

"No, I need my concentration. Too many cooks spoil the broth," Gina said,

shooing her away again.

"You don't know my cousin Gina like I know her," Monica said under her breath. "Once she makes up her mind, she won't change it."

"Goodness!" Adora said.

"My cousin is very possessive about her kitchen." "Yep, call me homemade Gina," Gina joked.

Soon the kitchen was suffused with the most delectable aroma, which drifted its way to the living room, drawing Charles like a magnet. He stuck his head through the doorway and smiled bashfully at his wife.

"Honey," he said gaily. "Something smells nice."

He inhaled the air deeply, and rubbed his copious stomach, standing at the threshold of the kitchen.

Gina waddled over to him and reached towards him. Standing on the tip of her toes she kissed the tip of his hairy chin. He bent his head towards her and nuzzled her face with his nose. He laughed and rubbed her protruding belly and his eyes shone with love as he bent slowly till his face was level with his wife's belly. He kissed her stomach gently, and then rubbed it slowly, while speaking in a very gentle tone to the fetus. For a moment, it seemed that he forgot all about the delectable aroma that drew him to the kitchen and the pair of eyes that watched them.

Adora tried to shrink into the background, feeling almost embarrassed at witnessing such a personal moment between husband and wife. She felt intrusive, as though she had no right to see them like that.

"Honey, what are you making?' Charles asked his wife, finally straightening up and drawing closer to the gas range, which was loaded with bubbling pots. "What isn't she making?" Monica said. If I didn't know any better, I would say that Gina was trying to get me fat, just like her."

"You need to put some meat on your bones anyway," Gina retorted saucily.

Charles laughed, and then seemed to notice Adora for the first time. A look of embarrassment showed upon his face, as he realized his errors, and he approached her slowly, panting from his effort.

"Please excuse me um------err."

"Adora," Gina reminded him. A frown furrowed her brows.

"It is about time you remembered your manners Charles," she added. "Pardon me Adora," he blustered, and directed a pleading look in the direction of his wife.

"So, what happened to soccer?" Gina teased, looking at her husband through narrowed eyes.

"Oh honey, you know, half time," he muttered, almost unintelligibly.

"You mean dinner time?" Gina teased.

Charles ignored his wife's jibes and lumbered to the refrigerator. He rummaged around until he came up with a bottle of Gulder beer. He grabbed a can opener from a drawer and patted his wife's belly again before returning to the living room. Both girls glanced at each other, and a look passed between them. Gina ignored their gestures and continued her earlier activities.

Before long, she ran out of steam and her movements slowed. Her breathing

quickened audibly, and tiny beads of perspiration stood out on her upper lip. The girls firmly maneuvered her to a kitchen table, where she sat back panting, her protuberant tummy sticking straight out in front of her. Monica frowned at her, shaking her fingers at her.

"Seriously Gina, you need to know when to stop. You can't do everything at once."

"Says who?" Gina retorted, fanning furiously at her face with her hand, almost panting out the words.

"She's right you know. Look at you, and listen to yourself," Adora said. She poured a cool glass of water from a pitcher in the refrigerator into a glass, and handed it to Gina, who downed it in a few rapid gulps. She replaced the glass on the kitchen table in front of her, and moments later, she was struggling to return to her feet. Adora shook her head fiercely at her and detained her in her seated position with a firm gesture of her hand.

"But I have to complete dinner," Gina complained, trying again to rise to from the chair.

Both girls stood over her, and blocked her way, frowning fiercely at her. Gina took one look at their faces and burst into laughter.

"Okay, okay, you both win, but I really haven't finished," she said, looking around in dismay at the dishes in the sink, the plastic preparation bowls on the countertop, and the remaining pots simmering on the stovetop.

"I have really turned into a slob. I normally clean up as I go along, but look at this mess," she said, waving expansively at the preparation area.

"We can both handle what's left," Monica said firmly.

"You've done most of the work anyway, all we need to do is to finish the salad, clean up and serve," Adora said, indicating the kitchen sink.

"I guess you're both right, thanks for your help," she said, expelling a blast of air through her mouth.

"I have to admit that I am sort of slowing down," she added, and remained reluctantly at the kitchen table while the two girls busied themselves putting the finishing touches on Gina's dinner.

Monica rinsed out the plastic preparation bowls and the dirty dishes and tossed them into the dishwasher, while Adora washed down the white granite kitchen counter with a cloth napkin and a spray wash. She glanced at Gina, who was glaring at them, as though she still wanted to take charge of the situation. She threw her a sharp look.

"Honestly Gina, I know that it is none of my business, but you really can't go on like

this in your condition. Now is the time for you to slow down a bit-----." "But I get my exercise this way. The doctor said that I need moderate exercise," Gina countered, interrupting Adora.

"Yes, the exercise is good, but you don't want to overdo it. Any extra exertion can bring on premature labor you know."

"How do you know all of that?" Gina challenged, apparently unwilling to give up the active life that she was accustomed to despite her doctor's advice. "My father is a physician-----he always tells his pregnant patients to get plenty of rest. Maybe your husband can help you out sometimes."

"Ha!" Gina snickered disdainfully. "My husband the couch potato. The day that my chauvinistic husband comes into the kitchen to help me, I will have to raise a gun salute."

"But I am here, I want to help" Monica stated tersely. "I like to work," Gina countered.

Adora stood over her, with her hands folded over her chest, glaring at her. "You need

to adjust your lifestyle a bit," she said. "You need to conserve that energy for when the baby arrives. Believe me you will need it,"

Monica replaced a glass jar in the cabinet and shut the door firmly. She placed her hands on her hips and turned to face Gina. "Adora you tell her," she said. "She doesn't listen to me."

"Honestly, you girls do not need to fuss so much over me just because I am expecting--," Gina began.

"Oh, yes we do," Monica retorted, standing over the stove, holding a wooden spatula poised over the steaming pots. She ladled out the savory looking mélange into ceramic tureens and set them on the dining table in front of Regina.

"You should put up your feet," she told Gina.

"That's right," Adora added and pulled up a chair, and hoisted Gina's legs over it. Gina looked dissatisfied. She pouted her lips and frowned at her cousin.

"Listen, I don't want you to think that I don't appreciate this, but I'm not used to a lot of fuss. I like to do what I have to."

"Well, you definitely need to adjust. I take care of you for a change. End of story," Monica said, dropping the napkin in her hand. She stood over her cousin and Adora took over from her, dishing out the foods into platters. "When that baby arrives, believe me you won't have the strength to do so much, and you will be needing my help," she said.

"Why don't you let me deal with it when the time comes?" Gina responded stubbornly, her jaws set in a firm line of determination.

"That is the trouble with you Gina Udensi, you never give in," Monica said in a voice bristling with irritation.

"What about you? You are just as stubborn Monica Udeh," Gina said hotly.

Adora stared at them in wonder. "Ladies, that's enough! Dinner is served," she said, planting her body firmly between the squabbling cousins. "Never mind us, we always argue like this, but we love each other anyway," Gina said with a smile.

"Yep! You can call us the cuddle some quarrelsome twosome," Monica quipped as she set the silverware on the kitchen table for two and then set the dining room table for Gina and her husband.

The food was savory and appetizing, and Adora found herself tucking in

eagerly, despite the fact that she had just eaten brunch a few hours ago. "Mm, scrumptious," she exclaimed, as she loosened the button on her jeans and bit into a succulent braised carrot. She resisted the urge to smack her lips and reached instead for a third piece of jumbo mushroom stuffed with peppers and onions. Monica nodded and continued to pick at her food.

"Mm, your cousin sure knows how to cook," she said again, rolling her eyes skyward. "You really need to try this," she added, pushing a platter of broiled fish at Monica. To her surprise, Monica agreed, and succumbed to the allure of the mouth-watering array of culinary delights on the table.

"Now you're talking," Adora said, watching with amusement as Monica put away the fish with wild abandon.

"Mm m," she said. "I'm afraid that I'll end up like Charles if I continue to stay here," she remarked.

"Shhh,," Adora cautioned. "Please don't say that about your in-law. He'll hear you."

"Then, let him lose   the weigh," Monica whispered, and giggled.

"Can you blame him? Your cousin can cook," Adora responded.

"Really, it's no wonder Charles put on so much weight. My cousin is eating for two but what's his excuse?" Monica retorted in a voice dripping with sarcasm.

Adora made a face and continued to concentrate on her food.

"You know," Monica began. "Charles wasn't always this heavy, but Gina told me that he started to gain a lot of weight right after she got pregnant, sort of keeping up with her own weight gain I suppose, but I dare say that I can't blame him because you are right. Gina sure can cook. So now you see why I try to be so careful. I have my work cut out and I have to constantly watch it" she said this with a horrified expression on her face.

"Charles promised her that he would lose the weight right along with her after the baby arrives," she continued.

Adora listened with interest. She did not necessarily agree with Charlie's method because he might have difficulty losing the weight afterward and she conveyed this to Monica, who speared at a piece of carrot from the vegetable mélange on her plate with her fork and popped it into her mouth. She munched thoughtfully.

"Mmmm," she said, closing her eyes with a bliss expression on her face. She took another bite and ate it with relish, then turned her attention on Adora. "Personally, I don't understand how my cousin can stand all that bulk. As for me, I prefer the tall athletic types, like you know who."

"Who?" Adora asked innocently, although she knew exactly where Monica was going.

Monica gave her an incredulous look and laughed uproariously.

"Oh, come off it now Adora, you know exactly whom I am referring to," she finally said with a sigh.

Adora fixed Monica with an innocent little stare. "Not really, who?" she said, trying not to laugh. Monica looked exasperated and rolled her eyes at Adora.

"Right!" she said sharply and stuck her tongue out at Adora like a schoolgirl. "Okay, okay, I concede," Adora said finally, giggling at the silly expression on Monica's face. Monica dropped her fork and joined in her laughter.

Monica closed her eyes and sighed audibly. When she opened her eyes, she had a dreamy, faraway look in her eyes.

"Oh Adora," she said softly, in a voice that was barely a whisper. "I just love a man who knows how to treat a lady. Nothing like the way Charles treats my cousin. Just look at the way that he took out his time to help us yesterday."

Adora gave Monica a sharp look. "How do you know that he always treats women like that? Don't you think that he was only trying to impress us? You forgot what Gina said about Charles' behavior before they were married?"

Monica dismissed Adora's words with a wave of her hands.

"Don't be such a wet blanket," she said petulantly. "Somehow, I just know that Randy will be different. Oh, I simply can't wait until Saturday. I am sure that he'll still remember us. Do you think that he will remember us?"

"Us?" Adora asked incredulously. "I don't recall mentioning that I had any intention of going to the party Saturday."

Tossing her hair impetuously, Monica stood up from the table and gathered up her empty plates and took them to the sink. She dropped them on the porcelain surface with a loud clatter and ran water noisily over them. "Suit yourself," she said. "But I am definitely going. You should see the outfit that I plan to wear."

Adora stared incredulously at Monica, who seemed hell bent on a self- destructive leap before you look mission. She was definitely getting irritated with her girlish impulsiveness.

"You're getting too carried away. We just met Randy------when? Only yesterday afternoon remember?"

"So what's the big deal?" Monica asked with a shrug. "How much do you know about this guy anyway?"

"I know that he is good looking and charming – a sharp dresser, and don't forget gallant---need I go on?"

"All superficial things. You haven't scratched the surface." "But Gina said-----------."

"Gina doesn't live with him. Besides, didn't I hear you mention what she said about his reputation with the ladies?"

"All rumors I'm sure," Monica said derisively. "How do you know that?"

Monica glared at Adora and placed her hands on her hips.

"I don't really care," she said heatedly. "I am sure that is just a bunch of talk about him. I do know that I like his style, and I wouldn't mind meeting him again."

Adora shrugged and said nothing further about the matter. Monica was an adult, accountable to only herself. Silently, she gathered the remnants of her meal and dumped them in the dustbin.

Chapter 14

"Wait till you see this," Monica declared as soon as the girls stepped into her room. It was a simple room, much smaller and plainer than Adora's room with white walls, a louvered window covered with blue patterned drapery and a full-size bed pushed against the wall. White sheets had been thrown over it in a hurry, and a brown suitcase sat in the middle of it, next to a smaller, matching valise.

"Wait till you see this," Monica repeated as soon as she dragged the brown suitcase off the bed and leaned it against the closet wall.

"Sit down," she told Adora, patting the bed.

Adora sat on the bed and moved the other valise closer to the wall. Monica rushed off to the small wall closet and rummaged around. She returned shortly with a sparkly red material in her hand, which threw off red sparks in the fading light that filtered through the blue window blind. It was a sequined red dress that looked about two sizes too small for Monica. She held the material against her body and did a flirty cat walk in front of the floor to ceiling mirror on her closet door. Upon closer inspection, Adora could see the dress had a plunging neckline, and an even lower cut back. Adora's eyes almost popped out of their sockets.

"Is that legal? Where's the rest of it? " She exclaimed incredulously, her eyes as wide as the plates that she just ate out of.

"Listen girrl, when you've got it, you flaunt it," Monica responded insouciantly.

"Flaunt it but just be careful, okay Monica," Adora cautioned.

Monica dismissed Adora's statement with a wave of the hand. "Enough of the lectures, school ma-am. I swear you sound exactly like my grandma. Keep this up and I promise you one day you'll wake up as old as gramma, still lecturing and still single. Who will want you then?" she retorted.

Adora ignored the barb.

"Monica, you're missing the point." she said slowly.

"You should live a little more my friend," Monica retorted saucily as she sauntered to the window, and drew the cream and blue flowered drapes, letting in a draft of air, which circulated sluggishly around the stuffy room. "Gosh, it's hot in here, she said, as she fanned herself with her hands, and walked towards the bed.

"Yep, a bit," Adora said.

"I'm going to need a fan. So, what do you intend to wear?" Monica placed the red dress on the bed, right next to Adora.

Adora sighed wearily. She was getting tired of Monica's stubborn refusal to accept the fact that she simply wanted to face her studies. Maybe Monica didn't have a father like hers, so she wouldn't understand. ""Monica, I thought I already told you. It depends upon how my schedule turns out. I really need to place priorities with my time.

"Aw, C'mon now-------," Monica began.

A light tap on the door interrupted her. She tossed the dress on the bed and ran to the door. Regina was standing behind it with a cordless phone in her hand.

"There's a call for you," she said handing the phone to Adora, who took the phone from her hands and mouthed "thank you" to her.

"Time to go," Adora announced after she hung up the phone. "Aww already? But you just got here," Monica complained.

"My family called from Enugu--my aunt says they'll call back in two hours so I have to go."

"Why don't you use this phone and call them back?" Monica suggested. "I'm sure Gina won't mind."

"But I will," Adora said, "But we will see each other again soon," she added as she descended the wide staircase with Monica in tow.

Gina was sitting in front of the television in the living room, knitting blue a baby bootie, and Charles was nowhere in sight. Adora sat next to her and hugged her fondly.

"Gina, it was such a pleasure. Thank you so much for your hospitality. I really had a good time." Gina dropped the needle and yarn on her lap and looked at Adora in dismay.

"You're leaving already?"

"My dad is going to call me back soon and I have to be there."

"Just let me get my keys. I'll drop you," Gina offered, but Adora shook her head firmly.

"Oh no Gina thanks. I will walk. I need that after the scrumptious supper you

made me eat. Besides, you need your rest. Don't forget everything I told you. Some things you just have to let go of. At least for the wellbeing of the baby. There will be time to push your point, but this is not the right time."

"Thanks Dr. Adora," Gina joked as she hugged Adora again.

"Then let me walk you half-way," Monica offered, pulling on her flats.

They parted company at the intersection of Toyin street, and Adora set off down the street at a jaunty pace. The sun was just beginning to descend on a bed of clouds for its nightly nap and the air was filled with the pungent scent of tropical flowers which were growing in abundance around the estates that she passed. She quickened her pace, ignoring the hoots, whistles, and catcalls that came from the direction of the estates, from the men sitting on benches, and some on the street. Cars horns honked in an attempt to catch her attention and Adora ignored them, keeping up a brisk pace.

At the intersection of Obafemi Way, a sleek white Jaguar purred to a smooth stop besides her. Adora kept walking, but the car crawled apace with her, and the tinted glass of the passenger side slid down smoothly. A cool blast of air-conditioned air escaped the white leather clad interior of the car, and hit the bare skin of her arms, sending a chill traveling up and down her spine.

'Would you like a lift to your destination?" the man in the car said in a voice that

sounded like gravel. He was dressed from head to toe in black, and his eyes were covered by dark aviator glasses. Adora shivered again. She wasn't sure if it was the cold blast of air that continued to assault her bare arms from his car or the sinister tone of his voice.

"No thanks," she said decisively, and crossed the street to the other side. The jaguar looked like it would make a U turn to her side. Not again, she thought uneasily to herself. She increased her pace to a near sprint, then noticed out of the corner of her eyes, that the man motioned to his driver, who straightened up the car, and sped off, amid screeching tires that raised blinding dust, swirling around for a while and making her cough before settling down on the pock marked, eroding asphalt road.

Slightly unnerved, Adora shivered involuntarily, and rubbed her arms briskly as she continued down the road at a brisk pace. The street was still bustling with activities. A woman, pushing a pram as her gurgling baby shook his toy rattle vigorously. A couple strolling arm in arm, stopping to nuzzle and kiss, cars breezing past her, some of the drivers waving at her.

At the gatehouse of a grand Mediterranean style house, a group of houseboys had gathered to chat and while away the afternoon. When they spotted Adora, they began to call at her in Pidgin English, each trying to outdo the other.

"Hey Yusuf! Look at that fine fine lady-o," said one, rushing towards the gate. The others followed him.

"*Ikenna, she fine well well. Eh, na me go marry this one-o*."

"*Fine lady, wetin be your name?*" said Yusuf.

"*Fine girl, na me go marry you-o*," said another one.

"*Abdul, na lie you de lie. Na my wife she be*," the one they called Ikenna said, making to open the gate.

"*Make you lef am Ikenna*," said Abdul said, snatching Ikenna's hands from the gate clasp.

"*Hey, I wish I fit friend this kine woman, pretty lady, you think say I fit friend you?*" another one said.

"*Mamoud, you dey craze. You think say you fit maintain am as she fine so? You know that Lagos girls*

need money." They trailed her to the other side of the fence, laughing and jabbering in Pidgin English.

"***Me I wan takam to my house oo. Hey fine lady, you go 'gree say make I take you out?***" Mamoud said, laughing boisterously.

Adora bristled with extreme annoyance as she increased her speed to a near sprint. What a crude bunch of foolish oafs, she thought angrily, as she waited for traffic to thin, and crossed to the other side of the street, quickening her pace even more. The boisterous laughter of the idiots followed her, carried by the wind. She kept up a brisk pace till their voices faded away.

A brisk evening breeze was fanning through the trees, ruffling her hair, and caressing her skin, which was burning from a combination of the warm rays of the waning, sun, the anger that had caused the hot blood to course through her veins, and the exertion of trying to get away from those bumbling fools.

She slowed her pace and took slow, deep breaths, trying to enjoy the stroll. Everything was so serene and peaceful. The sun was setting lower on the horizon, peeking through the fluffy bed of clouds, which were fiery shades of orange and sienna, reminding her of the fluffy balls of colored cotton balls in a crystal jar that still stood on her mother's dressing table. The clouds were playing hide and seek with the setting sun, which warmed her face and neck. She slowed her pace to a more leisurely gait, taking her time to enjoy the splendid setting.

At the intersection of Victoria Lake Drive, Adora glanced at the direction that her friend Gina had drawn up for her. Soon she would reach the front gate of her aunt's house.

It was then that she heard the muffled sound of footsteps behind her, and she increased her pace to a sprint, fighting the panic that began to engulf her, not daring to look back. By now, the sun had completed her descent into the west, and dusk was beginning to blanket the city, making eerie, elongated shadows from the trees across her path.

The only lights were coming from distant streetlights and the headlamps of the cars that zipped through the streets. The shadows lengthened on her path, turning the trees into silent sentinels. Adora's mind began to play tricks on her as her imagined stalker gained on her.

In panic, she began to sprint towards the familiar gate, but a familiar voice stopped her in her tracks. The very sound of that cultured voice sent shivers coursing up and down her spine.

"It couldn't possibly be," she though as she felt the familiar quickening of her pulse.

"Hey, if it isn't Adora Amadi, from yesterday," Randy said in his incredibly smooth voice. Adora's breath caught in her throat and she stopped dead in her tracks.

"Wha, what---a--- surprise!" she blustered, whirling around to face him.

"Sorry gorgeous, I did not mean to frighten you," he said in his smooth, cultured voice as he took in the panic, now ebbing from Adora's beautiful face.

"What, what are you doing here?' she began, then regained her composure in record time, and tossed her hair haughtily.

"Who said I was frightened?" she said with an impatient little toss of her head. Her eyes flicked over him, and she took in his tall, athletic form at one glance. He was dressed casually in baggy blue jeans, a jade green short sleeved polo shirt, and white running shoes. His shirt was unbuttoned one notch from the chest, revealing a hint of his chiseled chest underneath the pique material. Randy's curly hair was trimmed even shorter than she remembered it, and he had a cheeky grin on his face.

He looked devastatingly handsome and Adora's breath caught in her throat and she felt her heart skip a beat as she felt compelled to look into the velvet depths of his golden-brown eyes, which locked onto hers, and held an expression that she could not decipher. She felt the blood rushing to her face, and she averted her gaze from his eyes, afraid of what he may read in her eyes. Tenderly, he stroked an errant lock of hair from her face.

"I always knew that one day, my nightly stroll would yield a healthy surprise," he

quipped. "Honestly, didn't expect it to be so amazing," he added earnestly, his pleasure written all over his face.

Adora's heart fluttered nervously in her chest, and she felt tongue tied under the scrutiny of his steady gaze.

She shifted awkwardly from foot to foot and made a desperate attempt to find her tongue. She felt unreasonably awkward, like a gawky schoolgirl, and cleared her throat nervously.

"I didn't expect to see you here--- of all places----," she faltered, finding herself strangely under the spell of this handsome stranger.

"They say nice surprises come from the strangest places," he said, taking her hand. Her heart raced and she shivered involuntarily. Girl, pull yourself together, she chided herself.

Taking a deep breath, she gathered the remnants of her rapidly unraveling dignity and straightened herself to her fullest height.

"I have to run now," she said too quickly. She flashed a contrived smile at him, and pulled her hand away from his. Without waiting for his response, she turned on her heels and started walking briskly towards the imposing gate that fronted her aunt's estate.

"Hey, did I forget to thank you for your help yesterday? Well thanks again for your help," she threw impudently over her shoulders, not daring to look back, and not slowing her pace. Secretly, she was hoping that he would not walk away from her. He didn't.

He fell into step besides her, and touched her shoulder lightly, an action that sent little shivers of excitement running through her body.

"Hey Adora, why don't you let me walk you home?' he asked, keeping in easy stride with her own erratic ones.

"N,no thanks, I am almost there anyway," she responded glibly, wondering if he could see through her little act.

"Adora," he said out of the blues. "I'd like to see you again. Is that a possibility?" He locked his compelling brown eyes with hers again.

"Definitely not!" she snapped, annoyed that she was allowing this handsome stranger to get under her skin. "Listen, I can't dawdle any longer, I am expecting an important call and I have to go," she said with more vehemence than she meant to portray.

Randy's eyebrows shot up in surprise. He stared at her for a moment, then he shrugged.

"Have a nice evening then," he said with a mock bow, and within moments, he dissolved into the settling dusk.

Adora watched his retreating figure in dismay, feeling strangely bereft, abandoned, and angry that he did not insist on walking with her and piqued that he did nothing further to explore the idea of seeing her again.

Such colossal nerves. Who does he think he is anyway! She fumed silently and stalked towards the entrance to her aunt's gate, then she caught herself. Why did she have to care whether he insisted or not. The guy meant absolutely nothing to her and in all probabilities, she would never see him again in her life.

"Oh, how silly of me," she reprimanded herself as she thrust her finger into the round buzzer button. Her nail snagged on the button, and she winced in pain.

"Ouch!" she yelled crossly, blowing cool air at the tip of her finger. It smarted from the jagged red gash that tore a path into her skin.

The gatekeeper appeared behind the scrolled grill of the gate and gave her a funny look. She forced a bright smile on her face and greeted him with a cheer that she did not feel.

"You okay," he asked her.

"Fine, I'm fine Suleman," she replied.

When she reached the house, it was strangely quiet.

"I wonder where everybody is," she thought, walking towards the south windows. The high-pitched sound of Melissa's giggling accompanied by the sound of splashing water reached her ears faintly. She peered through the window in the direction of the pool, which was out of view, around the corner, but the light from the pool was on, and she opened the back door and followed the sound to the back of the house. The pool was brightly illuminated by a floodlight, which was attracting a lot of tropical fauna. They whizzed towards the bulb where they perched and sizzled instantly before falling into the collecting plate directly under the light.

Aunt Agatha was lying in a lounge chair by the pool wearing a white halter neck bathing suit, sipping lemonade from a tall ice-filled, frosted glass. A glossy high fashion magazine lay in a basket at her feet. Melissa was frolicking at the shallow end of the pool wearing a neon-pink bathing suite embellished with bits of frills at the hips. Her mother lay on the chaise, but she kept a sharp, eagle eye on her while she splashed.

Adora pulled up a chair next to Aunt Agatha.

"Is she okay in there by herself?" she asked as she watched goggle eyed, as Melissa dived under the water, and shot underwater like a fish, then she resurfaced near the edge of the pool, giggling and wiping the water dripping down her face. She dived into the water again, using perfect strokes, and threaded water, then she dived underwater again.

"Melissa has had swimming lessons since she was two. She is like a fish in the water," Aunt Agatha said, although she kept glancing anxiously in Melissa's direction.

She lay there, cool and beautiful, but her body language indicated that she was ready to pounce in case---.

"Oh, I can definitely see that," Adora mumbled in wonder, marveling at the incredible things that Melissa was doing in the water. Adora, who prided herself on her own swimming techniques had to agree that Melissa was a natural.

As if aware of the scrutiny, Melissa suddenly shot up from below the surface, saw Adora, and waved gaily. She clambered out of the pool and padded over to them, shivering, and dripping water all over the aqua colored floor tile. Her mother sat up and handed her a folded towel from the basket that held the magazine. Adora draped the towel around the little girl's tiny body and briskly rubbed her dry.

"Hi Adora," Melissa greeted, grinning happily.

"Melissa!" her mother reprimanded her in a sharp voice.

"What is it mommy?" the little girl queried, taking a sip of her mother's lemonade, and making a wry little face.

"Aw, mommy, I think it needs a little more sugar," she complained.

"It's sweet enough Melissa. You don't want cavities. Besides you're changing the topic. You address Adora as auntie Adora."

The little girl returned the lemonade glass to the floor and regarded her mother with genuine puzzlement.

"How come mommy?" she queried again. "Yestoday, em yesterday you told me that she is my cousin, and if she is my cousin, then how come she is also my auntie?" the little girl asked, genuinely puzzled at the conflicting rules that grow-ups imposed upon kids.

Adora smiled at her little cousin's questions. Aunt Agatha smiled too, but she sat up on her lounge chair and reached towards Melissa. Watching Aunt Agatha, Adora marveled at her aunt's washboard flat stomach, which seemed to belie the fact that she had given birth to two children. The only telltale signs were the faint networks of stretch marks that crisscrossed a tiny portion of her trim hips.

Aunt Agatha hoisted Melissa onto her laps and dried off her dripping hair. "Melissa, Adora is your cousin, but you have to address her as auntie as a sign of respect because she is a lot older than you."

The little girl's face was a study of puzzlement.

"Auntie Lola called her auntie, but Auntie Lola is older than her. I heard you say so yesterday," Melissa said triumphantly, jubilant that she had scored a point in this pointless protocol.

Aunt Agatha let out a soft sigh, and Adora thumbed through the fashion magazine, although she was curious about where this conversation would lead.

"Melissa, that is a cultural thing. Lola calls her that because Adora has a lot more education. It is her own way of showing respect."

"Oho," said Melissa, her eyes glittering with a look of determination. It was obvious that she was preparing for the offensive.

"But mommy, how come we don't call our teacher auntie? She is a lot older than us, and she also has more education."

"Your teacher already has a title of respect," said Aunt Agatha, gathering her cover-up around her body. You already call her Miss Dupe. If you call her auntie teacher, don't you think that will sound absurd?"

"Auntie teacher? Ha ha. That sounds really funny," said Melissa, doubling over with laughter.

Adora and Aunt Agatha joined in the laughter and Melissa turned to Adora, her eyes shining from excitement.

"Auntie, you wanna swim with me?"

"No slangs young lady. The proper thing to say is do you want to swim?" her mother corrected.

"Okay, do you want to swim with me?" Melissa said with a sigh.

"No thanks young lady, I would rather watch," Adora said, returning the fashion glossy to the basket.

Melissa screwed up her face in disappointment, and Adora smiled at her. "You're such a good swimmer," she complimented Melissa, whose face brightened up, and she smiled at Adora.

"Thank you Adora, oh, I mean auntie Adora," she said with a giggle, as she took off the huge beach towel that encircled her body and threw it on the floor. Her mother looked hard at her, and she giggled and picked up the towel and folded it neatly, then returned it to the basket.

She walked carefully to the edge of the pool and executed a graceful dive, slicing cleanly into the water with hardly a ripple, and resurfacing moments later at the other end of the pool. Adora stood up and applauded as she clambered up again and walked towards them. "See, I can dive," she said triumphantly.

"Very good Melissa," Adora said, clapping her hands.

"Thank you," Melissa shouted, as she took off towards the pool again.

With a loud whoop, she splashed into the shallow end of the pool, creating a huge wave, which deposited chlorinated water on her mother. The water swirled and eddied around Adora's feet, and she shrieked, jumping into the air to avoid getting soaked. When she landed on her feet again, she screamed in dismay as her sandal clad feet slid on the wet tiled floor and she fell on the wet floor in an undignified heap. Her aunt shrieked and rushed to her side as Melissa also scrambled out the water and ran to her.

"Are you okay? Aunt Agatha asked as she helped her to her feet and onto a lounge chair.

"Thanks auntie, I am going to be okay," Adora said, thoroughly shaken and embarrassed.

"Young lady, you see why you have to be more careful," Aunt Agatha remonstrated her daughter.

"I'm sorry Adora, um Auntie Adora," Melissa said, hanging her head.

"Don't worry Melissa, I will be fine," Adora said shakily, rubbing at her right ankle, which was throbbing with pain.

"Let me take you to the hospital," Aunt Agatha suggested.

"I think I am fine. I could place my weight on my ankle, so I don't think I broke or fractured anything," she responded. "I sometimes watch dad attend to his patients, so I know what to do.

The water swished around her feet, splashing the edge of her long denim skirt.

"Aw, Melissa," Adora shrieked, bending down to wring the spot on her skirt where it was dripping. Melissa giggled and dashed to the other end of the pool to execute her fancy strokes.

Aunt Agatha reached towards the basket and grabbed a towel. It was partly soaked, dripping water from one end. She wrung out the water from the towel and dabbed at her wet body, making a face. Adora stood up and reached for a towel, which was hanging on a rail that ran across the other end of the pool. She handed it to her aunt. "Here auntie, this one is dry," she offered.

"Thank you my dear," Aunt Agatha said with a grateful smile and started to dab at her perfectly curled hair, which was slightly damp from the melee. "That child, she can get a bit too boisterous," she complained, although her eyes sparkled with pride.

"Wow! Auntie, all I can say is that she has opened up quite nicely." Adora slipped off her wet sandals, dabbing at the wet spot on her skirt, and then concentrated on drying off her legs and feet with a towel.

"It was just a matter of a little time," Aunt Agatha responded, reaching around to dab at a wet spot behind her shoulder.

"Just wait till she gets even more accustomed to you," she continued with a grin. "You may have to pry her off you with a crowbar."

"I'll say," Adora said with a giggle.

Aunt Agatha gave Adora a long penetrating look.

"You know, Adora, I could have imagined it, but I could have sworn that you looked really flustered when you just came in. Anything wrong?"

"Oh no auntie, n, nothing at all," Adora responded too quickly, prompting her aunt to examine her face even more closely.

"It was probably the brisk walk," she added quickly. "You walked home?" her aunt quizzed.

"Monica's cousin Gina offered me a ride, but it was such a beautiful day outside," Adora responded.

"I know the neighborhood is very safe my dear, but it is late and you should have called me to send the driver for you," Aunt Agatha stated.

"I guess you are fight auntie," Adora

She moved her chair closer to the pool, watching Melissa shoot through the water like a mermaid.

Sitting by the edge of the pool, grateful to escape the scrutiny of her aunt's eagle eyes, Adora dipped a cautious toe into the cool azure water. Melissa swam underwater and grabbed her foot underneath the water. Adora let out a loud cry of surprise as she kicked her foot in the air, splashing more water on her skirt.

"Oh, that tickles," she whooped, kicking up her feet again, and wetting her skirt further.

Melissa was gone in a flash, but a moment later, she emerged on the other side of the pool, floating in the water, and giggling gleefully.

"Ha ha ha, auntie Adora, I got you bad," she laughed. The water streamed down her hair and onto her face and she flicked the water off her face, and continued in a sing song voice.

"I got you-u, I've got you-u."

Adora frowned at her in mock anger, then burst into laughter herself. "Oh, you naughty, naughty girl," she admonished Melissa playfully.

Aunt Agatha was not the least bit amused.

"Melissa, behave yourself or you will have to go upstairs to your room. Do you understand?" she admonished sternly.

"But mommy, I was only having fun," she said in a whining voice, then she began to cry.

"I don't want to go to my room," she said. She clambered out of the pool and ran to her mother, dripping water and pouting.

"But I don't want to go to my room mommy, please don't make me."

"You need to apologize right away to Adora," her mother admonished her sternly. "I'm really, really sorry Ado---um, Auntie Adora." She turned to her mother. "Please don't make me go to my room mommy please, I promise to be good."

"Very well then," said Aunt Agatha, patting a more contrite Melissa on the head.

"Yes mommy," Melissa responded happily, lowering her body slowly into the pool.

Chapter 15

She was wearing a full-length empire waist gown of a whisper soft gossamer fabric that shimmered in the moon light with every move that she made. Embellished with sprinklings of rhinestone and pearls at the bodice, the gown had a scattering of multi-colored stones that threw off psychedelic colored lights as she moved. It had a long train, like a wedding gown that floated behind her, shimmering in the hazy light of the moon like a mirage, and lending her an ethereal quality. The faint scent of freshly cut roses clung to her, lingering softly in the air.

She had a long, elegant neck and a regal carriage, and seemed to glide. When she moved there was the faint melody of chimes that tinkled softly, as though she was wearing tiny clusters of bells on her feet. She was going much too fast and Adora had to run, to keep up with her pace, which seemed effortless for her; she hardly seemed to be moving at all, yet Adora was panting, trying to keep up with her.

They were in an unfamiliar wooded area, with tree branches that hung so low that

the leaves brushed against Adora's cheeks, tickling her nose. The thorns from the bushes reached out and tore at her dress, scratching her skin. Adora pressed on stoically ahead, oblivious to her disconcerting surroundings, intent upon her goal, which was to catch up with the hazy, elusive figure that seemed intent on evanescing into the mist that hung heavily in the air.

"Stop," she implored softly, struggling to get the words out. Her jaws felt wired shut by invisible forces and she fought to open her mouth.

The figure in front of her did not seem to hear, or if she did, she did not react to her pleas. Her steps did not falter, and the bothersome thorns that tormented Adora seemed to part in her path and reach towards Adora as she approached.

"Pleaaase wait," Adora pleaded in a hoarse, disembodied voice that seemed to be coming from a distance. She tripped on a root and stumbled, falling slowly, endlessly, in slow motion. She landed on the soft, mossy earth, and clawed way up. Undeterred, she picked up herself, fighting the unseen forces that held her down, and scrambled after the rapidly vanishing figure.

Soon, they reached a clearing in the woods and suddenly, the woman whirled sharply around to face her.

The face that turned in her direction was incredibly beautiful, so indescribably that Adora could not bear to look upon such ethereal loveliness. She kept her eyes downcast, and reached out, trying to grab the nebulous figure.

"Oh mother, please wait," she implored earnestly with tears streaming down her face. With a heavy heart she cried out, "Take me with you mom and don't ever leave me."

The woman in front of her came to a standstill.

"No!" she commanded sharply in dulcet tones, clear as a bell with a musical lilt. It was the tinkling of many tiny chimes, the melody of cathedral organs. It was almost like part of the wind rustling through the tree branches. "Stop!" she repeated. She turned fiery eyes, blazing like fiery embers on a smithy's furnace towards Adora. If Adora had listened carefully enough, she could have detected a hint of steel in the bell-toned voice. Her voice turned soft again.

"You cannot come any further than this," she said.

But Adora was beyond caring now. She had finally found her beloved mother, and nothing was going to make her let go again.

"Mother," she cried in a voice choked with tears, rushing towards her. "I don't care

where you're going. You have to take me with you." She was so close now, within a hair's breadth reach, and she was not going to let her leave again. Never again!

Gleefully she took another leaping step, and her heart swelled with joy because her beloved mother was almost within her grasp. Another happy step and she gathered her beloved mother in her arms.

Immediately, her joy turned to bitter, earth shattering disappointment because her mother had dissolved into ether, vanished before her eyes and she was only hugging herself. Bereaved, confused and terrified beyond description, Adora threw herself on the ground and wept bitterly.

"Oh-- please-- come, come back mooom," she cried, beating the soft, mossy ground with her hands. Her hand came in contact with something hard, and a loud crash sounded very close to her.

She woke up with a startled gasp and discovered that her palm had hit the hard

surface of the night table, and she had knocked the phone off the table. Her heart was pounding, her body was covered with cold sweat, and she was still shaking with the intensity of the emotion that the sudden dream encounter invoked within her. Every detail of that dream was still vividly etched in her brain, and it seemed so real that she could still smell the scent of roses that clung around her mother's apparition.

Something wet trickled down her face onto her pillow, and her hand groped at the pillow like a blind person, making contact with the soft pillow, soaked with a combination of her sweat and tears. Only then did she realize that the tears were flowing down her cheeks directly from her dream state.

She heard a loud beeping sound, and her eyes followed the sound to the phone, still lying on the carpet, emitting a loud beeping signal. She picked up the handset, replaced it on the cradle, and returned the phone to the night table.

Her mind continued to reel from the experience, and she did the logical thing that she could think of. She knelt by her bed and prayed for God's supreme guidance. She prayed for her mother's soul, for God to keep it safe. She also prayed for God to ease the heavy sorrow of her desperately floundering father who was even more devastated by the loss than he was willing to divulge, and she prayed for her brothers who were suffering just as much as she was.

When she ended her prayers, she felt lighter, like an enormous load had been lifted off her shoulders. The anguish and bewilderment remained, but she felt that she could handle anything because of God's loving presence.

God had never left her side and she knew that he would never leave her as long as she continued to embrace him.

She glanced at the face of the digital clock by her bedside. It was already 6:30 in the morning and the lovely room was suffused with the soft twilight hues of early morning. Adora switched on her bedside lamp and read a passage from the King James Version Bible that she always kept by her bedside. It was about hope and faith and walking by faith and not by what we see. The passage gave her a measure of hope and comfort, and she rose from the bed.

By this time, it was already 6:45 am, and she pulled on her robe, and hurried to the bathroom for her morning shower. The warm water felt good, and as she lathered her skin with the fragrant white bar soap, she felt her troubles slipping away with the white foamy lather that drifted down the drain. When she emerged from the bathroom, the gloom that had settled upon her was easing somewhat, and she said a silent prayer of thanks to God for uplifting her.

The brick red shantung silk suit, which she had selected the night before was hanging neatly on her dresser door. The maid Chinasa had ironed it the night before, like Adora had requested. She donned the long sleeveless red jacket over the short skirt that ended just above her knees. The tailored jacket was slightly longer than the skirt and grazed her knees. Adora felt glad that she had selected that particular outfit. The bright color was a perfect foil to the dolorous mood that she carried with her this morning. She completed the look with a pair of suede high-heeled sandals in a matching shade of red, and applied just a touch of red lipstick to accentuate the look.

A glance in the mirror revealed a poised and polished woman with a cosmopolitan flair. She hoped that she felt as poised as she looked. The suit molded to her lithe figure, and the color did wonders for her complexion. She picked up her brown leather attaché, and hurried downstairs for breakfast.

Her aunt was already in the dining room, eating a bowl of warm cereal. Aunt

Agatha's husband Paul was sitting across from her, perusing the Daily Punch over a steaming mug of coffee. The table had been set for four with scrambled eggs, thick slices of buttered toast and stewed sardines. Chinasa stood over them, pouring steaming tea into their teacups from a silver teapot.

Paul glanced at her and cleared his voice. "Good morning my dear, do sit down, join us for breakfast." he said cordially. Nodding numbly, Adora sat on the empty chair next to her aunt, leaning her tan leather briefcase against her chair. In response to their greetings, she murmured a hoarse "good morning," followed by a muttered "how are you this morning and picked up a piece of toast, nibbling absently at it.

"Everything okay?" her aunt whispered, looking earnestly at her, with concern etched all over her face.

"Oh yes auntie," she lied, trying to infuse enthusiasm that she did not feel into her hoarse voice and forcing a bright smile upon her face.

Paul peered at her from above his tortoise shell framed glasses and asked. "You sure?"

"Of course," she replied, training her eyes on the glass of juice in her hand. Aunt Agatha's gaze was more penetrating, and Adora forced a bright smile that she didn't feel upon her face.

You look like you just saw a ghost," she informed her. "What is the matter?"

"I'm fine, just a bit nervous about my first day I guess."

"Relax, you have nothing to worry about," her aunt reassured her, turning her attention to her husband, who was flipping through the pages of his paper.

Paul flung down the paper on the marble floor and his wife glanced at him in alarm.

"They jailed that freedom fighter," he said, his voice pregnant with disgust and despair.

"They jailed him?" aunt Agatha responded with equal despair. "How cruel and barbaric."

"When will they realize that the people are ripe for true democracy in this crazy government system?" Paul lamented, scratching his head.

"Maybe not in this generation," Adora inserted, her voice filled with sadness. "Want some tea?" Aunt Agatha asked, and she nodded mutely. Her aunt

poured tea from a silver-plated teapot into her cup, while Adora patted creamy butter on another slice of bread.

"Is Melissa still in bed?" she asked her aunt, as she piled a significant amount of

scrambled eggs upon her plate. She had to maintain as much normalcy as possible to throw her aunt off her scent. She was also determined not to start off her first day at the University of Lagos with a deflated mood.

"She is upstairs with Lola, getting ready for school."

As if on cue, Melissa burst into the dining room, wearing a navy-blue pinafore dress of cotton twill, which contrasted sharply with the crisp white blouse that peeked out underneath the jumper. The breast pocket of the pinafore was emblazoned with her school crest in gold and red embroidery, which offset the gold ribbons that decorated the two long plaits on her hair. She skipped excitedly to the table, threw her book satchel across the table, and flung her arms around her father's neck, giving him a wet, noisy kiss on the tip of his nose. His eyes lit up immediately, and he returned the kiss noisily, giving her a tight hug.

"Ohhh daddy, I can't breathe," she squealed melodramatically, pushing him away. He tickled her tummy, and the room was filled with her excited giggle, which gave way to a shrill squeal of delight. Her face shone like the moon, and she gazed adoringly at her father.

"Oh daddy, you are so funny," she said.

Then as though noticing the others for the first time, she extricated herself from her father, and went first to her mother, and then to Adora.

"Good morning mommy," she greeted her mother, who gave her another tight hug. She made a face and giggled. Her mother fussed around with her dress, patting it here and there, and straightening the bow on her hair.

"Ow mommy, that hurts!" Melissa complained, squeezing up her face into a tight knot. "Okay, then let's make that feel better," her mother said, and with a few deft movements of her fingers, she loosened the tight base of the braids. Melissa's face relaxed into a smile, and she turned her attention to Adora. "Good morning auntie Adora," she greeted, taking a seat right next to her. "Morning Melissa," she responded, smiling cheerfully at the little girl. "Auntie Adora, I like your outfit, you look so pretty," Melissa announced, touching the silky hem of the fabric gingerly.

"Thank you, Melissa, and you do look smashing in your school uniform," she responded, tweaking Melissa's ribbon.

Melissa made a wry little face and commented between mouthfuls of scrambled

eggs. "I don't like to wear it because I don't like school much because I don't like to leave my dad and there's this boy named Stephen in my class, and I don't like to go to school because he sits behind me, and teases me, and pulls my hair, and makes faces at me when Ms. Dupe is not looking and he makes me cry and he always lies to Ms. Dupe that he did not pull my hair, but he did, because I don't like him!"

Melissa hardly came up for air, causing her mother to look up in alarm from a quite conversation with her husband.

"Melissa!" she said sternly. "Yes mommy."

"You know better than to talk with food in your mouth."

"Yes mother, I should not talk with food in my mouth." she said contritely, hanging her head.

Adora handed her a glass of water, and she shook her head vehemently, and reached for the pitcher of fresh orange juice with both hands. Adora poured it for her, and she took a small sip, then pursed her tiny lips into a pout. She waited till her mother's attention was reverted from her, then she whispered fiercely to Adora.

"Really I don't like Stephen."

"Maybe Stephen teases you because he likes you, and wants to be your friend," Adora offered helpfully.

"I don't like him," she repeated then turned to her mother. "Mommy, I don't have food in my mouth," she informed her mother, then returned her attention to Adora without missing a beat. "I don't like him at all, I told him so," she said fiercely, screwing up her face into an expression of disdain. "But Melissa, maybe if you were a little nicer to him, he probably won't tease you so much. I think that you should say hello to him. That would probably encourage him to stop teasing you. What do you think?"

Melissa mulled over this last piece of information for a while, her face a study of concentration. She nibbled thoughtfully on a piece of buttered toast, washed it down with some more orange juice, and nodded her head.

"Okay, she agreed.

"I will say hello to him today. I will share my lunch with him, and I will play with him at the playground."

"Now that's a very good girl," Adora said, patting a beaming Melissa on the head.

Paul concluded his conversation with his wife and kissed her tenderly on the side of her lips. Their eyes locked briefly, and Adora averted her eyes for a fraction of a second. When she looked up, her aunt was straightening up her husband's tie. He picked up his briefcase and looked at Melissa.

"Okay now big girl, we have to get going. Say goodbye to your mom and Adora."

Reluctantly, Melissa stood up and hugged her mother and Adora goodbye. She put her little hand in her father's big hand and they walked hand in hand to the side door that led to the indoor garage. Adora followed them and helped Melissa into the back seat of the black Mercedes sedan, and buckled the lap belt around Melissa's tiny frame. Patting her gently on the cheek, she leaned closer and whispered conspiratorially in her ears.

"Don't forget what I told you about being a little nicer to Stephen okay?" "Okay," Melissa responded as she settled into the plush leather seat of the car.

"I will say hello to him as soon as I see him," she said with a nod. Melissa hugged Adora tightly.

"I love you auntie," she said with a big smile on her face. Adora hugged her back.

"I love you too bunny," she responded, kissing her lightly on the cheek, and

straightening up.

Melissa giggled, and waved through the open door of the car.

Outside, in the driveway, Aunt Agatha was waiting behind the wheels of the white Acura Legend. She tapped her long nails on the steering wheel as Adora let herself into the passenger seat.

The sun was out in its full glory, and Adora could appreciate the air-conditioned

interior of her aunt's luxury car. They drove through the swank Victoria Island neighborhood, in light traffic. By the time that they approached the outskirts of the Island, traffic was thickening, and by the approach to Third Mainland Bridge, traffic had crawled to a stop.

Aunt Agatha threw her hands up in despair and glanced impatiently at her watch. It was already 8:30 am. Motorists honked their horns impatiently.

Others tried to maneuver their cars through whatever gap they could find. Hawkers lined the sides of the expressway, darting through the slow-moving traffic, and displaying their colorful wares to the motorists.

The driver of a beat up Molue bus on the lane to the left of the Legend zipped in front of them and careened towards the curb in a zealous attempt to catch a passenger, who was running into the traffic melee. The passenger darted through the tight line of cars and jumped into the slowly moving Molue bus. Aunt Agatha slammed on her brakes narrowly missing the bus, which had stalled in front of her.

"Goodness!" she exclaimed, as she swerved to the left, and passed them.

The sweaty driver of the bus had restarted his engine, and was bearing down on them seemingly intent on trying to bully her out of her lane. She honked a warning signal at the guy, and he retaliated by spitting in her direction. The brown tinged spit flew through the air and landed on the road inches shy of the car window.

"Oloriburuku!" the driver cursed at her in vernacular, making her eyes to widen in utter embarrassment.

"Cretin!" she gritted through clenched teeth as her fists tightened its hold on the steering wheel.

Her eyes blazed, and Adora could see that she was fighting to maintain a tenuous

hold on her frayed temper. Adora had never seen her aunt lose her temper like this before, and she reached out and patted her gently on the shoulders. Aunt Agatha released a blast of pent-up air and relaxed her hold on the steering wheel.

The man continued to shout and gesticulate at her, jabbing at the air with his forefinger for emphasis. The vein stood out on his sweat soaked neck, and his dingy crooked brown teeth flashed dully in the bright morning sunshine. Aunt Agatha responded by pressing the up button on the automatic power window console, effectively cutting off any further verbal exchange with him.

"What a filthy louse," she stated tersely, jabbing at the switch on the console with her French manicured fingers, an action that produced a refreshing swish of cold air from the car air conditioner. The French white tip of her perfectly lacquered shell pink nail showed a jagged chip and aunt Agatha stared at it for a split second.

"Oh no," she said in horror, her eyes glancing briefly at the ruined nail before returning her attention to the road ahead of her.

The Molue bus driver switched lane again, and rattled past them, its battered exhaust pipe spewing a choking cloud of black emission smoke. The conductor of the bus hung on to the door of the bus, his dirty shirt which was half in and half out of his ill-fitting pants flapping forlornly in the wind.

Thankfully, the Ebute-Metta exit sign loomed before them, and Aunt Agatha maneuvered the Legend into the exit ramp. Only then did her tensed- up body relax. The traffic lightened, and she inserted a compact disc into the slot on the console, and within moments, the hidden speakers in the car piped in a relaxing meld of jazz and pop recording by South African jazz composer Hugh Masekela.

"What did that mean?" Adora asked.

"The instrumentals? – oh, you mean the bus driver? Trust me, my dear. You don't want to know," said Aunt Agatha, who had a fluent command of the Yoruba language. She shook her head slowly.

"Whatever that means, I guess it goes to show his lack of polish," Adora said as a means of comfort.

"Polish? What does a person like that care about polish?" Aunt Agatha stated tersely.

Once they got off the bridge, the flow of traffic thinned, and Adora allowed her mind to wander to what lay ahead for her. A million unanswered questions jostled around in her head for attention, and she took a deep breath, and tried to focus instead on the soft strains of jazz music coming from the car stereo.

As though sensing her discomfort, her aunt smiled and placed a cool hand on her shoulder.

"Don't worry my dear," she reassured her. "It is not as bad as you think. Believe me, you will readjust to your new environment in no time." Adora smiled gratefully, thankful for her aunt's insight.

"What is the school really like?" she asked anxiously, glancing out the window at the turbid waters of the Lagos Lagoon that snaked underneath them like a thick twisted length of gleaming glass.

Aunt Agatha smoothed her hand over her chic bob.

"You already know that it has one to the best curriculum in the country, and it has international repute, so it should come as no surprise to you that it is highly competitive, but then that scholarship was highly competitive, and you snagged it."

"I sure hope that I can measure up," Adora breathed apprehensively.

Aunt Agatha threw back her head, and laughed uproariously, revealing a neat row of even white teeth.

"Don't be silly child," she finally said, as they slowed to a traffic police signal.

"Of course, you can do it. You graduated from high school with distinction, and you were class valedictorian. You are much too modest. Your record speaks for itself. My dear, the fact that you won a scholarship into the school alone -- just do your best. I am sure that Chidi is not expecting you to be superhuman. The important thing is to make the effort."

Adora blinked at the reference of her father's first name. Most people addressed her father by his title while others called him sir. It was refreshing to hear his name, the way she remembered her mom calling him. Aunt Agatha patted her gently on the arm, as though she noted Adora's mood shift.

Presently they approached an imposing structure surrounded by scores of large buildings, all enclosed by an iron fence that seemed to stretch out to infinity. A short, thin man, wearing a baggy brown khaki uniform sprang out of the gatehouse and snapped to attention. His movements were quick and spry, but upon closer inspection, he appeared to be in his late seventies. His wizened old face, lined with time and the tribal mark that crisscrossed his sunken cheeks, was beaming as though lit from within.

He doffed his hat and waved them through.

"Good morning Mallam," Aunt Agatha responded cheerily, maneuvering the car through the widely flung gate. Mallam shifted around on his legs and looked expectantly at Aunt Agatha. His gaze came to rest upon Adora, and he waved at her.

"Adora is my niece, and she will be attending school here," Aunt Agatha said as a means of introduction, and in response to the non-verbal question on Mallam's face.

"Hello fine miss," he said, smiling at Adora, and revealing badly aligned teeth, stained brown from chewing too many kola nuts.

"Hello sir," she responded pleasantly, and Mallam returned his attention to her aunt.

"Madam, you are looking younger every day, I would have thought that she was your twin sister."

With a deft movement, he produced a rag from his pant pocket, and began to make a show of polishing the already clean windscreen. Aunt Agatha retrieved a crisp one thousand Naira bill from her leather handbag and handed it discreetly to Mallam. His face broke into a wide smile, and he practically fell over himself, waving vigorously as they drove past the gate to the school grounds.

"Thank you, madam, thank you very much, he said loudly, his face reflecting his pleasure. Another car rolled towards the gate, and Mallam sprang spryly towards it, no doubt for a repeat performance.

Chapter 16

They parked the car next to a line of cars at the outdoor school grounds and walked towards the bank of buildings to the History faculty building. Adora followed her aunt through a long, confusing maze of corridors, and they finally stopped in front of a door with a golden plaque which had the words, "Agatha Adekunle, History Professor." inscribed in italics.

Aunt Agatha swept through the door into an outer office where a hefty woman with breasts the size of watermelons sat behind a desk with a manual typewriter, which sat next to a plastic filing tray that overflowed with papers. A black telephone with blinking buttons sat next to the typewriter. The woman behind the desk was wearing an Asheoke bubo and wrapper in an iridescent hue of purple interwoven with golden threads. Her head was artfully wrapped in a shiny cloth of a similar material, which was fastened with a winking rhinestone clasp.

With the exception of the forefinger, every finger of her left hand was bedecked with various sized stone-encrusted rings and her wrists were overloaded with gold bracelets and bangles, which jangled discordantly with every move of her expressive hands. Her face was quite pretty, but it looked incongruous sitting upon that mammoth body. She probably would have looked less heavy if she didn't seem to have such an unfortunate taste for loud clothing that drew attention to her outsize body.

Ignoring the blinking lights, she was chatting on the phone in vernacular in a loud boisterous voice that somehow jarred on Adora's frayed nerves. She punctuated every other word with wild gesticulations, punching the air with her plump fingers on which winked many colored rays, producing that jarringly flat clang of metal hitting metal. She stopped mid-sentence when Adora entered the room with her aunt.

"Kemesia," she said, dismissing her caller in Ibo, and replacing the phone with a loud clang.

"Good morning Prof.," she said raucously, settling her plump rump more comfortably on the chair, an action that was accompanied by the jiggling of her enormous breasts and the clanging metals of her bracelets.

"Good morning Stella." aunt Agatha responded, sighing and dropping her briefcase and the manila envelope on the black cushioned couch that reposed in a corner of the room.

"This must be your niece that you spoke about," Stella said, heaving her bulky body off the chair and coming towards them with great effort.

"Yes, this is Adora," aunt Agatha said, as she picked up her briefcase again. "Pleased to meet you," Stella said as she offered her hand to Adora.

Her handshake was soft and sweaty, and the scent of White Linen perfume clung strongly to her, intermingled with a faint odor of sweat. "Your aunt has been bragging so much about you, and it is a pleasure to finally meet you," Stella said loudly, laughing huskily, a deep sound that rolled deep within the recesses of her throat.

She struggled back to her seat and plopped her rump onto the wide cushioned chair. She let off an audible sigh of relief and belched softly, covering her mouth with her hands. She excused herself and tore off a piece of paper from the message pad on the desk and handed it to her boss. "Madam," she said. "Professor Ibikunle called at 8:45 am. She wanted to meet you for lunch at 1:00 p.m. today. The rest of your messages are in here," she said as she handed her boss a pile of pink paper.

"Thank you very much Stella," aunt Agatha said, leading Adora into the adjoining room.

It was a sparsely furnished room dominated by an immense oak desk upon which reposed a wire tray overflowing with papers. In the middle of the desk was a brass-framed photo of herself with Paul and their two kids. The stark, white wall behind the behind the desk was decorated with plaques, citations, and framed copies of her numerous awards and certificates.

There was a large frame window, bare, and letting the rays of the sun stream in, illuminating the large potted palm tree that stood close by, its broad green leaves swaying slowly to the gentle zephyr that blew in from the open window.

Adora finally verbalized her unspoken thoughts.

"How on earth do you put up with that woman?" She's so loud," she commented, as soon as her aunt shut the adjoining door. Stella's loud voice could still be heard, laughing raucously, talking loudly in Ibo. Aunt Agatha sighed, and dropped her bags on the desk.

"Part of daily living. You just do it."

"Pity," Adora said as her aunt waved her to a chair.

She perched on the chair, and her aunt sat on the brown swivel chair behind her desk. She handed Adora a copy of the school prospectus and Adora glanced through it, while her aunt sorted through her lesson plans for the day.

"I'll be just a moment my dear, please keep yourself occupied meanwhile. I just need to check a few things."

Finally, she gathered some papers from her desk, and stuffed them back into her briefcase.

"That's about it for now. Come along now my dear," she instructed as she rose from her desk and Adora followed her back to the outer office. There was no sign of Stella, but her distinct perfume still lingered in the air.

They walked along a bewildering maze of corridors, up two flights of stairs, finally arriving at a cavernous lobby, which was abuzz with sounds and activities. Students were milling about, chatting, and greeting each other, checking out the various bulletin boards posted on the walls. Others sat on the metal chairs that lined the walls, glancing at their watches, filling out forms, or just chattering in animated voices with their friends, glad to see each other after the long vacation.

A young girl of about twenty-six approached them with a bright smile on her beautiful face. She was wearing a black and white polka dot silk blouse, tucked into a white micro mini skirt, high above her knees and very tight. "Good morning Prof., had a good holiday?" She greeted as she stared curiously at Adora, and whispered something to her friend, who smiled sweetly, and greeted Aunt Agatha. A young man of about twenty-five joined them. He was handsome in a dashing way, dressed casually in carpenter style blue jeans and a light blue chambray work shirt.

"Good morning Mrs. Ade," he said, glancing at Adora with open interest. "Good morning Kunle. How's your mom?"

"Momsie is fine. She sent her greetings." "Did you guys enjoy California?"

"Man! California was a blast. Lots of fun--- pretty girls - --- He caught himself as one of the girls nudged him and changed the topic.

"I brought you a souvenir ma," he began.

"Kunle, you're only a student, you shouldn't have" Aunt Agatha protested, as Kunle handed her a package. She removed the crinkled white paper that covered the package and pulled out a metal key chain inscribed with a picture of a beach surrounded by swaying palm trees.

"This will come in handy, thanks Kunle," she said with a delighted smile. "No sweat," Kunle said, and hurried off, followed by the young girl in the mini skirt, who rushed after him, shouting.

"Hey Kunle, wait for me you hothead."

Aunt Agatha led Adora to the registration department, located at the right end of the lobby. They entered a large room filled with students standing on line, waiting for a male clerk who attended to them with a bored look on his face. A closed door off to the left of the room displayed a plaque that proclaimed, "Thomas Hardy," in large letters, and "Dean of admissions" in smaller lettering.

Aunt Agatha walked briskly towards that door with Adora in tow and stopped briefly at the secretary's desk in a small outer room. A compact, petite woman of about thirty-three sat behind the desk, wearing a short black silk skirt suit, which contrasted sharply with her pecan skin tones, tapping slowly at the keys of the typewriter with her long, manicured nails.

Her hair was done in an upswept style with swirling tendrils, and her thinly plucked eyebrows were penciled into a very high arch- way above her natural brow line- lending a perpetual startled expression to her perfectly made up face.

She stopped tapping at the typewriter, picked up a stack of papers, and walked towards a metal filing cabinet, revealing perfectly proportioned legs which were encased in black silk stockings and high stiletto pumps that did nothing for her diminutive appearance. Adora found herself wondering two things. How the lady could manage to walk in such impossibly high heels, and how she could type with those long nails, which she was tapping right now on the rim of the cabinet drawer.

She smiled sweetly when they entered the room and turned to face them. "Good morning Prof.," she greeted in a pleasant voice that dripped honey.

Aunt Agatha composed her face into a pleasant smile.

"Good morning Adamma, is Dean Hardy in yet?"

Adamma paused between leafing through files and flashed a vibrant smile.

"Yes, he is, go right ahead Prof. I believe he is expecting you," Adamma said, fluffing her hair with her fingers. The scent of her perfume, which smelled very expensive, filled the air.

"Thank you Adamma, this is my niece Adora," aunt Agatha said pleasantly. "Your niece?" Cool as cucumber Adamma sputtered, clearly flabbergasted. "I could have sworn that she was your younger sister, but your niece?" Her face took on an earnest expression.

"So, tell me Prof., what is your secret fountain of youth?"

"Aw, come off it now," Aunt Agatha said breezily, and swept through the door into Dean Hardy's office.

Dean Hardy's office was slightly larger than Aunt Agatha's, dominated by a large

oak desk, which sat in the middle of the room, cluttered with papers, a black phone, and a three-tier metal filing trays, overflowing with more papers. Among all that clutter reposed a large, ceramic ashtray overflowing with ashes, and a plump brown cigar with a charred end was stuck in the ashtray. Arranged in an L shape next to the desk was a smaller desk, which held a Dell™ computer with a flickering screen that threw off an eerie glow against the pole of a basketball hoop that hung in one corner of the room, suspended over a wastebasket, which was overflowing with balled up pieces of paper.

Dean Thomas Hardy sat behind the computer, tapping at the keys as he ran his hands against a sheet of paper that lay by the computer. He rose as they entered the room and seemed to take up the space with his height. He was a lanky, forty-something Caucasian man with sandy colored hair cut into a crew cut above steely gray eyes. His skin was fair, sprinkled with a generous amount of freckles. There were creases around his eyes and around the corners of his mouth and when he smiled, the creases around his eyes deepened. He was tall and gangly in a loose-limbed sort of way and was wearing a light blue cotton poplin dress shirt with the sleeves rolled up, over khaki colored cotton twill pants, and no tie. He had been rummaging through a file cabinet in another corner of the room, and was on his way back to his desk, whistling a tune when he became aware of his visitors.

A startled look crossed his face as his eyes swept from Aunt Agatha to Adora and

his jaws literally dropped.

"Put your eyes back in their socket Hardy," Aunt Agatha joked, laughing at the expression of pleasure that spread across Dean Hardy's face.

"Hark, what vision of loveliness stands before me," he said dramatically with a theatrical flourish in a clipped British intonation, as he walked around from behind the cabinet to meet them.

"Remember the niece that I told you about?" aunt Agatha said, laughing at the dean's theatricals.

"Of course. You said she was brainy, but you never warned me that she would turn out to be such a stunner — oh, I get it," he said, smacking his forehead. "Genetics don't lie I guess," he said.

He took Adora's hand and raised it to his lips, brushing the back of her hand ever so lightly with his lips.

"Nice to meet you, Dean Hardy," she said crisply, burning under his open scrutiny.

"Believe me, the pleasure is all mine," he said, offering them a seat with a wave of his hands.

"And please call me Tom, everybody does," he continued in his British intonation as he sank into his massive brown swivel chair. He swiveled his chair to face the computer. "Let's see now," he said, his face taking on a pensive expression.

The dean sat behind the computer, tapping at the keys. He looked up from the screen, and his face had a puzzled expression. "Wait a minute, yes, I got it."

He tapped a series of commands into the keyboard, ran a printout of the information that flickered across the screen, and handed Adora a sheaf of forms and questionnaires, attached to a clipboard.

Adora sat back on the sofa and crossed her legs as she placed the clipboard on her laps. Tom's gray eyes flickered across her legs, and lingered a little too long there, even as he bantered banally with her aunt. Adora ignored his gaze, focusing on the contents of the forms that she was filling out. She finished quickly and handed the completed forms to him, watching him as he transferred the information into the computer, while quizzing her on the contents of the questionnaire for clarification.

He picked up his phone handset and jabbed his finger at the intercom button. Adamma's cool voice came over the speaker.

"Adamma," he said.

"Yes, dean Hardy," Adamma breathed.

A quiet smile tugged at Adora's lips as the dean's face turned beet red. He turned off the speaker and instructed her to run Adora's schedule on her printer. He balled up the questionnaire in his fist, swiveled his chair to face the wastebasket, and aimed the bunched-up paper at the hoop over the wastebasket. The balled paper sailed through the air, missed its mark by a wide margin, and landed some eight inches from the trash.

Tom let out an audible groan of disappointment and ran his hand through his sandy shag.

"Aw, missed again," he muttered half to himself. Then he smiled apologetically at the women.

Aunt Agatha's eyes shone with mischief and the corners of her mouth twitched. She let out a light laughter.

"Let's just put it this way Dean Tom Hardy," she said humorously. " Don't quit your daytime job yet."

Dean Hardy let out a loud guffaw, sprinted to the corner of the room and picked up the errant paper. He stuck his hand through the hoop, and dropped the paper, which landed into the wastebasket. He gave a little bow and went back to his desk.

"Keep practicing," Aunt Agatha said.

"And someday, who knows, you may make it into the American NBA."

Tom Hardy guffawed out loud and ran his fingers through his sandy hair. "Gosh by Jove, I know that I am supposed to have a passion for soccer as a red-blooded Briton, but--all those years in LA got me hooked on basketball." "I know, I love the game myself," Aunt Agatha said, and stood up to leave.

Dean Hardy showed them out, and Adora thanked him for his help. He winked at her and went back to his desk.

Adamma was waiting for them at the outer office with Adora's schedule. "Looks like our Tom gave you the once over," she said coolly, noting the look of distaste that still lingered on Adora's face.

"Don't mind Tom a bit," she laughed. "His bark is worse than his bite. He means no harm at all. It is just that he likes to exercise his freedom to commit lookery. But trust me, he has an impeccable reputation, and is happily married.

"Thanks, Adamma," she said, taking the schedule from her.

When they were out of earshot, she confided to her aunt how uncomfortable Mr. Hardy's scrutiny made her feel.

"What a lecher," she said angrily. He reminded me of professor Maduka at the Nsukka campus. He was staring more than lecturing and had a reputation for dating female students. I couldn't wait to finish his course." Aunt Agatha laughed mildly.

"Relax, I am not condoning his behavior, but Tom is really a harmless soul. He is happily married, and there has not been a hint of scandal or gossip generated about him around here. Besides, you won't have to deal with him again," aunt Agatha said comfortingly.

"Thank God for that, and I feel sorry for his wife if that is the way he chooses to conduct himself," Adora said scathingly.

◆ ◆ ◆

Her first class of the day, English Composition 1, was scheduled to start at 10:00 am at Room 800. Aunt Agatha led her to the English department, and they stopped at a door labeled "Room 800."

"This is it Adora, good luck. I will meet you in my office at 5:00 pm, I am sure that you can find your way back to the history department. If you can't find it, simply ask for directions. I have to rush now because I have a lecture scheduled in about ten minutes."

Aunt Agatha hugged her briefly, and rushed off, leaving Adora standing in front of room 800.

Adora stood outside the door for a few moments, her hand frozen on the door knob, petrified with fear and uncertainty, fighting to conquer the sudden panic that rushed at her. She glanced at the watch on her wrist, the gold Lanvine one that her father had given her when she first entered college. The gold Roman numeral indicator read 9:47. She took a deep breath, held her head erect, and stepped into the room, making a great effort to infuse confidence into her faltering steps.

Glancing at her schedule, she took the first empty seat she could find, at the third row next to a large glass window that looked out to a vista of rolling green lawn and a bank of parked cars. Twenty-five pair of eyes fixed upon her, and she fought the rising panic that suddenly engulfed her by busying herself with her leather briefcase, fiddling with the latch, and taking her time to retrieve her pen and notebook.

She glanced at the lecturer, who was standing by the blackboard, jotting down information. He glanced at her and gave her a curt little nod as their eyes met, then sat at his desk, and began to peruse his notes. Adora swallowed the lump in her throat, and nodded back before dropping her eyes, and fiddling again with her pen.

The Professor was a tall, lanky man in his late thirties with an intense face offset by fiery eyes, intensified by a pair of fierce, bushy eyebrows that almost met at his furrowed brow. A pair of wire rimmed glasses were perched at the bridge of his sharp beak of a nose and he peered at the class over the rim. His white dress oxford shirts were unbuttoned at the neck although all the windows in the classroom were wide open, letting in a slight breeze. He had an air of easy confidence that stemmed no doubt from years in front of a classroom full of adults.

He took off his glasses, polished it with a folded white handkerchief that he extracted from his pants pocket, and waited for the class to fill up. In a few more moments, the class was filled with apprehensive looking students some of who seemed lost amongst the sea of new faces like Adora. Those who seemed to know each other sat in tight little cliques and whispered in hushed tones.

At precisely 10:05 am, the Lecturer stood up, cleared his throat, and started to address the class in a flat monotonous tone.

"Good morning students, my name is Dapo Oludapo, and I am your English Professor for the rest of the term. It is my pleasure to meet all of you. Many of you are coming here for the first time, although I see a few familiar faces, and one or two recurring faces, and to you I address this question. 'Why are you still here?"

This last comment elicited a few titters from the class, and Professor Oludapo banged a ruler on his desk. The laughter died down and without missing a beat, the professor continued.

"Many of you already know each other, but as a matter of courtesy, I would like each of you to stand up and introduce yourselves to the class with a brief capitulation of your background and why you think that you can benefit from taking this class. This way, we can eliminate all the constrictions that normally accompany the transition into a new environment and get on with the business of taking this course."

His eyes swept across the room and rested on the student sitting at the corner of the first row. Nobody in the first row moved. The professor looked around the room again and cleared his throat.

"I like to run my class democratically, and I leave it to you to decide. Who would like to begin?" he said, looking around the room.

A wiry, bespectacled young man of about twenty-five stood up immediately, and strode confidently to the front of the class. He cleared his throat ostentatiously and began to talk in a very loud voice.

"It is my pleasure to make my acquaintance with all of you. My name is Taiwo, Taiwo Ogunleye, but you can address me as Tai. The name Taiwo means that I am one of a set of twins. My twin sister Kehinde also attends this school. As I look across the classroom, I can observe that we are comprised of a multi-cultural cross-section. For that very reason, let me take the liberty to educate you that in the Yoruba culture, Taiwo is the only name that I could ever go by. This is because in the Yoruba culture twins are always named Taiwo and Kehinde. Anyway, I graduated with distinction from Government College right here in the heart of Lagos. I obtained my Bachelor's degree in marketing right here from this illustrious institution, and I am majoring in finance. I am taking this course because I believe that everyone should be well versed in the art of English Language regardless of his or her field of endeavor. I look forward to the knowledge that I can hopefully garner from this learned gentleman," he said as he gestured with a flourish at Professor Oludapo.

"I also look forward to taking this course with all of you, and I hope that my association with all of you will prove to be most profitable."

He finished his speech with a theatrical flourish, taking a dramatic half bow, and looked expectantly at Professor Oludapo for approval, perhaps a pat on the back. He was greeted instead with an icy glare, which froze him in his tracks.

"Are you done, or would you like to include the Theater Arts amongst your repertoire of achievements?" the Professor asked in a voice that barely concealed his impatience.

This caused the class to erupt in laughter, and Professor Oludapo rapped impatiently at his desk with his ever-present ruler.

"Quiet class," he boomed, rapping the ruler sharply against his desk for emphasis.

"That will be all sir, thank you sir," concluded Taiwo, not the least beat perturbed by the Lecturer's frosty reaction. He gave another slight bow and pranced confidently back to his seat.

In his exaggerated confidence, he sat too close to the edge of the chair and crashed to the floor with a loud clatter. There was a loud commotion of shifting chairs as the students closest to him moved simultaneously, some to get out of his way, and some to help him. He got up with some assistance, sat gingerly on his seat, and brushed some imaginary dust off his gray pants legs. Another student handed him his glasses, and he thanked him, and examined the glasses, running his fingers along the lens. Then, satisfied that it was not affected by the fray, he replaced the spectacle on the bridge of his nose.

"I am okay," he said with a slight quaver in his voice and shrugged off the concern of the other students.

"I am sure that Taiwo is fine," Professor Oludapo said in a serious voice. His piercing brown eyes swept across the class.

"Would anybody like to top that?" he asked with a perfectly straight face, although his voice was tinged with humor.

The entire classroom erupted in a paroxysm of laughter, and the tension that had had hung so palpably upon several members of the class seemed to dissipate with this last exchange. One by one, the students stood up and introduced themselves. Midway through the introductions, the door opened and a short, stocky man of about thirty-seven burst into the room. His entire demeanor was one of nervousness. He was dressed in a shoddy gray shirt, which was at least two sizes too small, and seemed to defy all his attempts to keep the tails tucked in. His badly creased pants were an indeterminate shade between gray and brown, and his worn canvas shoes, which could have started out as white, were a drab gray color with dirty brown scuff marks all over it.

His features were coarse and plain, and his shiny, acne streaked face had a steady stream of perspiration that kept popping out despite his best effort to stem the flow with the sleeve of his dirty shirt. It ran down his chin, and soaked his dingy, brown/ gray shirt. A pungent odor of sweat and suffering clung to him mingled with the faint odor of cheap soap. The young man slunk to the back of the class, plopped himself in the only remaining empty chair, and wiped off the steady stream of sweat that popped off his brows with a sodden piece of raggedy cloth that he pulled out of his pocket.

A hush fell upon the class, and half the class regarded the newcomer with a mixture of curiosity and amusement. Adora stared at him, feeling a wave of pity for the poor creature. She could see that the newcomer was encumbered with a hard life, and perhaps her aunt could help him with a part time job or something. There had to be something that could be done, and she couldn't just turn the other way.

He stood up, and shifted uncomfortably on his legs.

"Sorry sir," he panted. "My bus was caught in traffic, and......" "Silence," Professor Oludapo interrupted in a voice that sounded like the crack of a whip.

"One of my rules for this class includes stringent adherence to punctuality. I have no tolerance for tardiness in any form. I make absolutely no exceptions. This classroom is not a playground, and I will not tolerate any disruptions to my sessions.

He paused in his pacing, and turned to the rest of the class, his eyes flashing with anger.

"To anybody here who takes exception to this or thinks he or she cannot abide by these simple rules I suggest they pick up their bags right now and never come back."

He looked around the classroom again, and nobody moved. "Do I make myself perfectly clear?"

The newcomer nodded silently and hunched very low in his seat in a futile attempt to appear invisible.

Professor Oludapo took off his spectacles, examined the clear glass, and returned it to his face. He turned to the newcomer and gave him a piercing look.

"Now do you care to introduce yourself?" he asked in a chilly tone of voice.

The young man bolted up from his chair and opened his mouth. No sound came out. He cleared his throat, and began in a quavering nasal voice. He sounded like he had something in his mouth and was trying to talk at the same time.

"Err--eh-- I am--uh--I mean, my name is Edwin Effiong, and um-- eh--I hail from a small town named Ikot Ekpene, near Calabar.

◆ ◆ ◆

Edwin Effiong had good reasons to feel out of his elements amongst this group of younger, smartly dressed students whose biggest problem in life probably involved making a decision about what to wear to school each day. Edwin had bigger problems than that. In fact, his looming problems seemed to have no end. The oldest of five children, Edwin came from a family of poverty-stricken cassava farmers who could not afford to put a decent meal on the table. Edwin had never known anything but` gnawing poverty all his life.

He had never known the luxury of wearing anything brand new. All his clothes were second hand, or hand me down from some affluent relative. Nobody in Edwin's family had ever made it past elementary school. Their father had more use of them in the farm than frittering his hard-earned money on school fees and books, not to talk of the needed uniforms. Despite the insurmountable odds piled up against him, Edwin was determined. He would be the one to deliver his family from the debilitating depths of poverty that held them in its ugly grips. He obtained a job in Calabar, working as a houseboy and handyman for a wealthy family while putting himself through school.

Edwin arrived in Lagos with only the clothes on his back. He squatted for three months with his childhood friend Paul Obot, who worked a cook for an expatriate British family. Through Paul Obot's cousin's friend, Edwin obtained a job as a gardener and a handyman for a television actress, a temperamental woman, who gave him the job in exchange for room and board and meager wages. Edwin worked long hard hours, and after three years with his employer, he had finally saved up enough money to go to college.

His work was hard and backbreaking, and his employer, exacting and demanding. Edwin was expected to be at the disposal of his employer at a moment's notice, and the only day he was allowed off was Sunday, much of which he spent in church. Somehow, he managed to squeeze in study time between his packed schedule. His work involved more than being a gardener. In addition to mowing the lawn, and clipping the hedges, he was also expected to clean the yard, tend the pool, run errands, and pitch in wherever heavy work was needed. In exchange for all that backbreaking work, he received the equivalent of one hundred American dollars per month, three decent meals a day, and a bare room in the boy's quarters, where he had to sleep on a lumpy threadbare mattress vacated by the previous house boy. The housekeeper told him that their mistress had fired the last houseboy in a fit of temper.

From his meager earnings, he would have to squeeze in enough for his old parents back home, and for his Molue fare to and from school.

Although Calabar was a large city in its own rights, the metropolis of Lagos was totally out of Edwin's scope, with its bright lights, nonstop traffic and twenty-four-hour enterprise, which combined to inspire awe in him.

In this classroom, amongst this group of confident, well-dressed young college students, he felt totally out of his league. Their spiffy, well- coordinated outfits were in such sharp contrast to his drab shoddy clothes. Most of them probably drove to school in their own cars. Edwin had to make the trip in a Molue, those makeshift, rickety ill maintained and ill-ventilated buses that plied the routes of Lagos, contributing to the air pollution with their smoke emissions.

This morning, like every other morning, Edwin had to wake up at the crack of dawn and complete his morning duties. He had to walk three miles to the nearest bus depot since his employer lived in Ikoyi, a swanky, upscale neighborhood where most residents were chauffeur driven, and had no use for public transportation. By seven am, Edwin was waiting at the Ikorodu bus depot for his bus. By the time that the Molue rattled to a stop, accompanied by a choking cloud of black exhaust, the depot was filled with other would be passengers.

As the passengers in front of him filed into the bus, Edwin realized to his dismay that the bus was already filled to capacity.

"Come on get in, there's still space," the conductor said sharply, encouraging the desperate passengers, who squeezed in, and found gravity defying ways to cramp their bodies inside the box like interior of the bus. Edwin almost made it. Then a sweating fat woman in a loud iridescent bubo edged him out, cursing loudly at him Pidgin English.

The bus finally drove off emitting another cloud of choking black cloud, which left Edwin sputtering and coughing, and made his eyes water.

After another forty-five minutes, another bus finally pulled in, and he scrambled in amongst the sweating passengers, pressed against the bony hips of a middle-aged woman, who kept shoving him with her bony elbows. The bus rattled slowly in slow moving traffic, stopping every now and then to illegally pick up and discharge passengers, a practice that further compounded the traffic jam. When the bus finally arrived at his stop, he realized that he had to walk another two miles to the school.

As Edwin sat there in mortification, trying to take in the lecturer's droning speech, he felt hopeless, defeated. How could explain all of that to the professor? How could any of the students in the class relate to his life experience with their fancy clothes and expensive shoes? Edwin always had to scramble for whatever honest means of survival he could lay his hands on. He could not afford such luxuries as deodorants and colognes. After his long struggle in the hot sun, just trying to get to school, his entire body was saturated by a pervasive odor-caused by a combination of sweat, dust, and emission smoke, which clung to his clothes. He cringed and tried to appear as invisible as possible. He could feel the eyes of his classmates on him, as they shrank surreptitiously from him. Edwin was a very clean person. He always showered twice a day, and did his best to keep his clothes clean, but no amount of washing could erase the smell of sweat and suffering that clung to him or improve the appearance of clothes that were threadbare and discolored from too many washings. Perspiration soaked through Edwin's shirt, and ran down his sides, making his skin to crawl. Tiny beads of perspiration formed on his shaven upper lip, and he resisted the strong urge to scratch his armpits, which were itching from the extra shot of adrenaline that coursed along his veins.

At 12:30 p.m., Professor Oludapo dismissed the class, and Adora went off in search of her next class, "African Writers series." The rest of the day passed quickly and uneventfully for Adora, and at 4:30 p.m., she walked out of her last class for the day. Stella was chatting on the phone again when Adora walked into the reception area. She placed the caller on hold to inform Adora that her aunt was still in her last class for the day and ushered her into the office where she offered her a bottle of coke. Adora

gratefully accepted the cold drink and sank into the sofa by the corner of her aunt's office. As she sipped the cold liquid, she spread her notes on her laps, and reviewed her notes for the day.

Alone with her thoughts for the first time that day, she let her mind drift off and her previous day's serendipitous encounter with Randy strayed unbidden into her muse. Without giving conscious thoughts to why, she felt the return of anger about his arrogant reaction to her rebuff. "*Such a pompous ass! The least he could have done was to insist on walking me home instead of acquiescing so readily,*" she fumed silently to herself. She forced her wandering mind back to her notes, but she was chagrined to discover that she could not concentrate on the contents although she honestly tried. Images of Randy's handsome face kept popping stubbornly into her mind, taking precedence over the notes that she was trying to study.

Thoroughly disgusted with herself, Adora closed her notebook with a thwacking sound. The door flew open, and her aunt walked into the room holding her briefcase in one hand and clutching a stack of papers in the other. "First day of class, I'm glad it's finally over," she sighed, and plopped herself on her swivel chair, dropping her briefcase and the stack of papers on her desk. She kicked off her high-heeled pumps and sighed.

"Tell me about it," Adora said, relieved for the interlude that her aunt's presence presented from her rampaging thoughts. Aunt Agatha spread some paper on her desk and began to scribble notes on one of the papers.

"My dear, it is always like this on the first day of the school term. Lessons to prepare, new students to break in ---how was your first day?"

Adora sat back on her chair and proceeded to regale her aunt with stories about her day. Her aunt laughed gaily about Taiwo's antics, but her face clouded over with concern when Adora told her about Edwin.

"Do, do you think that there is anything that could be done--- to help him, that is?" she asked.

"My dear, I understand your concern, but what do you really know about him?"

"Just about enough," Adora insisted. "You had to see him. You would feel just as bad."

"I'll see what I can do," aunt Agatha said, a secret smile tweaking at the corner of her lips.

Her niece was exactly like her late sister, always going out of her way to help the less fortunate.

"Electra is throwing a surprise party for her son Randy. He is turning twenty-nine this month," Aunt Agatha said out of the blues, taking Adora by surprise. They were sitting in evening traffic, and Adora took a little while to respond.

"Electra has a son?" Adora asked, feigning innocence.

"Yeah, Randy Okere. He is the Vice President of Air One."

"Vice President?"

"Randy is a sharp businessman. Paul has gained so much from his association with Air One."

"Hmm," Adora said.

"I hope you can come with us," Aunt Agatha said. "Come with you, where?"

"To the party, my dear. They throw such great parties, the Okere's. Their parties are always gala events. You will have a good time if you---- WHAT IS HE DOING?" Aunt Agatha exploded in the next breath, slamming on her brakes. She jabbed at the horn button impatiently at the taxi in front of them, which had stopped in the middle of traffic to pick up a passenger. The taxi driver made an illegal left turn, narrowly missing a gray Peugeot, which veered in front of Aunt Agatha's car.

"Phew, can you imagine the way some people drive?" she seethed, slamming on her brakes.

The driver of the Peugeot stuck his head out of the window and proceeded to berate the taxi driver with a barrage of unprintable diatribes. "Where did you steal your license? From Balogun market, or did you buy it from Alade market?" he screamed in unbridled anger. The taxi driver craned his neck towards the Peugeot and cursed the driver in Pidgin English, then drove off.

"Lagos drivers, so annoying and frustrating!" Aunt Agatha said, letting out a shallow puff of air. Adora nodded her head in sympathy and they drove on in silence.

Finally, the traffic eased up, and Aunt Agatha released her foot from the brake.

"I hope you will come with us dear, you will have fun if you do," Aunt Agatha stated, picking up the thread of their last conversation as she drummed her shell pink fingernail on the steering wheel, in time to the strains of Onyeka Onwenu from the car stereo, careful not to aggravate her broken nail, which was now swathed in a plastic tape.

"Where aunty?" Adora asked feigning innocence. "Electra's party. It's the talk of the town," Aunt Agatha responded.

"I rarely go to parties these days, but I plan to go to this one." she concluded.

"I don't know auntie, I guess I will just have to think about it. I have school to think about now," Adora responded with a small sigh.

"That's entirely your decision my dear, but school is just starting and the workload for now is a breeze. I have your syllabus and school schedule, so I know."

"Look out," Adora screamed as a young child of about fourteen seemed to appear from nowhere and darted in front of the car, rushing to cross to the other side of the wide road. Aunt Agatha honked desperately and stepped hard on the brakes, grabbing the steering wheel so hard that the veins stood out on the back of her hands. The tires squealed its protest as Aunt Agatha turned the wheel sharply to the right, missing the child by mere inches.

The car veered to the right, and stopped abruptly in the pedestrian walkway as the people on the walkway scattered in every direction trying to get out of harm's way. Adora screamed in agony as her head whipped back and snapped forward, hitting the airbag, and then snapping sideways. She felt her head explode as her neck snapped to the side and her head made impact with the side glass window. Something warm coursed down her face and she realized that she was bleeding from her temple.

From a distance, she heard the voice of a woman calling her name. It sounded like her aunt, or was it her mother? She tried to answer, and her mouth felt like it had been stuffed with cotton. A desperate scream ricocheted in her ears, and she reached out for her mother, who reached out to her through a gauzy white haze. She cried out her mother's name and reached towards her as she retreated into the fog. She tried to run after her but her feet felt like they had been bolted to the floor. She screamed and shuddered and fought as she felt herself being sucked into a thick black, eerily silent pit.

Excerpt from Book 11

A Three-Way Street Called Love

"Excuse me lovely, would you like to dance?" Monica Umeh whirred around and stared at the burly form of the Federal Minister of External Affairs. She knew who he was because his pictures often appeared on the evening news. He was dressed nattily in a black two-piece suit paired with a white shirt that contrasted sharply with the lustrous geometric patterned silk blue tie that encircled his neck. His black oxford shoes gleamed like newly laid out coal tar.

"Dance? I don't think your wife would like that," Monica said scathingly, in a voice that barely disguised her contempt. The Federal Commissioner's wife was a well-known newscaster for a local television station and Monica had spotted them earlier, arguing loudly at their table, while sampling the delectable array of snacks that the waiters passed around. The wife was complaining loudly about his roving eyes, and he was telling her how much he loved her. The commissioner sidled closer to Monica. Apparently, he missed the sarcasm in her voice.

"My wife?" he said vaguely, glancing nervously behind his back.

"I'm sure she would prefer for you to dance with her," Monica stated tersely, grating her teeth in disgust at the way that his eyes slid hungrily up and down her form in her tight little red dress.

"She's too fat. I would rather dance with you lovely," the commissioner said, smiling and placing a chubby paw on her hip. Monica fumed silently. The man was old enough to be her father for Chris sake's. Didn't he have any shame at all? Hiding her contempt, she placed a sweet smile on her face.

"Sir," she said slowly, staring at the gaily dressed people behind him. "I think I see your wife coming now." She fought an urge to laugh out loud as the commissioner's head swiveled behind him, followed quickly by his chubby body. She turned away from him with a haughty toss of her head.

"You okay?" A voice close to her said.

"Charles!" she exclaimed in relief. "Thank goodness you came. I am getting tired of this." A waiter passed them, carrying a tray filled with glasses of champagne. Monica grabbed a glass and tossed it back and sighed, as the bubbly liquid tickled her nose. She giggled and turned her back on the commissioner, who was now locked in a heated conversation with his wife.

"Why don't we dance?" Charles asked her.

Why don't we?" Monica replied, moving her body in time to the beat of the music. Charles followed her, lumbering around the floor like a beached whale. Poor Gina, Monica found herself thinking. My poor cousin, her husband is pregnant right along with her. She swayed her body slowly to the music coming from the live band, which played an eclectic blend of pop, jazz, and Afro Funk, taking their cue from   the deejay, who stood by the bandleader. The music switched to an upbeat dance number and Charles ran out of steam.

"No------no more," he stuttered, out of breath.

"It's good exercise Charles, and you really need it," Monica said tactlessly, dancing in a circle around him. Charles ignored her barb and mopped his brow with his handkerchief.

"I'm going to sit down, he wheezed and stalked off.

"I'm going to circulate some more," Monica said as she danced away from him.

She felt a light tap on her shoulder and turned to see young man of about thirty-five smiling at her.

"I couldn't help but notice you from across the room. Do you have any idea how beautiful you are?" His eyes flicked up and down her long lithe form in her bare little red dress. Monica stared straight through him, but he continued to talk.

"May I introduce myself? I am Felix Aham. Would you like to dance?"

"Not right now," Monica said mockingly, tossing her head haughtily. Felix handed her his card. It was a beautifully embossed card in gold filigree that read, Felix Aham, President. Surge Oil Drilling LTD.

"You are extremely pretty," he repeated.

"I'd like to get to know you better---you can call me anytime," he said smoothly. When toads grow wings, Monica thought angrily, walking away from him. The man was wearing a wedding band for goodness sake. "Call me anyway," Felix called out, over the din of music and the hum of voices.

"Yeah right," she said under her breath. Monica was getting irritated.

The same thing all night. All these married men surging around her, vying for her attention. It was truly atrocious. She knew that she was a hit in her little red dress but there was only one person in the room that she was hoping would pay her that kind of attention and he was nowhere to be found. She knew that she would catch Randy's attention the moment he set eyes on her. After all she had spent forty minutes dressing with care, applying her make-up and combing and re-arranging her hair just for him. She had not seen him all night because the grand hall was crowded with luminaries, but the night was young, and she had time.

A tall dark-skinned man, wearing a dark gray suit and black wing tip shoes sidled up to her.

"Hello beautiful, what's your name." He looked late twenties or early thirties and had a bulky, muscled body underneath the expensive suit. An expensive brand of cologne clung to him.

"Monica," she said idly, although she was not inclined to talk.

"Lovely name Monica," he said, scratching his beard thoughtfully.

"Thanks," she said blandly.

"Would you care to dance? My name is Phillip."

"Why not?" Monica said impulsively and stepped towards the dance floor with Phillip in tow. A short, plump woman in a tight blue dress barreled towards them. She had small mean eyes and a bright yellow complexion, and her face sat on her neck, jutting out like a charging bull. Her eyes flicked coldly over Monica, like she was an insect and she pinched her scarlet painted mouth, which looked like a vivid red gash in her face, into a tight line of disapproval and grabbed Phillip by the shirtsleeve.

"Phillip, you are having fun again without me?" she complained loudly.

"N, no honey," Phillip said shakily. "I've been--- looking for you." She marched off in a huff, scolding Phillip, who scampered after her like a child. "Looking for me? I guess you are looking for me up the skirt of every young bimbo that catches your eyes. Keep going after those young sluts and I'll take away that flashy car that you love so much and cut you off without a red kobo," she spat out, within earshot of everyone who cared to listen.

Monica marched off in the opposite direction, feeling no pity for Phillip. "Frig them both," she thought, as her eyes scanned the vast ballroom, looking for Randy.